## *"He's coming this way! Head him off!"*

The drought-dry lilacs were crushed to the ground. In front of Glennys, gasping, heaving, was a horse—a stallion. A dark, chestnut-colored stallion, with a lightning blaze down his face.

A slim boy, clean and bright as gold, stood out in front of the stallion. Everyone silenced and backed off except for the boy—and Glennys. The boy whistled and chirped. Glennys talked to the horse, praised him in a murmur entirely different from any language she'd ever spoken outside her dreams.

The stallion stood solidly on all four legs. His neck stretched out just a little. His ears, at first laid back, began to twitch, then pointed directly at her! He danced his front legs, shook his long, graceful neck, tossed his flossy mane. He took a hesitant step forward. Glennys wanted to feel that soft nose in her hand more than she had ever wanted anything.

He came to her . . .

*Ace Fantasy Specials*

# THE HORSEGIRL

## CONSTANCE ASH

ACE BOOKS, NEW YORK

This book is an Ace original
edition, and has never been
previously published.

THE HORSEGIRL

An Ace Book / published by arrangement with
the author

PRINTING HISTORY
Ace edition / October 1988

ISBN: 0-441-34275-2

Ace Books are published by The Berkley Publishing Group,
200 Madison Avenue, New York, New York 10016.
The name ''ACE'' and the ''A'' logo are trademarks
belonging to Charter Communications, Inc.

PRINTED IN THE UNITED STATES OF AMERICA

10 9 8 7 6 5 4 3 2 1

*Ned Sublette*
*was the leader of the band.*

*Lou Stathis and Kathy Sagan*
*were the special guests.*

*Tamar Kotoske and Keith Rawls*
*provided the technical support.*

*Thanks, guys.*

*The Horse*: Beware the horse, accomplice of sorcery and witchcraft of all kinds, emblem of insistent lechery, a symbol of instinct gone berserk.

*Alaminite Bestiary*

# ONE

The girl staggered under the weight of the buckets hanging from the yoke over her shoulders. Filling the buckets to the top wasn't one of her parents' rules. But she hated carrying the buckets, and she'd counted. With them only half-filled it took more than a hundred trips, back and forth, over the two furlongs between the garden and the well to do the job.

As she walked, the water slopped over the slats of the buckets, ran down her scratched calves, and splashed onto her bare feet. Though she did her best to keep her skirts neatly tucked up around her hips, they always came down. Stains from the rusty bands binding the bucket slats marked her clothes like old blood. The girl pushed her toes into the powdery caliche soil. It was the fourth week of summer and there had been no rain.

As the girl worked, she talked to herself. Words splashed in the well of her imagination and spilled over into the air around her. She preached, told stories, made up songs about what she saw.

"I'm not gonna grow up and have a husband and babies and a house. I'm *never* gonna have a garden." The water spilled over the sides of the buckets in a back-and-forth slope, sloshing in rhythm under her words.

"Dirt, nothing but dirt, hot dirt. Weeds, weeds, pull the weeds, kill the weeds. Bugs and worms, pick them from the leaves, squish them, cut them. Cut the cutworms, I hate cutworms. Haul the water, pour the water, hoe the dirt, pick the beans."

Her voice got louder and louder over the drag of the swaying weight of water. "*Squash* the bugs, *smash* the beans!"

The well was between the barn and the house. A voice of admonition, louder than the girl's chanting, came through the open shutters of the kitchen window.

*1*

"Sissy, Sissy, you hush your mouth. Stop dawdling, do your work, and shut up. Girls that can't keep quiet generally find more trouble than they like."

The girl quit walking. She put the buckets on the ground.

The voice from the house became more cajoling. "Mary, Mary, quite contrary, how does your garden grow?"

The girl whispered, "I hate the garden."

Alarmed by what she'd just said, she looked through the first and fourth fingers of her right hand at the rows of corn, hills of potatoes, ruffles of carrots, lace of dill. She tried to ward off her own bad wishing with the gesture. The family needed the food that came out of the huge plot. She hadn't meant to badspeak it.

"Don't be a bad girl," she said to herself.

She tossed her head as she peered through the guidelines made by her grubby fingers with their broken nails. She'd felt light-headed when her mother had awakened her at dawn. By the time the pretty part of the morning was over she'd felt sick to her stomach, but it came and went. Now her lower back hurt.

All of her body was keenly aware of the brassy, clear sky above the northern march of Nolan. The sharp line of the horizon was breaking up as noon approached, becoming a shimmering, wavering mist as the heat of the sun was reflected back from the baked earth. The land was no stranger to periods of drought. But this was the first time she'd experienced one.

She couldn't remember feeling sick like this before, either. She put her hands to her back as she'd seen her mother do many times every day. The world spun out from under her for a moment and everything went black. That was scary. She hated feeling afraid more than anything. She began her personal litany against fright. They were the words she'd learned to repeat with the other children on her first day at Queen's School.

"In the world of Mittania I live in the nation of Nolan. Leon Eidel the Fourteenth is King in Nolan. The capital of Nolan is St. Lucien, where sits King Leon. I live in County Soudaka. I go to school and kirk in the village of Dephi. The Baron Fulk is the King's Justice in Soudaka. As citizens of Nolan we owe him respect and obedience. The signs of his authority are the horses of the Eidel Kings, which Baron Fulk has in his care.''

Thus the girl attempted to locate herself back into her world. But this time the litany didn't work. She was old enough now to understand that those she lived among didn't respect the Baron or the Eidel Kings—and that they thought horses were filthy and evil. The Alaminite congregations here on the northern boundary of Nolan didn't consider themselves a part of the Dominion, even though they were forced to harbor the King's Justice and the King's horses, pay the King's taxes and fight in the King's armies. All that was Old Nolan and it had nothing to do with them.

The girl thought of her mother and father and her two sisters. She thought about the three baby brothers born dead. She thought about her mother's belly big with child once again. Her sickness and dizziness became insistent. She said out loud, ''I am *not* gonna have a man and babies and a garden and go to kirk.''

The first time she'd said those words was at a Gatherin three years ago. Her father had thrown her outside of Grandfather's house and spanked her so hard she couldn't sit for days. Her mother's words from that Gatherin rolled around inside her head. ''What are you going to have, what are you going to do? All girls grow up, you know.''

The girl responded again to those words as she had that day. ''I am going to have horses and ride them.'' Her mother said it was impossible. She wondered why adults pretended everything was so hard, when it was clear they could do whatever they wanted.

The voice of admonition spoke again from the kitchen window. ''Sissy, Sissy, where are you with your pa's tomatoes? You haven't been to the well for the last ten minutes. Get a move on!''

The girl dumped the water over the roots of the rustling corn. She wondered if she were hearing the corn grow. There wasn't the slightest bit of breeze. The stalks and leaves were still green because she'd been pouring water into the corn hills for weeks. Every day, morning and evening. She took another few minutes to squish the mud between her toes before heading back to the artesian well. She knew by the time she got back to the row the mud would have turned into a damp smudge.

A warning came from the kitchen window. "Sissy, you'd better not be daydreaming. Move!"

Back to the well she went, and back to the garden. She bent over under the hot sun. Her knees were weak, her legs trembled. The tomato vines tied to their stakes were taller than she was. Between the overgrown rows of plants there was no air. Their musty, thick odor made her feel sicker as she walked through the rows. One of the ripe fruits had fallen and split. It looked like something wounded and bleeding. She felt as though something sharp had jabbed her in the center of her body. She saw visions of the slaughter of table meat, the killing of useless farm stock. Her knees folded up under her.

"Sissy, what are you doing lying down there? Daydreaming? This time of day? Sissy, you get up from there. You got lots to do."

The girl opened her eyes. She could see tiny black ants. Her face in the dirt was a barricade against their work. The ants were dragging bits of stuff across the floor of the garden. She wondered if the ants ever got tired or were bothered by the drought or cared about anything but their work. Reverend Tuescher approved of ants. She saw her mother staring at her through a snarl of tomato vines.

"You sick?"

"My stomach hurts."

Impatient, her mother sniffed. "How can your stomach hurt? It's summer, no sickness about. You had food this morning, praise Alam. How can you be sick?" her mother demanded.

"I don't know," the girl said, expecting a slap. "It's the smell . . . these vines . . . they make me dizzy. And the sun. He's so hot."

The woman pushed her daughter with her foot. "You are the most obstinate thing! I've told you and I've told you not to call the sun 'he'! Only the Nolanese Aristos name Alam's creation 'he' or 'him' like the heathen they are. You might have to do that in Queen's School sometimes, but you *don't* talk like that around your own kind. You're a member of a good Alaminite family, so why do you want to fool yourself that you're like one of them? Them! They only care for themselves. Now, will you get up and pick those tomatoes? You can wait on the watering, until it cools towards evening.''

"Ma, honest, I don't think I can. My stomach hurts too much. I don't think I can walk. The tops of my legs hurt too.''

The girl moaned and then retched some bile. An odd thought flitted by like a grasshopper on the wing. At that moment she couldn't tell if the sickness was real or if she'd brought it upon herself because she'd said she was sick.

The girl's mother pulled her to her feet, not roughly, but not gently either. She peered into her daughter's face. The girl's clear cheeks were pale under the dusting of sun freckles. Her forehead was clammy and chill under her mother's hand.

"Shouldn't be cool-like on a day hot as this. Well, then Sissy, you go up to the house and look after your sisters. I'll pick the tomatoes myself,'' she said. "But you listen to me good, girl. If you're faking this, pretending to be sick when you're not so you can get out of your work, I'll make your bottom as red as these fruits. You hear?''

She gave a swat to her daughter's back skirts. "Now, Sissy, what have you done, sat on some of the fruit and squashed it and got it all over your clothes and we can't spare the time for washing until regular day, though we have the water, Lord of Light be thanked, there's others as doesn't, and you don't have enough clothes as it is, you growing so fast and times being so hard.''

The girl loathed being handled that way, as if she didn't belong to herself. She hated it when her mother started one of those sermons in which complaint, threat, and religion jumbled all together. She tried to pull away.

"Hold still and let me see this.''

She felt her mother's hand in her back clothes, heard her gasp. Suddenly she was spun around by her shoulders and the blow she'd anticipated earlier and thought she'd escaped landed with a stinging crack across her cheeks.

"It's too soon for you to have blood. You're only in your tenth summer; it can't have come to you yet.''

What did her mother mean?

"You wicked, wicked girl. How could you do this to me

too on top of everything else I have to bear this summer? You shouldn't start bleeding for another three, four years. But no, I always get punished with whatever bad luck is going around.''

There were tears on her mother's face. The girl backed away and ran up to the house. Running away from chastisement brought at least a spanking, if not a real beating. But she had to get away. She knew she was the bad luck and her mother's punishment.

In the decently curtained alcove that concealed the family chamber pots, she lifted her skirts above her thighs and cautiously examined herself. There was a red slickness between her legs, slender red threads that ran down to her knees. The heaviest red had soaked through her skirts while she'd lain in the garden dirt. Was she going to die? The pains and nausea were still with her. She should get some cold water from the well and soak her bloodied clothes in it. She couldn't make herself do it. She wondered if she would ever be able to go outside again.

It took all her courage to ask, when her mother returned to the house, ''Why am I bleeding from there?''

The woman turned a bleak smile upon her daughter. ''Don't mind what I said in the garden. It isn't your fault, really. It happens to all girls when they grow up. Don't mind what I said.''

Her look of embarrassment was turned down to her own gravid belly. ''My mother slapped me too, the first time. It's to show you're a woman. You have to do this so you can have babies.''

The girl stared at her mother. Distaste and skepticism showed in equal measure on her face.

''It's just that you're so young it doesn't seem natural.'' The mother's voice dropped, taking on a sad tone that the girl hated. ''I had thought that when their time came I wouldn't do to my girls what my mother did to me, but I was caught by surprise. I had no idea you were growing so fast.''

She shook her head. ''Your father will most likely say some woman like old Mabley turned an evil eye this way. But it's not witchcraft. This house doesn't hold with superstition. It's only the woman's curse. You're not sick and you'll still keep working.''

Her mother opened the parlor. It was shut up most of the

time, kept for company. The room was dim and seemed cooler than the rest of the house. She spread a piece of old sheeting over the sofa and told her daughter to take off her soiled clothes. She got the girl a fresh chemise and told her to lie down. A moment later she brought in a stone mug of squeezed tomato juice.

"Drink this, Glennys," her mother said. "And bind these cloths between your legs. Here, I'll do it for you this first time."

Mother and daughter were both uncomfortable. Anger was more familiar to them.

Glennys pretended to put the mug to her lips. Her mother hadn't spoken so kindly in a long time. But the smell of the red liquid with the suspended yellow seeds made her stomach turn over.

Her mother compulsively examined the furniture for dust. She paused in front of a large embroidery that decorated the wall over the fireplace. The hanging was older than Glennys and contained a mystery. Blue silk threads twined subtly among green to depict a meadow full of long, deep grass. A silver and blue stream ran through the meadow. Clumps of trees, low and broad and very green, swept towards brilliantly colored flowers in the grass. In the background was a mass of grey, blue, and black. It might have been clouds or a city.

Once during spring cleaning, while the hanging in its frame was on the floor, Glennys had seen the back side. Pondering over the mystery that made embroidery a smooth design in front and a mass of knots in back, she saw an outline on the back side of a mare and foal. The public face of the embroidery was empty of horses. Already fascinated by the forbidden, Glennys asked her mother about it.

All she answered was, "I decided to pull those threads out." Her tone of voice put the question in the same category as those about where babies came from.

There were no meadows, as such, in Soudaka. The embroidery showed Glennys a different place than the harsh land into which she had been born. She loved to look at it, and make up tales that might take place in such a country—tales full of horses.

Her mother was talking about babies and boys and husbands. Glennys understood that part. She'd put in several seasons of barn work by now. She didn't listen to the parts about ladylike behavior, housekeeping, or childcare. She'd heard it all before.

Her mother concluded with, "You aren't an Aristo girl, so don't think you can spend five days out of every moon cycle lying down, taking care of your pretty little hands and having someone wait on you like this time." She went out of the parlor, shutting the door behind her.

Glennys hated the feel of the rough cloth binding between her legs. She didn't think she'd like going through this every month, even if her mother had said it wouldn't hurt next time.

But—her mother had called her by her name, called her Glennys. That must mean something significant had happened. Hardly anyone except the Schoolmaster Muran ever called her Glennys. She liked Schoolmaster Muran, and she loved the Queen's School, which most of the Alaminite children would have been glad to skip. At school she learned interesting things that she heard nowhere else. At school she was away from her father.

Her first day the Schoolmaster had asked for her name and those of her mother and father. She'd said that her father was of the Kolkiss clan and her mother's name was Stella Heitkamp. From the boys' side of the schoolroom one of Reverend Tuescher's sons sneered, "Yah, that one's ma ain't got no family at all. She used to work for the Baron's wife before the old sow kicked off. Stella thought she was too good for Dephi and went and lived in Nolan with Fulk's folks."

The boy put a spin of derision into his voice, as though the words were stones thrown at Muran and herself. Milton Tuescher snickered. "Yah, Stella came back here in the end. But your old pa wishes she didn't. None of her boychildrens live."

That was when she first heard that her mother had been in Old Nolan, in horse country. Her mother never would talk about the days before she married Glennys's father. The wonder of it didn't leave Glennys, even after she tried to fight Jerold and Milton Tuescher for sneering at her mother.

Remembering that day, Glennys turned on her side and faced the embroidery. She spread her fingers under her cheek, and pulled her knees up to her belly.

The Queen's School had been established for less than a

full generation in their County. It had taken a royal edict, backed by Baron Fulk's men and the instruments of law, to get girls on the school benches. Old ideas die hard in hard communities, the Schoolmaster often had told her.

Even now, at Gatherins and from the kirk pulpit, there were railings against the Dowager Queen whom the Alaminites held responsible for getting the 'owd King' to insist that girls be educated. There were quite a few who preferred that there be no school at all for boys or girls, except kirk school.

The kitchen door slammed and heavy footsteps crossed the floor, announcing her father was home from the fields. "Stella, where in hell is that girl? I was going to knock over the old ox cow and I want the girl to hold the cow's head. I don't see her anywhere. She didn't move the sheep this morning either, like I told her to."

Glennys heard her mother reply. "I told her not to move the sheep because they've already chewed the grass too short on the east side." The rest of the words were too soft for Glennys to hear. A hot flood of revulsion ran through Glennys's limbs as she realized her mother was telling him about what had come on his daughter.

"Who cares the girl's bleeding unless you can marry her off now and get her out of here. But who's gonna catch the blood while the ox bleeds?"

Stella's voice was reasonable. She suggested her husband get his father, Kolkiss, or one of his brothers to help him butcher the ox.

"They're hunting down a dog pack. What else is *she* good for anyhow?"

Glennys tensed against her father's entry into the parlor. In the dreamy state induced by her pain, she admitted she didn't like her father. She thought she didn't like any of the men she saw often, especially Grandfather Kolkiss and Reverend Tuescher. Her father didn't come into the parlor after all and Glennys fell asleep.

It was late in the afternoon when she woke. Unaccustomed both to sleeping during the day and to being in the parlor, she was confused. Then she remembered. The binding had soaked through to the chemise, but hadn't stained the sheet because she'd slept with her legs drawn up. The sickness had passed.

She felt exhilarated, as though the old life had been cleansed out of her body. Things had changed.

She folded the sheet and put it on the shelf, the same shelf that held the old cloths. She knew what those rags were for now, where previously she'd hardly noticed them. She changed into her oldest clothes, those that had been put aside for the rag bag. She felt as though she'd gotten capable. She felt her hands knew how to manage things themselves.

Outside, the best time of the day had begun. Her mother was sitting down, a pillow behind her back, cutting up the long green beans. Debbie, the three-year-old, played quietly under the table. The baby, Becky, was crowing because she'd learned to pull herself to her feet by whatever she could get her tiny grasp on. Debbie encouraged her to stand whenever she plopped to the floor.

"I'm well, Mother. I'll go out and do the watering now."

Glennys stood shy and proud in the doorway. The clothes she'd put on were too small for her. The sight made Stella smile. "Now this is how I like to see my big girl," she said. She chuckled as she used to do before there were three tiny cremations in the sacred fire of Alam behind the kirk.

"I took some of my egg money and paid the Reverend's oldest boy, Ezekial, to do the watering for this evening. Why don't you take the babies outside? They haven't been able to be in the yard all day. Soon enough their playtime will be over and then they can help you and me."

Stella smiled again as she saw Glennys imitate her own manner with the younger children. She murmured to herself, "Perhaps this was good luck after all." Her oldest daughter had never displayed the least bit of interest in babies before. She'd never volunteered to do anything before either. She'd always had to be told to do her work.

The cats had returned from whatever business kept them out of sight during the hot hours. Alaminites admired cats because they destroyed vermin. They needed no special care, no attention, to do their job. But the kirk's sanction or not, cats will scratch babies that pull their tails. Both of Glennys's sisters needed to be watched every second.

A loud shout broke the peace of late afternoon; then more shouts, yells, cries. Men were running through the garden and the field behind it, men on *horses* racing to the front of their house.

A sound of power. Was it like the deep-toned gong in the kirk? No, it wasn't like anything Glennys had ever heard. But it had to be what she thought it was.

"He's coming this way! Head him off! We can corner him behind the house!"

The drought-dry lilacs were crushed to the ground. In front of her, gasping, heaving, was a horse—a stallion. A dark, chestnut-colored stallion, with a lightning blaze down his face.

Glennys forgot her sisters.

Stella gathered the two terrified children into her arms and hustled them into the house. The small yard was crowded with men carrying prods and ropes. Glennys noticed them hardly more than she had noticed her mother or sisters.

The stallion's coat gleamed where sweat had washed through the dust. He shivered and rolled his eyes, showing white, then stood on his hind legs and cried out. His tail shook like a whipped thunderhead as he reared again. He pushed his front legs against the air, and hopped against the lilac bush stems.

A slim boy, clean and bright as gold, stood out in front of the stallion. Everyone silenced and backed off except for the boy—and Glennys. The boy whistled and chirped. Glennys talked to the horse, praised him in a murmur entirely different from any language she'd ever spoken outside her dreams.

The stallion stood solidly on all four legs. His neck stretched out just a little. His ears, at first laid back, began to twitch, then pointed directly at her! He danced his front legs, shook his long, graceful neck, tossed his flossy mane. He took a hesitant step forward. Glennys wanted to feel that soft nose in her hand more than she had ever wanted anything. He came to her.

The sleekness of his cheeks felt smoother and finer to her fingers than her mother's embroidery thread. In a moment the stallion was haltered and the boy asked Glennys to give him a leg up.

"I've never done it before," she said. "Do you mean like this?"

She squatted, then put her two hands together and boosted

his foot. His boot had a tiny gold emblem of three trees on its cuff.

She stood for a golden time in the golden part of the day, her hands on the stallion's neck, breathing deeply the smell of the horse, trying to get as much to remember as she could. She tried to tell the stallion that the long, ugly tear that oozed scarlet drops across his chest would get better.

The man who seemed to be the boss, firmly, though not roughly, moved the girl away from the horse by her shoulders. He examined the gash. "I don't think he did that escaping from his stall. This happened later, maybe with a Lighter billhook. It's going to leave a scar and the King's groom is going to give me a lecture."

Glennys's father had grudgingly broken out a barrel of beer for the Baron's men and for his neighbors who'd run to investigate the excitement.

The man said to the boy, "Hengst, ride him out of this crowd."

Glennys paced the horse as though bewitched. "Please, can I sit on him? What's his name? I've never been this close to a horse before. I've never touched one. I've never ridden one."

Hengst gaped at her. "You never rode a horse?" She might have said she had two heads. He couldn't have exhibited more disbelief.

The man who'd ordered Hengst to take the horse away didn't drink with the rest. He looked at Glennys and said, "This one's work name is Speed. He's a racer from King Leon's personal stud. He's not the property of the Baron. I can't take a chance and let you on him."

Hengst, who was a couple of years older than Glennys, felt sympathetic. He dismounted and turned the King's horse over to the man, who walked him back and forth to cool him down.

"He's the Stablemaster, and when it comes to horses everyone has to do what he says. But if you come to Three Trees I'll show you around. We're not so fussy about who sits on our horses. We raise war horses, not racers. I'll let you ride my horse. He's a gelding named Smoky."

"What's a gelding?" asked Glennys.

"You don't know anything, do you?" Hengst said. "A

gelding is a male horse who's been fixed. You know, like you turn a bull into a steer?''

"Did you say I could come to Three Trees? Can I?"

Hengst smiled and winked at her.

Glennys tried to think of a way that a ten-year-old girl could run off from her work and enter the forbidden promised land. She watched on the road, heedless of Stella's commands to come into the house and help with supper, until Speed, Hengst, and the Baron's men faded out of sight. She heard the Stablemaster's voice carry back over the distance, reprimanding one of his grooms for riding in an Alaminite grain field.

After midnight Stella awakened to the boom of thunder. Lightning trees budded, bloomed, and split open the sky. The long-prayed-for rain poured down. She could hardly rejoice, remembering as she did the enraptured expression on her daughter's face as the horse dipped his nose into her hand.

# TWO

Muran, Schoolmaster for the village of Dephi, thanked the Lady Eve that Elder Bohn was still mindful of his duties to the Eidel throne. He'd brought the school a load of coal from the Badlands before the days got really cold. It had been Bohn's turn to supply the school with fuel during the eleventh month. Muran had learned not to count on coal, oil, or repairs appearing when it was another Elder's turn.

Muran restoked the classroom stove and lit the whale oil lamps. Though it was only the middle of the afternoon, night's skirts were already gathered, about to flare out over the northern march of Nolan. It got dark so early now and Harvest Gatherin still hadn't been held. Muran shuddered.

"Glennys, if you like, you may take the book home with

you. Your mother must be waiting." He spoke softly, reluctant to disturb the girl's peace, or his own.

Glennys raised her head, her tawny-colored hair a tangle of flyaway snarls. There was a purple bruise around her left eye. She put her hand on the big open volume as though she were caressing the pages. She looked at Muran but he wasn't sure she saw him.

He pushed back the forelock of dark golden curls that insisted on covering his eyes. He was a young man, but he carried enough weight on him to back up the blows with which he disciplined the Alaminite boys. Many of them were as tall as he was.

"Glennys, you are going to have to learn to control your temper. Your folks aren't going to like seeing their daughter come home with a black eye."

Glennys's face showed she had come back to Dephi from wherever she'd been gathering dreams. It became a fierce mask, as Muran had seen it do many times.

She said, "The boys shouldn't have been talking about me. I can't help it that I'm growing up." She looked down involuntarily to her budding breasts and blushed.

Muran hesitated, "Maybe you should tell your folks that you fell down on your way to school."

She said matter-of-factly, "My pa knows where black eyes come from."

It was true. On any one day at least one of Muran's pupils had an eye swollen and discolored. Many Alaminite fathers, sons, and brothers feuded among themselves as fiercely as the cocks in a poultry yard.

"Master," asked Glennys, "why do the Queen's School books say there are no such things as familiars and witches when these other books tell stories about them? At kirk school we learn about witches, and the devil, too."

None of Muran's other students would have asked him that. None of the other students would have read the book she had in front of her either.

"You're reading *The Chronicle Book*. That one repeats stories from mythology. It tells how centuries ago the Stallion Queens and their, their—husbands—rode into Old Nolan out of the Saquave Desert and defeated the demons who held the land along the Setham River. Nowadays we call stories like that myths. Myths are an invention, just like poetry, to help understand the past and to remember it. Myths are true like storybooks are true, and not real in the same way. Did that make sense to you?''

Glennys looked skeptical, but obviously didn't want to hurt Muran's feelings. She grinned blankly and nodded. Muran, however, continued. Who else was there to talk to?

"No matter how the story's told, the Nolanese tribes on horses way back then really did conquer what you Alaminites call Old Nolan and the people who lived there first. The Alaminites were one of those peoples. Mythology is one way to boast of how we Nolanese conquered other peoples and took their country because we had horses. In fact, that's one of the things people like me study at the Seven Universities. But none of this stops those tales from giving pleasure to people who read them. So why don't you take the book home, read it to your sisters?''

Glennys shrugged. She wasn't willing to humor him anymore. "Mother's sick and I have to do a lot. Besides, my pa would throw the book into the fire faster than you can say 'Alam's Lord of Light.' He's gonna be mad enough as it is. I'm late.''

But she made no move from her bench. "Maybe there really are witches though," she said. "My father says that my baby brother was witched by the Eidel King's stallion that ran to Mother's farm last summer. That's why that baby died like all my other brothers.''

Muran sighed and rubbed his hands over his afternoon beard. So that was what she'd been thinking about.

"There are *no* witches and *no* witcheries. When will you Alaminites accept that? That's why this school is so important. Your people are good, hardworking folks, but there are too many things about which you're obstinately determined to believe lies. It holds you back. It's an old, old business, this thing about horses and witchcraft. We took the land you call Old Nolan from you a long time ago because we had horses and rode them into battle, and Alaminites didn't. So to keep your pride, you decided horses were a power from the devil. Otherwise you'd not have lost the fight and the land. You Alaminites have made that into a dogma.''

He paused to ask the girl if she understood that word, *dogma*.

Glennys nodded her head. Dogma was an important word in the kirk catechism, one of those you memorized along with its meaning. She never had any trouble memorizing anything. Reverend Tuescher's youngest boys could hardly remember how to spell their own names.

"Now the way I see it, Glennys," Muran said slowly, "is that the Alaminite kirk has made it a dogma that it's wrong for a man and a beast to be as close to each other as they must be if one rides the other into battle. You've all feared and hated horses for so long that you can't imagine anything else. It's spilled over into all parts of your lives. For instance, all of you keep sheep, but you won't use dogs to help. You'd have to understand the animal's mind to do that, and he'd have to understand yours."

And, he reflected to himself, their practice of shunning horses and anything to do with them made these Alaminites the tribe who had never assimilated with the Nolanese. Though there was a cross-breed fringe—Lighter women did get pregnant at times from Nolanese men, and not always through rape—County Soudaka kept its religion and its separate identity. Muran, born poor and obscure in Old Nolan, had a grudging respect for that.

Glennys said, "Alaminites hate dogs almost as much as horses, yah. The kirk Elders burned our dog lady, old Mrs. Mabley. They'd told her and told her to get rid of her dogs and start coming to kirk again. But she wouldn't."

Muran's guts lurched. "When did that happen?"

"At the end of summer. Before you came back from Old Nolan."

He wanted her to keep talking. "I've heard that Alaminites used to burn witches," he said, "but I don't think it's true anymore. Our King doesn't allow that."

"They did too burn a witch. I'm not lying. It was Grandfather Kolkiss and the Coals of the Lord, the men who don't have any wives or farms of their own and live with their pas' families. The stallion came to my house and Mother's baby died when it was born. Speed came to see *me*. Grandfather Kolkiss said so. And that was because Mrs. Mabley did it to make Grandfather and Pa look bad to Reverend Tuescher. So she conjured the devil and came to my house inside a horse.''

If she's telling the truth, Muran thought, the Baron had better know what's started going on here while he's stayed away so long.

"Glennys," he asked, "do you believe horses are from the devil?"

Her face was hard as a stone and she didn't bother to think about the question. Her voice was high and shrill. "Horses are the most beautiful things in the world. They aren't evil. Anyway, I don't care. I don't care what those people think."

She whispered because this was a real secret. "I don't care what my father says or my grandfather. My mother told them and told them that the baby died because it was Alam's will, not because of a witching. She wouldn't go to the burning and she kept me home with her, even though Grandfather said it was for us. Reverend Tuescher sure was mad about that. He's still mad and I'm glad!"

This is an opportunity, Muran thought, if I know what to do with it. "Glennys, listen to me, this is very important and I want you to remember it. Don't say another word about witches or horses to the Elders or anyone, not even to your family. Both of us could get into trouble. There's no one to help us except Baron Fulk and he's not here."

Glennys said, "The Baron's not here but his son is."

"Stogar's at Three Trees?"

"Who's Stogar?" she asked. "I mean Hengst. He used to live in St. Lucien but he's been here since spring. He's got his own horse. His sister's coming too. They have to stay on Three Trees until they're grown-up."

"How do *you* know this?" Muran questioned.

"Hengst came to my mother's farm to help catch Speed. When my mother was sick having my dead brother I sneaked off to visit him and his horse. He asked me to."

Glennys carefully put *The Chronicle Book* in its place on the long shelves. She was ten years old going on eleven. After a point adults made no sense; even Muran got silly. But she liked him anyway.

She stared at the map of Old Nolan on the wall. "Where's the Saquave Desert? I wanna go there one day."

Muran laughed. He wasn't expecting that. "If you ever

went to the Saquave, you wouldn't like it. What happened here in the summer was a drought. The Saquave is hot and dry all summer, every summer. There's no coal, like you have in the Badlands, so what would you cook on? There's even less wood than here. It's flat and it goes on forever there behind the Rain Shadow Mountains. The Nolanese are much better off in the river valley of Old Nolan than that place. We send criminals and crazy people to the Saquave to punish them."

"It sounds like a great place to be—it doesn't get cold. And there are wild horses there. The books say so. I could catch one."

"A weird kind of horse, that's right. A horse that no one ever sees, so none's ever been caught. We've got plenty of horses right here, the best horses in the world."

"Not on my mother's farm," Glennys said.

After she left, Muran went through the door behind his desk to his living quarters. He looked at his reflection in the shaving mirror. Big and burly, a well-educated man. He still had years of bondage ahead. The only way he'd been able to attend the Seven Universities was to sign a contract to teach Alaminite children one year for every term of his tuition. He'd chosen Soudaka because, bad as it was, it had an advantage that a place in Nolan's Dominion Outremere didn't—he could go back to the Seven Universities in the summer, visit St. Lucien, stay in touch with the shifts of political climate. And here his only friend was a rebellious Lighter girl who belonged in this community no more than he did. He hoped he could do her some good. Lighters. They burned their witches and they burned their dead. He began to shave. If he walked fast he could get to Three Trees in time for supper.

Glennys picked her way through the fields. The overcast sky was as unfriendly as the scowl that always was on her father's face. The grain stubble pricked her hard, bare feet. Her mother had been too sick this year to fight with her father about winter shoes. She was clumsy and gawky in layers of ill-fitting skirts and jackets. Her tangled hair stood out like a truant halo around the scarf over her ears.

In her imagination she was a majestic stallion who skimmed

over the ground in company with a whole herd of horses that belonged to her. She whinnied and blew through her nostrils, imitating the horses she saw on Three Trees the day she'd been there. She reared on her hind legs and pawed the air, like Speed had done in front of the lilac bushes. But she was better than Speed. The Glennys-stallion lived in the Saquave Desert and was the freest, fleetest creature in the world. Nobody could see her.

At her house the Glennys-horse pulled up sharply and went away. The girl recognized the booming tones of Reverend Tuescher coming through the walls. He was the loudest man in the world, she thought. The kitchen door stood open. Something was wrong. All the way from the parlor, old Tuescher's sharp eyes spied Glennys on the back steps to the kitchen.

"So, you've finally chosen to come home. You've kept us waiting, girl. Get in here."

Though he was old, Tuescher was big and powerful and moved quick as a boy. He took her painfully by the shoulders because she'd not obeyed quickly enough. He propelled her into the parlor. Her mother was crying in a chair pushed into a corner where it wasn't supposed to be. Her father was standing in front of the fireplace in his everyday work clothes. His boots were dirty, though Tuescher's clothes and boots were not. Her father's head hung down, his hands in his pockets.

Tuescher addressed her father. "Tomorrow at the crossroads have your wife and your firstborn wait for us. It already may be too late to save them from abomination, but Alam is our strength, and we shall try."

He jerked Glennys around to face him. He pulled her head back by the hair. "I've heard you say it more than once in kirk school that Alam doesn't talk to you. God loves you, child, and if the kirk must beat that into you so that you understand, we will. Those the Lord loveth, he chastiseth. It's for your own good and peace of soul. You are part of the instrument that teaches women not to question the kirk and its Elders. Your mother is not a proper woman these days because she questions and does not accept. Women who ask questions let the devil into them."

"Are you going to burn us like you did Mrs. Mabley?" Glennys demanded with a reckless defiance.

"We are saving you." He slapped her chest. "Just because you've got a woman's tits don't think you have the right to question your father and the kirk."

In the girls' room off the kitchen Becky began to wail. She was scared. Tuescher restrained Stella and Glennys from going to the crying child.

"Alam knows of your secret sins, the Aristo love you caught from your mother."

He turned his eyes back to Stella. "The Lord of Light knows your blood is tainted. If it were clean your boychildren would live and your girl wouldn't have her head full of Aristo heathen ways and you wouldn't have fallen into the sin of despair."

Stella's tears continued to flow as she rocked back and forth on the hard, wooden chair. "Look at me, woman, when I talk to you. Stop that caterwauling now!"

Glennys's lips curled away from her teeth. The tendons in her neck swelled, just like Tuescher's. "You're a bully. You hate Aristos because they're richer and stronger than you are so you pick on my mother instead. It's not fair to pick on somebody who can't fight back!"

"It's for her family's own good!" Tuescher backhanded Glennys across her face, blackening the other eye.

He said solemnly, "You're a horse-lover. You must be saved. Tomorrow your kirk will save you."

After Alaminite authority took its leave, Glennys's father lifted his head. Her mother remained on the chair. She didn't make a move to pick up the mugs and plates that had been set out for the men, just as she no longer took any interest in selling her eggs, or working with needles and thread.

"Stella, why didn't you obey me? If men think there's witchery about it's not the place of the weak vessel to tell them nay. Why didn't you join all of us at the witch burning? Now the congregation thinks I'm a sorry husband, a weak man who can't control his wife."

In a sudden fury her father swept all the crockery off the table. "Look at this house. Nothing is the way a decent Alaminite home should be. Those brats cry and want something every minute. That girl should be at home instead of at that school all day stuffing herself with Aristo heathen ways, just like you did.''

He glared at Glennys. ''Nothing's what it was ever since that devil horse showed up last summer. It was your fault that horse came here. You court temptation. Before, even though your mother didn't give me sons to help in the fields, at least she kept my house in order and brought in cash money. Now she don't do nothin' but sit around and bawl like a weaned calf all day. If she'd gone to the burnin' and got cleansed she'd have got better instead of worse.''

Glennys began to clear up the mess on the floor. Her mother's blue milk jug, the one Stella had had since she was a little girl, was broken. Glennys washed Becky, who had soiled herself. Her mother kept rocking back and forth on her chair. Glennys made some porridge for all of them. Her father sat muttering in the parlor and drank what was left in the beer jar.

Glennys put the slops from the parlor with the scraps from the scanty supper she'd made. She threw them to the sleepy chickens who hadn't been fed or watered. It was a relief to be out of the house, taking care of the animals.

Her mother was sharp and impatient, quick to chide and quick to enforce her chidings with a blow. But Glennys couldn't hate her as she hated her father. If he'd been sick, the household would have continued smoothly. Even heavy in pregnancy her mother had worked in the house, the fields, the barn, the garden. She brought in cash from selling her eggs, from her needlework, from her spinning. If she hardly ever stopped talking at Glennys about working more, working harder, well, no one worked as much and as hard as she did. Glennys didn't want to be like her mother. But she respected her more than anyone else in the world. Her mother could fix anything that was broken. She was very good, like Glennys could never be.

Just before noon the next day, Dephi's congregation was gathered at the crossroads east of the village. The southern turn led to the Baron's seat of Three Trees. The west road led to Dephi, through congregational Soudaka and the Badlands. The north road would eventually take a traveller to the icy nation of Andacac.

Glennys could barely walk, her anger was so strong. Her father had finally beat her last night, after finishing the beer. Her body, feverish from the beating and her rage, welcomed the chilly wind whipping from the sea far to the north. Her mother trembled, her face a white set mask. She did whatever she was told, said what she was told to say. She said it over and over again.

"Forgive me, please forgive me."

The Elders' Council distributed sticks to the congregation. Even her classmates, too young to take the sacraments, had sticks.

Reverend Tuescher gave Stella a large, round stone. The one Glennys had to carry was smaller.

"These stones are the burdens of your sins. Hold and touch what will drag you down to the devil, if you don't repent and mend your ways. Carry your stones to the kirk. If you stumble, hesitate, or fall, your congregation will strike you to your feet."

She saw the Schoolmaster standing next to Hengst. Muran held the reins to Smoky's bit in his fingers. Shame flooded through her. The people she wanted to like her saw her being punished.

Stella fell often over the road marked by three milestones. Glennys, healthier and younger, stayed on her feet. She was afraid if she fell she'd attack whoever struck her. That would be a dangerous thing to do. They were there to be punished, to be shamed. The congregation wasn't going to kill them, not today.

"It's a hard road we must walk to arrive at Alam's House and be received in loving-kindness," Reverend Tuescher preached in front of the kirk. This ordeal wasn't yet complete. Now they had to go inside.

In the nave at the front of the gathered congregation, Stella again had to beg forgiveness for setting her will against theirs, for separating herself. She kissed all the sticks and thanked those who had chastised her. Reverend Tuescher then gave her the sacraments. Glennys, too young to receive them, watched on her knees from the stone floor.

Reverend Tuescher preached one of his interminable sermons. "This woman standing before us today refused to attend the witch's release from the devil. She kept her daughters at home. She said we were the ones who'd done sin. She said such a thing wasn't fit for children to see.''

He enumerated Stella's pregnancies. He named each dead infant. As the names were called off, Stella wailed. He complained that her daughters lived and were healthy, appropriating the substance of the husband, stealing it from the sons that were rightfully his to have. He spoke of the sinister significance of an Eidel stallion appearing in her backyard.

''The devil didn't show himself in our yard, but in hers, a place open to it because her oldest daughter has allowed herself, through her own perverted desire, to be witched by the horse's glamor.''

He went on repeating what was heard in many Sabbath sermons, what was in all the kirk books: women are weak; women pollute the Light; women tend toward bestiality; women lose distinction between the beasts and the noble being, man, created in Alam's own image.

The congregation swayed in rhythm to Tuescher's measured statements and declarations. They gave response in unison and canon. The words dug into Glennys's mind like a pitchfork that separated the dirty straw from the clean. She clung to the image of the stallion who had emerged out of the lilacs last summer, held on to it as the congregation chanted the words that also appeared, carved in stone, above the altar: ''The horse and his rider the Lord of Light shall cast into the burning pit.''

Her mother was a good woman. She didn't gossip or dress wantonly. She worked hard. Animals bore well for her, showing Alam's favor. The horse and rider hadn't been thrown into the pit. . . .

When the ordeal finally was over, the congregation scattered to the Coach Inn and each other's houses to talk over the great doings of the day. Stella lay on the stone floor. Glennys sat next to her. Her father was not to be seen. Glennys could not think how she was to get to the farm, harness the oxen to the wagon, and come back for her mother. There was no one to care for them, and her father wasn't doing it.

She moved her mother's head into her lap, and cradled it. Down the front of her dirty clothes she could see her own breasts. She could see her mother's too. She hated breasts, she hated everything.

When the kirk doors opened, two figures stood before her in a swirl of frigid air. It had gotten dark outside. She was too stiff and sore to talk or move. One of the figures lit candles. It was Hengst. He held his candle high and moved it about.

"What an awful place a kirk is." His voice bounced off the stone walls and the stone floor and got lost against the wooden roof.

Muran wrapped Glennys and her mother in blankets. He looked into Glennys's eyes, blazing in the reflection of the candlelight. "You really ran into it this time," he said. Wisely, he said nothing else. He helped them out of the kirk and into the back of a pony cart.

Hengst shook a leather-bound bottle. "My father won't mind this use of his brandy. He's going to hear about this when he comes home for St. Lucien's Eve. There'll be someone in this town who's going to be sorry. Did they really burn somebody? I wish the First Horses, the ones ridden by the Stallion Queens, really existed. I'd turn them loose on Dephi and on that Tuescher and the Elders and see how they liked that!"

Muran hushed the boy. "Responding to ignorance on its own terms makes you just like them. But your father does have to hear about this and about the poor woman who was burned. This is a symptom of rebellion on Nolan's border. Our job is to check that and tell your father as quickly as possible. Public punishments of any kind, for any reason, are the prerogative of the throne, which in Soudaka means your father and no one else."

Glennys's youthful resilience responded to Muran's ministrations. It was such a relief to have someone who wanted to protect her from the kirk. She choked from the fumes of the first spirits she'd ever touched.

Glennys said bitterly, "Thank you." She couldn't help it, she had to say it out loud now. "I hate him. I hate my father. He wanted Reverend Tuescher to do this. He should be taking care of my mother, not leaving it for others to do. Even the congregation said she was clean now. They gave her the sacraments."

Muran didn't know but he guessed. "Your father's probably too ashamed."

Stella shifted in her blankets. Her voice was weak, barely audible, but Glennys heard it. "He should have been here."

Glennys began to cry. It was the first time Muran had ever seen her do that. "I wish you and Hengst hadn't seen us. What can I do?"

"I don't know. I wish I could do something more than drive you home. It takes a lot of money to get along in this world—money and important friends. And I have neither."

Hengst said, "You can come and live with me."

Muran smiled in the darkness. As he moved the cart over to the side of the road to give right of way to the Post Stage that ran from Old Nolan, he continued to smile. He could write a good letter, and he knew how to get it delivered. He'd have to pay for it, but he was eager to gamble his postage money.

# THREE

Glennys wasn't expecting any gifts on the night before her eleventh birthday. It was as though carrying the heavy stone to the kirk door had relieved her mother of a burden. Stella had become herself again. But her father hadn't gotten over what had happened in his family. These days, when the fields no longer demanded sunup to sundown labor, her father spent most of his time drinking with the Coals of the Lord in the public room of the Coach Inn. He wasn't home tonight either. That was gift enough for Glennys.

Tonight was the night of Alam's Fire, the celebration of the great battle against the devil and the dark. At Harvest Gatherin, Dephi's congregation had started to prepare for the Great Night. In Nolan this night was known as St. Lucien's Eve, the most uncommon of Nolan's Days and Nights. The school possessed a volume called the *Book of Uncommon Days*, each holiday illustrated by a woodcut and a caption underneath. Glennys always thrilled to read the one under St. Lucien's Eve:

> *Lady Eve brought the Stallion Queens before the gates of St. Lucien City. They danced with their horses on the ice of River Setham. The horses were given ale, to make them wild and fiery for the Dance. That night none could think of other than horses and swords. In their Dance they took St. Lucien City and made the country all their own.*

Glennys had finished doing the barn chores. The cattle, sheep, and pigs were munching their extra rations given in honor of the Great Night. They were content now that they'd excreted into the new straw.

Before working in the barn, she'd been baking with Stella. Her nose wrinkled at the whiffs she caught of herself, an odd combination of pumpkin pie and pig shit. She stared out the barn door to the west.

Her work done, she had a few moments to herself. She dropped easily into her dream. She ran with a herd of wild, fierce horses that her fantasy shaped out of the cloud bank on the western horizon. She hadn't decided if this time she was the stallion himself, or if she was the one possessing him.

A long blue shadow crept towards her feet. A horse and rider approached across the west field. It was a stallion, carrying a man dressed in black fur. Hengst had described his father's favorite mount to her. The stallion had to be Deadly, and the man with weapons bristling about his body had to be Baron Fulk. Her heart almost stopped beating.

The chill of her feet, standing on the frozen barnyard runoff, was forgotten as she felt the heat that rose from Deadly's body. He lipped the corn she pulled out of her pocket. His breath seared the stiff fingers poking out of her mitts. He snorted, pawed the ice. One of his front hooves, shod with heavy, rough-filed plates, struck out against the stone water trough. Sparks flew when steel hit stone.

"I've never seen anything like you before," she murmured to the black head that was longer than her own arm. Deadly's coat was as without sheen as charcoal. He was cobby in the body, his hindquarters as high as his shoulders and almost as heavily muscled. The twitch of his body under fur and leather put his forehand muscles flickering in sharp definition to each other. His mane was roached, the hairs stiff as the wire teeth in a wool carding comb. His neck, though thick like the rest of his conformation, arched in a sinuous curve, his nose almost touching his chest.

He wasn't beautiful in the elegant, slender manner of a racing stud. He was built for power and dexterity in equal measure. He was a horse that went to war.

After the stallion accepted the grain, Glennys looked at the man on Deadly's back and said, "You're Hengst's father—aren't you?"

The Baron laughed. "So his mother told me."

"Hengst said it takes a thousand years to get a horse like Deadly."

The Baron chuckled. "It's almost true. Deadly's pedigree is longer than my sword." He pulled the long blade out of its scabbard in a smooth flourish. The sword glittered for just a moment in the last rosy chill of sunset.

He resheathed his weapon and dismounted. "It's said that on St. Lucien's Eve the animals can talk to you. That is, if you're one of those who can hear them. Is that why you're out here and not in your warm house? Are you talking to the sheep?"

"I just finished the chores."

The Baron asked, "Is your father out here too?"

"No, he's not home tonight."

The Baron grunted. "I know where he is then. Kolkiss never was smart."

Glennys wondered if the Baron was thinking of the stories her father told with relish at the supper table. The Elders permitted a local Alaminite clan, the Prochnows, to own the Coach Inn, which handled the Post Stage traffic that came out of Old Nolan. They paid a triple tithe to the kirk because the Coach serviced the horse teams there. Whenever the Baron brought soldiers to Soudaka, some were quartered at the Coach. The congregation always resented their presence with unconcealed hostility. Many of those the Baron had with him this winter were new to their business, horses and men alike. The horses weren't always as well secured as they should have been. It seemed that some had wandered off and when they'd been found, they were dead. Though it looked as if wild dogs had been responsible, Glennys's father had hinted he knew better.

The Baron picked up the lantern she'd been using and led Deadly into the barn. "Let the Coals of the Lord have the Coach to themselves tonight. All of my men are at Three Trees. Alam's Fire for the Lighters, the Dance for us!"

He draped the oversaddle fur on the stallion's neck. Casually, he said, "I would punish the men who shamed my wife and daughter. I wouldn't collaborate with them."

Glennys, partly gratified, partly ashamed at what he said, was sure again that the only man she hated more than Reverend Tuescher was her father.

The Baron shut the barn door, damming off the currents of frigid air to a curling trickle. The pigs looked up curiously; the sheep looked stupidly; the cattle patiently. The cats, cautiously, came to investigate this strange thing, a horse inside a Lighter barn. The two humans stood still in a narrow pool of light.

The Baron looked at Glennys for a long time. Her eyes soon sidled away from his to stare at the war stallion. His tail was getting shaggy, growing out of the short campaign clip. She was about to go to the horse, even though she knew the Baron expected her to remain still when he put down the lantern and took off his gauntlets.

He pulled the scarf from Glennys's hair. He undid her coat and pushed it down around her shoulders. He held up the lantern over her head while taking her jaw in his other hand. When her neck was at an angle under the light that pleased him, he gathered the fine, tattered locks of her hair in his hand. He pulled until she felt a tugging at the corners of her eyes.

Her stomach muscles tightened at the feel of the Baron's hands on her, so different from those of others who'd handled her. He stepped back and said, "Take off your boots and coat and pull up your skirts." When she obeyed him, he walked with the lantern to another part of the barn. She was in the dark, her eyes riveted to the light trickling through the lantern's fireguard. She could feel the fresh straw she'd put down for Alam's Fire pricking against the skin of her calves. She wasn't at all cold, though she should have been.

He returned with a fleece and told her to stand on it. He felt the muscles along her calves. He lifted one of her legs and rotated the knee gently, then did the same with the other leg. He pulled the stockings from her feet. Pushing and pulling at her ankles, he arranged her feet several inches apart, toes pointed slightly away from each other. She straightened her back and tensed her buttocks involuntarily, which slightly shifted her weight and balance. The Baron slapped her across both cheeks through the layers of chemise decently covering her private parts.

"Good. You're whole and well-made. If you'd been riding there might be more of you down here," he said. "Drop your skirts." He ran his hands down her ribs. She winced when his investigation touched the last rib on her left side.

"How did that happen?"

She was ashamed to tell him that her father had given her a beating. "Skating," she said. "It hardly hurts at all."

He squeezed her waist. "You've got more hair than flesh, I think."

He took both of her hands in one of his palms. His own hand was scaly with callouses and a scab from a nearly healed wound. He worked her fingers and palms, both together and separately. "Flexible," he said. "Let's see how sensitive."

He whistled three notes and Deadly came to stand at his shoulder. He took the reins and threaded them between her fingers. He spoke very softly. "You want Deadly to look toward the swine. Tell him to do it with your fingers."

She chirped at the horse. A slight tremor ran from her forearm to her wrists to the tips of her fingers. It didn't go far enough. Deadly twitched his ears at her, wary, but willing. The leather reins shivered again and the horse turned his head after a feather touch reached the metal in his mouth. He didn't like the smell of pig.

The barn was dark, except around the lantern. There wasn't enough light to see different colors, only tones of grey and white. For a breath Glennys saw the white patches on the pigs glow brilliantly from a point of view that wasn't hers. She sneezed at the swine's strong odor. Deadly turned his head from them and she saw him with her own eyes.

The Baron took the reins away and looked at her hands

once more. "Very good. And I don't think you hurt yourself skating on the Shoatkill Crick."

He kissed both her hands and her entire body leaped.

"You must learn to accept courtesy, Glennys."

He pulled a piece of pie dough out of the tangle of her hair. "No doubt Stella's had you baking and roasting. Let's eat what you've made, in honor of the war horse."

He picked up the lantern and he picked up Glennys as well. She was glad he remembered to shut the barn door behind them as they left.

In the kitchen, Stella said, "Are you alone, Sir Fulk?"

"Certainly. The day I can't travel without a guard in Soudaka is the day I'd better turn over the Barony to Stogar. I couldn't bring Hengst along on this little expedition. If I hadn't found what I was looking for he'd have been too disappointed," the Baron said, with a nod toward Glennys.

Stella spared a glance of disapproval for her daughter. "Go clean yourself. There's hot water on the kitchen hearth. Put on your new dress and brush your hair clean and straight. Tie it back with the red ribbon. This way, Fulk. Come into the parlor."

Glennys was astonished. Stella was looking at the Baron out of the corner of one eye while she curtsied, and she was smiling in a way that Glennys had never seen her mother smile. It was almost as though the Baron were a friend. Sometimes she visited with the Bohn wives—Elder Bohn had more wives than anybody, thought Glennys—but it was always formal, not just running in and out, like some of the women did. Outside of this house, her mother didn't have even a relative of her own, only the Kolkiss kin. The idea of her mother having a friend of her own, and one that wasn't only a man, but a Nolanese Aristo, startled Glennys so much that for a moment she forgot there was a horse in the barn.

That evening the parlor was a cheerful room. It was like Stella to arrange something nice for a special occasion, but this looked as though she'd expected company. A table was laid at one side of the fireplace, where an expensive coal was burning hot and clean in holiday splendor. Her mother must have set the fire and laid the table while Glennys was out doing chores. Debbie and Becky, both dressed in their new winter dresses, investigated Fulk in much the same way as the cats had stepped and sniffed around Deadly's hooves.

The Baron, divested of his outdoor clothes and most of his weapons, seemed smaller and not at all the presence he'd been in the barn. The front of his scalp was innocent of hair, but on the back of his head the hair cascaded, thick and curling, past his shoulders.

Fulk asked Stella, "Do you still have bruises from the Lighter rods?"

Stella held a firescreen before her face—almost as though it were a fan. "Some bruises last a whole life long, Baron, even if you can't see them."

The Baron was standing in front of the embroidery. He scooped Rebecca into his arms and tossed her gently. She was delighted, not frightened. He put her down and touched the embroidery in its center with a big, prominently veined finger. "I seem to remember this from when you were younger, but it was a little different then." This time he took Debbie into his arms. She was older, already full of matronly dignity, so he didn't toss her. He looked carefully into her face, and then back at Glennys standing in the doorway. He gave her another quick nod, as though they shared something the others didn't.

"Stella," he said, "how did you come to have a daughter with nothing of Lighter ways about her?"

"Only Alam, Lord of Light, can answer that, Sir Fulk. I shan't try."

"Or you won't. You could be more stubborn than a whole team of mules when it suited you. You haven't changed in that respect."

"You think I've changed then?" she said with composure.

He touched Glennys's hair. Though still damp, with the lines of her hairbrush running through it, it was much lighter than that of her sisters. He tugged on the red ribbon that pulled it out of her face.

"A woman who has children isn't the same as she was before, everyone knows that," he said. "Why did you run back to this forsaken county, Stella? Even though my wife was dead there could have been a place for you in my sister-in-law's townhouse. Abigail appreciated your skills with the needle."

Stella busied herself with the cask of Fire Ale, specially brewed for this night. She said easily, "The Light called me back. The strength of my 'forsaken' land, as you call it, can be ignored but not denied. You make use of it yourself, to make strong horses that die for Old Nolan. The rider and horse can stumble and fall, but a man in the hand of Alam has a support that's greater than Kings or horses. Aristos, who have only chance and luck to believe in, can't understand this."

"You haven't changed in that respect," said the Baron. "You're still as stubborn about that religion of yours as you ever were."

Stella poured out three bumpers of ale, and two smaller cups for the little ones. "My father was dying when I came back. I was needed here." She indicated that Glennys should take one of the mugs of ale to the Baron before drinking her own. Glennys felt shy, awkward, as she hadn't in the barn, among this adult business.

The Baron said, "So how long did it take before Kolkiss lost the cooperage business after your father wasn't around to run it anymore?"

"Not long," Glennys's mother said shortly. "Alam be thanked, there was still the farm. The Lord knows that I'll never let this place go. I'll give the last breath in my body, and that of my children, to keep my farm."

It was as though her mother spoke a foreign language. Why would anyone want to stay on a Lighter farm when she could have lived in Nolan, where there are horses wherever you look, Glennys wondered.

"Come sit down, Baron," Stella invited.

He winked at Glennys over the rim of his mug. He pulled some papers out of his pocket and dropped them on Stella's plate.

"Yes," she said in a businesslike manner. "The reason you've joined us in our holiday cheer."

Fulk grinned. "Oh, yes indeed. Everything they said about her is true. I'm your Eve guest and I have the first toast. We drink this to my son Hengst, my Stablemaster Powell, and the Schoolmaster Muran. They found me a Horsegirl in the heart of Alam's country. Someone born and bred right here, like

Powell, to take over when the time comes. Drink up, Glennys. You're coming to Three Trees' stables where you belong.''

This was some grown-up game, she thought. They were fooling her. But Stella said, ''The congregation will forbid it.'' The expression on her face was the same as when she bargained to get a better offer for her eggs or her sewing. She was looking over the papers very carefully.

My mother knows how to read and write, Glennys thought with pride.

''There's another hurdle to get over, Baron,'' Stella said. ''My husband will object to losing her labor. He'll want a larger price than a waiver of apprentice fee to agree.''

The Baron gestured expansively over his plate. For some reason that Glennys couldn't fathom in the least, he was enjoying this very much. ''War, my dear lady, is a complicated and expensive thing. But war also makes some things easy when you act in the King's name. Too many Lighters are trying the same old tricks again, trying to make the Alaminites' Council of Elders the masters of Soudaka. So I'm going to have to conscript some members of this community. It'll be just like cutting the balls off a stallion. There'll be no more trouble after that. A list of names is being put together for me out of the congregations. I'll be bloody surprised if Kolkiss isn't on it. If he's not, I'll put him there.''

If Stella was startled to hear this, she kept it to herself. She paused a moment, then said, ''This puts a different face on things, Baron. Under the circumstances perhaps Glennys should stay here with me.''

''Hengst wants her. My daughter, Thurlow, has been complaining for weeks that she's going to die of loneliness on Three Trees. Your girl's strong in mind and body. It'll be good for Thurlow to have someone about who's younger than she but able to stand up to her—attitude. Powell wants an apprentice and your girl *wants* to come. Ask her.''

Stella said, ''Well, Glennys do you want to go and shovel shit at Three Trees when you could do it right here?''

The night was full of shocks. She'd never heard her mother use that word, ever. She blurted, ''But—it would be horse shit!''

''See, Stella?'' laughed the Baron, highly pleased with himself. ''She wants to go.''

"If she's going to be your children's companion as well as a paid hand, she should have more than this." Stella slapped the papers.

"I've already waived the apprentice fee. I'll give her a quarterly wage like any other hand, increasing as her skills increase. I'll hand it directly over to you," he said slyly.

"A companion for your own flesh and blood, Baron? Shouldn't she get more? Aristos always think a little cash covers everything. I remember what fine young ladies are like."

"She can work with the Dancemaster. She can study with Muran." He held up a hand to forestall what Stella was going to say. "Muran's going to tutor Hengst and Thurlow. He's eager, very eager. He's also willing to take on liaison secretary duties here between Three Trees and Sace-Cothberg, where I'm going."

"Then you're getting a tutor, a governess, and a secretary all for the price of one. You can afford to increase Glennys's wages. Not only does my farm lose her hands, but my husband's hands as well. It's too big to run alone," Stella declared.

"All right! Stop nagging! I'll give you enough to hire someone." The Baron charred a splinter of wood from the kindling basket. He wrote a number on the back side of one of the contract papers Stella was looking at. "Will that be acceptable?" he asked.

"Done, Sir Fulk," she said and kissed his hand. She got up from the table to get a pen and ink. "I want this on the contract in ink, and written out properly," she said.

So Glennys was apprenticed to Three Trees' Stablemaster for five years. Just like that. She was stunned. Stella had been planning this already and she'd never guessed. How well her mother could keep secrets. And her mother didn't seem at all sorry that Pa was going to be taken away. Well, Glennys wasn't sorry either.

# FOUR

Outside the kitchen, Stella hugged Glennys hard while the Baron lashed her bundle of clothes and sewing kit on Deadly's hindquarters. Fulk mounted, and pulled the girl up behind him. Stella took hold of Glennys's foot.

"You work hard and you do what you're told."

Fulk interrupted her. "If Kolkiss tries to punish you because Glennys is at Three Trees, tell him this. There hasn't been a horse execution in Soudaka since my grandfather's day. But we're still allowed to cut off his nuts. In the name of the Eidel Kings, I can do it myself."

Stella said, "When Glennys sees what the world of the Horsegirl is, she may wish to leave you, Baron. She's allowed to come back to her mother. That's the bargain I made with her."

The Baron gave Deadly the slightest touch of spur. The stallion leaped over the snow. The Baron's words came back to where they'd been. "There's nothing that will send your firstborn back to a Lighter farm!"

The weather had turned while they'd been inside. Hanging on tightly to the Baron, Glennys began to feel hot in her winter clothes. The wind had stilled. She leaned back and looked up at the stars. She gloated over the swiftness with which the world behind her receded. A cloud bank, low and heavy, massed in the north. She knew what that forecast. So did the Baron.

"A blizzard's getting ready to take Soudaka. It will hold off some hours yet." He spoke as though the weather obeyed his commands.

The man settled into the ride. It was clear that Glennys wasn't to disturb his thoughts. She was a piece of business that, now concluded, was forgotten. He was excited, but she knew it had nothing to do with her. His detachment made the ride an even greater enchantment, as though she'd entered one of the tales out of *The Chronicle Book*.

The old stories were alive on the grounds of Three Trees. Regimental standards and family pennants were planted in the hard earth. The colors on the horses' harness and in the jewels worn by the men reflected the snap and glow of the fires. The numbers of men and horses made Glennys understand that the estate had been deserted when she'd been here last summer.

The Baron swung out of Deadly's saddle and disappeared. She was glad to see Hengst's familiar face, even though he was showing off in unfamiliar regalia of spurred boots, sword, and baldric. He picked Glennys up and swung her around and then lunged for Deadly's reins. The stallion squealed.

"I said you should come and live here, and here you are!"

She felt like an outsider, despite all the horses around.

"Drink some of this so you don't get cold. I got some of Dad's brandy."

It was the second time she had tasted brandy.

"Stogar's in St. Lucien buying stuff for the Sace-Cothberg campaign, so I'm Dad's esquire while he's home. You want to help me give Deadly his corn and ale and get him ready for the Dance? I hate this part of the job. He wants to fight all the time. Stogar hates him. Except for Dad, the only other person Deadly likes is Powell."

Glennys put some brandy on her fingers so Deadly could lick it off.

Hengst pursed his lips. He said, "*You* can take his reins then. I'm warning you though, he *likes* to kick people in the head."

At that moment the Stablemaster appeared. He took Glennys's things and threw them to someone he called Cook. She was startled to see how much Powell looked like the Baron. His voice growled in the same timbre as Fulk's.

"Get away from your father's horse, boy, since you can't be calm around him. Deadly's got hard work ahead. You and the girl get out of here. There's nothing for you to do tonight except stay out of the way."

Hengst jerked his chin to his collarbone. "Yes, sir!" He grabbed Glennys's hand and pulled her away from Long Stable, out across the exercise yard. He whispered, "Powell's Dad's bastard half-Alaminite brother. He gets rough sometimes now that Dad's back on the place."

• • •

On the dance ground they were surrounded by men and horses who were eating and drinking. Other men warmed up their sword arms and their horses' muscles. In the big compound that included the stables and the exercise yard, great bonfires burned. Glennys's Alaminite-instilled frugality was impressed by the huge amount of wood heaped over the Badlands' coal. Carcasses of pigs, deer, and sheep were spitted through. At smaller fires rabbits, poultry, and pheasants roasted. Packs of sight hounds raced through the crowd, tangled in knots of mock battle and others that were real.

A big horse jostled Glennys and she absentmindedly patted its flank. She stepped back from a friendly retriever hound. Hengst said, "See, he just wants someone to pull his ears. I'd forgotten you Alaminites don't like dogs."

Hengst gave the golden-haired dog a push with his foot. Grinning foolishly, the dog rolled on his back, all four legs in the air.

"*I'm* not a bloody Lighter," Glennys said, carefully scratching the hound's golden belly.

Drums rolled. Fifes wailed high and sweet. Hengst caught his breath. "It's starting. Let's get a good place to watch."

Barechested men and barebacked horses circled the compound where all the snow had been cleared away. Four lines of four men each began to ride across the exercise yard in the *pas de quatre*. The horses led from the right foreleg in unison. They turned like wheels around the pivot of their hindquarters. The figure opened to quarter the yard when the horses changed lead to the left fore. Glennys thought she'd die. She'd never seen anything so perfect. The horses performed an extended trot, their legs pausing just before touching hoof to earth. The point of shoulder, knee, fetlock, all the horse's joints moved in precision—each horse in unison with the others. They moved so smoothly that they seemed to float and not touch the ground at all.

The men who circled the yard had their horses in hand. They stamped their feet and their horses stamped theirs. First the right side, then the left. Those inside the circle began a pattern that Hengst said was a "quadrille." There was a momentary silence and everyone halted. A roar went up to the sharp stars.

"For the war stallion! For Eve, the Stallion Queen! For St. Lucien, Queen of the world!"

Glennys asked, thinking of the woodcut in the *Book of Uncommon Days,* "Aren't any ladies going to dance?"

Hengst was puzzled. "Of course not. There aren't any more Stallion Queens."

A man, stripped down to leather breast shield, studded leather wrist gauntlets, finger guards, thigh pieces, and cod protector, mounted his stallion. The man was well-oiled with bear fat against the cold. The horse and rider made a running leap over the shifting circle of men with horses in hand. He stood on the back of his horse in the center of the yard, his blade naked and rampant.

"That's Wildan, Assistant First Rider, and Dad's aide. Dad's always First Rider," Hengst informed her.

Wildan sang, *"Where is the man who dares bid me stand?"*

Another horse and rider leaped into the center and answered the challenge. *"I am the man who bids you stand."*

The rest of the company gave its response:

> *Now throw your good sword bare*
> *And wave the blade high in the air*
> *Aim your strokes well when you fight*
> *Some man or beast will bleed tonight.*

All of them pulled out their blades. Their scabbards and baldrics dropped to the ground one by one smoothly, like the ripples that flowed through a length of silk when it was shaken. The horses bent their front knees, putting their heads to the ground, and the men leaped to their backs. The music began and the horses charged for the center.

The men fenced with each other. They tossed themselves over their horses. They were never all on the ground or all mounted at the same moment. They jumped head over heels, twisting their bodies while at the apex of the leap. If they landed on the ground they fenced with another man on the ground. If they landed on the back of a sweating stallion, the horse feinted with another stallion, using its front legs.

Glennys stamped her feet and picked up the responses with her voice. Her face was greasy from eating hunks of meat. Hengst kept offering her his flask of brandy. The strange words that Wildan called out, *courbette, curvet, passade, pirouette, levade,* began to be legible, as though the movements were formed in letters on a page.

The patterned repetition knitted the senses of her body with those of the horse. The noise, the heat, the strong aroma of sweat and piss, opened something in her that had always been shut, except during moments of anger or daydreaming. She could hear, see, and smell by herself or with the horses. Sometimes she thought she would gag. There were so many layers and currents of smell that there was no room for her to breathe. Then a new development in the yard would make the gagging pass.

A voice hammered through the smoke.

> *The King of Three Trees comes*
> *The King of Three Trees I!*
> *Is there a knight who bids me fight,*
> *Is there a man who dares to stand,*
> *Who dares to challenge ME?*

Deadly and the Baron vaulted through the shifting pattern.

The men formed two groups on a diagonal. All on horseback, Wildan's and Fulk's divisions rode into patterns of stars, squares, and triangles. The men held their blades horizontal to the ground. The men in Fulk's division braided their swords into a locked rose around Fulk and Deadly. A man from Wildan's side rode his horse to the locked rose, leaped to the platform, and thrust his sword at Fulk. Fulk beat with the flat of his blade at each challenger. He bellowed out the same lines, as each of them was thrown off the locked rose.

> *Don't lay the blame on me*
> *You awful villains all.*
> *I'm sure mine eyes were shut*
> *When this man did fall.*

The smell of blood began to mix with the other odors. There was a lot of blood, blood from shallow cuts and slashes, blood from men, and blood from horses. The wilder the Dance became, the more aggressively the riders and horses slammed into each other, broke and bled. There was no silken, graceful precision about them now.

A stallion, his chestnut coat heavily lathered, drew Glennys's attention. He and his rider were in hot pursuit of Fulk and Deadly. Time and time again they were forced away from the inner circle of dancers. They'd pull themselves around and try again. The chestnut stallion's will to pound Deadly into the ground was hard as a rock.

The wind had returned, bending the bonfires in streamers to the south. A sudden slap of sleet obscured the Dance. A veering gust tore the sleet shield away. The chestnut challenger stallion was on the ground. Blood poured out of the gash in his belly.

Everyone stopped, except Fulk. Quickly, he jumped from Deadly's back and cut the fallen stallion's throat. The Dance was finished.

Hengst pinched Glennys's arm. "Gordon's Luck! The first real Sword Dance done on Three Trees in my father's time and my brother, the heir, didn't get to see it! This is how the real thing is supposed to end, a lucky accident. The stallion's tail will be part of the regimental standard. All of us have to taste his blood now to honor him."

The first stinging blows of snow buffeted the men as they cooled out their horses, saw to their hurts, rubbed them down, fed them. It took a long time and was hard to do because it was so cold now. Powell led a mare through the central passage of Long Stable. Hengst told Glennys, "She's in season even though the daylight hours are so short. Another good piece of luck. Powell's taking her to Deadly. If she catches, it will be Great Luck for Three Trees."

"Catches?" asked Glennys.

"Gets in foal," said Hengst. Glennys followed Powell. She wanted to see this.

Another chestnut stallion, still lathering though combat was over, trumpeted a challenge for the mare. Fulk smashed the chestnut's rider on the side of his jaw. "You know better than to bring him to this end of the stable. Get out of here. She belongs to Deadly."

The Baron reached out one of his broad, long-fingered hands that seemed too big for his narrow frame. He pulled over the woman who had been walking with the challenger's rider. "Come with me."

Someone urged Glennys away from the circle surrounding Fulk, the woman, Deadly, and the mare. It was a girl dressed in a cloud of white fur. She seemed out of place. She led Glennys over to Hengst, who was standing with Muran and another man, who was short and old. Vaguely, Glennys recollected seeing him direct the drum and fife players.

The girl said, "Our father's crude as a stallion himself, keeping up that old custom."

Hengst responded mildly, as though he'd long ago learned the futility of argument with her. "What he is, is a *man.*"

"Much you know about it, little brother," said Thurlow.

The old man was Rampalli, the Dancemaster. He made an intricate bow, ludicrous in a stable, especially with the sounds coming from the other end. He began to lecture in learned tones.

"To the best Sword Dancer traditionally go all the spoils. In the ancient days of your people the Stallion Queen would accept him into her bed and hope for a girl child."

"These aren't the ancient days, however," Thurlow returned.

Glennys's blue eyes turned in wonder towards this girl, who was different from anyone she'd ever seen. "You're lucky to have a father like him."

Thurlow's dark hair was tucked neatly under her fur cap, except for curling escapees on her brow and cheeks. Her big violet eyes looked over Glennys. "You think so? He's your Baron. I'd have thought you'd hate him. He'll bed anything. He'd even take you if there weren't anything better at hand."

"Me? I'm too young!"

Thurlow looked at Glennys's dress, which had torn across her chest sometime during the Dance. One breast was nearly exposed. Glennys felt frozen and wondered what had happened to her cloak. If it were lost her mother would be very angry. It had just been made.

Thurlow smiled sweetly and said, "I don't think so." She waved her hand and asked the surrounding air, "Where is this, this—Horsegirl—going to sleep?"

"My room's big enough for two," grinned Hengst.

Thurlow giggled. "I don't think so. *You're* too young."

"I am not. I mean—that's not what I meant. This isn't St. Lucien and Glennys isn't like one of those silly girls you giggled with in Aunt Abigail's house. Gordon's Balls! No wonder our Dad decided to take you out of the city until he finds someone to marry you. You're as low as a bitch crawling in heat."

Muran intervened. He had more color in his face than Glennys had ever seen there. His eyes sparkled. There was a blur of red across one cuff. He must have tasted the stallion's blood too.

"Glennys is Powell's apprentice. Like Powell, she sleeps up at the Big House. Glennys is going to have her mother's old room, the one off the Lady's chamber, where you sleep, Thurlow."

"He's certainly made himself at home here, hasn't he?" Thurlow observed, as Muran went off muttering about Cook and fires built in cold rooms.

Glennys waded with Hengst and Thurlow through the blizzard to the Big House. On the wide porch, while the snow roared about them, Thurlow kissed Glennys on the cheek. There was a fragrance about the girl in white fur that was foreign and pleasant.

She whispered to Glennys, "We'd better be friends. There're no other girls here for us to talk to. And I'm almost as new to this place as you are."

In the small, warm room where Glennys tried to sleep, her mind dashed about in confusion. The stables outside were filled with flesh and blood horses. It was impossible for her to create the visionary herds that had been her bedtime companions for all her life. She tried to sort out the horses she'd seen tonight. Thurlow's face and those of other people kept getting in the way of her memories of the stallions and the Baron in the Sword Dance.

Nolanese people and ways were harder to understand than horses. Were stallions like those in the Dance really going to be her work? She missed her mother only a little.

It was storming in the pre-dawn of the first day of her eleventh year. Glennys felt a twinge of apprehension. Maybe getting what she'd always wanted might not be what she'd imagined. The apprehension evaporated like the first tiny flake of snow. She descended into a dream where she was the rider that Deadly obeyed and the Baron said she was the best girl in the world.

# FIVE

"I'm not supposed to do *this!* I'm a Horsegirl!"

Glennys's fingers were scraped raw from scrubbing heavy kettles and skillets in the cold, greasy water. Cook had dragooned her that afternoon when she'd emerged into the kitchen from the cellar tunnel that connected the Big House to the outdoors.

Glennys's understanding of Three Trees' layout wasn't instinctive yet and she had to think about what she was doing all the time. It was dangerous going in the blizzard, keeping a grip on the guideropes, and pushing back against the wind. Guideropes that kept people from getting lost in a snowstorm were something she'd grown up with. But here everything was farther away and there were more places to go than on her mother's farm. Blue ropes took you to the King's Stable; red ropes to Long Stable where the war horses were; green led to the brood mares' stable. Orange went to the barn housing the work horses, the ponies, the mules, and the oxen. Black ropes went to the stablehands' barracks and the cottages of Three Trees' staff. If Glennys hadn't been numb from hard work and trying to remember it all, she would have resisted the Cook.

Glennys had taken comfort in the fact that even though Powell had put her to work in the barn, it was with the draft horses and ponies, not the cattle or the mules. The House staff took care of the poultry coops. That Cook had conscripted her for the kitchen added insult to the injury done her pride when she'd found herself working in a barn, not a stable.

"It's not fair!" Hengst got to work in Long Stable where Deadly was.

But working with any kind of horse was better than this foul task. If her fingers got bruised carrying buckets of icy water to the ponies, scratched from pitching forks of hay to the draft horses, well, that was to be expected. That was what she was *supposed* to do, not clean up after people. She might as well still be on the farm with her father.

Glennys wasn't the only one in a vile state of mind that afternoon of the blizzard's second day. The storm had prevented the men from getting back to their quarters at the Coach Inn or in public houses throughout the County. The Big House strained to accommodate the hungover men, and the small staff was overworked.

Glennys chanted to herself. "I'm gonna get you, Lowell, you Cook. I'm gonna get Deadly when this blizzard's blown out. I'm gonna ride into your kitchen and ride over you, you—bloody Lighter!"

Too late Glennys realized she'd been talking out loud. Too late she remembered that Cook was sovereign in his domain and that like Powell, he was a half-Nolanese, half-Alaminite bastard. She ducked, barely in time, out of the way of the roasting grill Cook threw at her dish tub. The slimy water splashed her face, soaked her already cold, damp belly.

Cook, who was tall, long-boned, and white-haired, advanced on her. His face promised big trouble. She remembered Stella's warnings. Her mother would say her daughter should apologize and get right back to work scrubbing pots and pans.

Glennys stood there, trying to make herself say she was sorry. The pot of grey soap slipped out of her fingers. She decided to make a stand. She threw the scrub brush after the soap.

"I'm a Horsegirl. You're a Houseman. You don't do my work. I don't do yours."

She pointed to the pendulum bell clock. One of its counterparts in another part of the house bonged the hour. "It's almost time for me to go back outside for third shift stable duty. When I come back I'm not comin' back to this here dish tub."

"Horsegirl, yah? Little Horsegirls get dirty mouths out there in the mucky stables. Time you got cleaned up."

Glennys fought hard but Cook pushed her face closer and closer to the water in the dish tub.

"You ever bob for apples, Horsegirl? I'll bet a Lighter who thinks she's a Horsegirl hasn't even heard of that good old Nolanese custom, hey?"

Cook's people started to laugh.

Strands of Glennys's hair were floating on the scummy surface of the water.

"Bob me up a frying pan in your teeth, Horsegirl."

"Let her go, Cook."

Thurlow's voice curled through the hoots and hollers of the kitchen staff like a draft flowing through storm shutters. Her voice implied that Cook was engaged in nonsense he'd wish he'd never started. Glennys felt the pressure on the back of her head recede.

"It's hard, but we all have to get along." Glennys, breathing the fumes of sour water, recognized Schoolmaster Muran's quiet, determined voice, the one that made Alaminite boys pay attention even though they preferred not to. Cook's hands let go of her neck and shoulders. Glennys rubbed them, feeling a little like one of her mother's pullets spared from the pot.

"Something's out of tune in here," said Rampalli, shaking his head, sending his sparse, perfumed curls bobbing. "Let me see what I can do." He spun in a demented pirouette and took out his kit, a pocket violin, from the pouch at his belt. As the kitchen staff stood openmouthed, he played a jig while executing steps that made him look like a clownish farmer who came to Dephi four times a year. He leered at one of the women and bowed in front of her.

"That one's called 'The Lighter Country Clod.' " Don't you think I look as silly as our young Glennys over there?"

Even Glennys began to laugh as Rampalli capered over to the dish tub, miming Glennys's threshing legs and windmilling arms while his face caricatured Cook's outraged pride. But he never came close to tripping over his sword scabbard. Glennys decided that Rampalli was as far from being a fool as Deadly was from being a work horse. When Rampalli's back was to the rest of the people in the kitchen, he winked at her. So he wasn't making fun of her after all—or at least not only of her.

She'd never seen anyone among the congregations who resembled this man. She'd already learned that Rampalli wasn't a Nolanese. He came from Langano, which was over the sea. She was glad he was on her side. In a way, Rampalli reminded her of Powell. She hated to have the wicked side of Powell's tongue used on her and she'd hate it equally if

Rampalli went against her. Ruefully, she realized that Cook Lowell's job was hard. She didn't want him against her either.

Muran said, "Glennys isn't a hired hand. She's been apprenticed to Powell to learn his job. She's not available for kitchen work because she's got too much to do with the horses. So, why don't you, Lowell, and you, Glennys, shake hands and forget about this?"

The dining hall clock gonged the hour now. The Baron's men started to come through the kitchen, heading for the cellar and the tunnel and the ropes outside. It was time to take care of the horses again.

Fulk's and Powell's voices came before them, continuing the argument they had begun in the Library office and pursued through the front hall, the drawing room, the dining hall, and now the kitchen.

Powell said, "If there is grain left over you can sell it."

"That's more work for me," snapped the Baron.

Powell said bluntly, "I don't care about that. I care that the Three Trees teams don't get shorted because your men's horses ate it all. The war horses are going to have to eat a little less grain."

Powell talked back to the Baron! Glennys waited for Fulk to throw one of his outsized hands against the Stablemaster's head. But her Baron just ran his fingers through his pale-gold curls, then put on his hat.

"Well, half-brother, you live here. I don't. But Deadly's an exception and I'm going out myself to see he gets fed everything he needs."

Fulk took notice of the gathered company for the first time. "So here's where Stella's girl has got to. Get your gear, Horsegirl, and come with me. After we've taken care of Deadly we'll go to the barn with Powell and look at the teams. The storm's going to blow out tonight. Tomorrow we'll have to start clearing the roads."

Glennys ran past him to the cellar where her work clothes were. Both Fulk and Powell wrinkled their noses as she went by.

Fulk said, "Thurlow, do something about how that girl looks and smells. Make sure she's presentable by the time we ride to Dephi on Justice Day."

Thurlow narrowed her eyes but she said simply, "Certainly, Daddy."

Fulk pushed some of Thurlow's stray curls back behind the little pearls hanging from her ears. "Think you're capable of running a Big House, Thurlow? Learn all you can here because the household of the man you're going to marry is bigger than this one."

Thurlow pulled her head away from Fulk's fingers. Her hand, the one concealed from her father in her skirts, balled into a fist, the middle finger standing up.

The Library office had a modern stove, like the Queen's School, and it drew Muran and Rampalli like a magnet now that the Baron had left it for the stables. Except for the kitchen, all the hearths in the House were out during the storm. The unpredictable blizzard winds could suck flames as well as smoke up the flues and set the roof on fire.

Muran turned over some old St. Lucien periodicals. The current ones were on the order of *Equine News*, which listed horse auctions and carried notices for studs standing to mares outside their owners' lines. Muran was fascinated by this room. The Big House's past was exposed here in layers of paper just like Mittania's past was exposed in the cliffs around St. Lucien.

Rampalli, who entertained himself when there was no one else to amuse, stopped plucking a burlesque cavalry charge on his kit. He listened attentively to something outside.

He said, "Thurlow's going to join us. She's coming through the front hall. The girl walks well even in snow boots. I'll bet she's a natural dancer. Teaching her may not be unpleasant business."

Muran pushed back his forelock. "The girl is very intelligent, just like her brother. Anyone can enjoy instructing her—as long as it's what she wants to know. But I imagine that won't be a problem—for you. It might be more difficult for me."

Thurlow came in and warmed her hands at the stove, but soon moved to the big lounge by the cold fireplace. Old journals, records from earlier periods of Three Trees, were stacked on the lounge arms and the floor. A pouch full of correspondence from the last three months lay open on the desk and drew her attention. She flipped through the papers. One thin sheet with big margins caught her eye.

She slapped the desk top. "He never told me." Her eyes filled with angry tears.

Muran asked, "Have you lost a friend, Miss Thurlow? You look exceedingly distressed."

"A letter he got while he was still in St. Lucien." She held it up. "My governess says, 'My health has suffered a sudden reversal. It is, with deep regret, my duty to inform you that I will not be able to fulfill the responsibilities in your County for which you condescended to engage me.' Bitch! She's just afraid of the boredom."

She rapidly scanned the rest of the letters. "And there's nothing in here about finding anyone to replace her."

Rampalli shot a look at Muran. This wasn't news to either of them. He tried to soothe her. "The Baron's been very busy. He's got a great deal on his mind, between Justice Day and the Sace-Cothberg campaign."

"I think I understand my father's mind very well, thank you. He's never liked paying a wage to a governess. Except where his own amusements are concerned, and Three Trees' horses, he's a miser. He wants me to be an old-fashioned girl with all the old-fashioned virtues and none of the modern frills." Thurlow threw herself on the horsehair lounge in front of the dead fireplace. "I'm going to die, just die, out here, all by myself with no one to talk to and nothing to do except housekeeping!"

Muran said, "You can collect plant specimens and make sketches and drawings of them. I'll be happy to help you."

"You've got both of us for your amusement, my dear," responded Rampalli.

Scornful, she hissed, "Two old men, a stupid younger brother, and a girl who has tits bigger than her brain and can't think about anything but horses! Tolerable enough for a weekend in the country, I suppose, but not as my only companions until I'm eighteen. Then I'm supposed to marry a man older than my own father and go and live in another place like this one and be brood mare for the perpetuation of an old Aristo bloodline."

She ignored Muran's respectful correction that he was twenty-two and not an old man at all.

She hunched over her knees, sulking. She said bitterly, "My father paid more money to Glennys's mother than he'd have had to pay a governess. That's probably what he did with the money he should have spent on me. Why's that girl here anyway?"

Muran said, "Glennys wants to be here, Miss Thurlow. She's going to be a valuable, skilled horse trainer like Powell—who won't live forever. Good horse people, like governesses, are hard to get into Soudaka, harder to keep here, and very expensive."

Hengst ran into the Library. "And besides, Thurlow, she's better company than you are." He put his backside as close to the stove as he could get without burning it.

"Did you change your clothes after you came in from Long Stable?" Thurlow demanded. "It doesn't smell like it to me."

"Dad didn't change either, so there. He's in the hall right now with the seniors, drinking. The food platters were being filled in the kitchen and there wasn't time for clothes. I just came in here to tell you. You know how Cook is. Everyone's got to be seated before he'll let the food come out of the kitchen."

"Then Glennys won't have changed either and she sits next to me." Thurlow groaned a most tragic groan.

Hengst said, "Glennys isn't afraid of a little stink. I don't think she's afraid of anything. Did you hear about how she talked back to Cook?"

"I was there," Thurlow said. "That was a bit of diversion on a boring, horrible day. Glennys wasn't afraid because she doesn't know better. But it's true, she's not afraid of Deadly, like you are."

"Am not."

"Yes, Hengst. You're a fraidy-frog."

"Am not."

"You are too."

"Am not."

Rampalli looked at Muran and Muran looked at him. They understood each other perfectly. Thurlow was afraid of dying of boredom? What about them?

# SIX

"Stablemaster, if you tell me where the hoof pick is I'll get it for you. I can find it faster than one of the stableboys," Glennys said.

"And I won't run," she promised. The Rule was the Rule; around horses you talk quietly and move deliberately.

Powell released the seventeen-hand draft gelding's foreleg from his hands. He spoke softly. "Bring Nomad a double ration of grain too. One of the boys dropped a pick by the muck heap when we brought the teams in from the Coach Road. Do you know what a pick looks like?"

"Yes," Glennys lied.

She figured she'd know it when she saw it. The pick would be slender and hooked on one end. Everyone thought she was stupid because she didn't know the names of tack and equipment or where things were kept.

Glennys returned more quickly than Powell expected. She'd brought the corn and Nomad's blanket as well. It was a heavy, awkward load for someone of her size, so she'd put the blanket in an empty grain sack and pulled it behind her. The girl was stronger than she looked, Powell thought. She took the pick out of her pocket. The fingertips poking out of her mitts were as blue-white with cold as his own.

Powell blew on his fingers and held them close to the lantern before he nudged Nomad's shoulder with his own, and ran one hand down to the fetlock. "Lift," he said, and then took the hoof in the palm of his hand.

The girl was so eager to learn that it was a pleasure to teach her—as long as it was something she wanted to know. She wanted to work with the hotbloods and she was too green for that. She had to be trained up right, from the bottom, which meant working with the drafts and ponies. It was safer for her and for the horses.

"You're not very interested in the ponies or the cold-bloods, are you, Glennys?"

"Ponies, work horses—they're dull. Maybe ponies are too short and the work horses are too tall, but I can't hear them and they can't hear me, like Deadly does."

Under his cap, Powell's eyebrows shot up to his hairline when she said that. He wondered what odd thing she'd say next. He got back to the business at hand.

"You hold the lantern now. You see this soft, fleshy part of the inner hoof? Some call it the frog but we hold to the old language here and call it the swallow. The hoof carries all the weight of the horse—pony, draft, or horse of the blood, it doesn't matter—a horse is only as good as its hooves. The swallow is the center of a horse's ability to work and if it's not kept clean and healthy the horse is useless."

He had the right words. "And it also hurts the horse." He knew she would remember that. In the four days he'd watched her, she was never anything but kind and gentle to animals. He worked at the huge hoof with deft, neat movements.

When Nomad stood again on all four feet, Glennys up-turned a bucket to stand on. She was too short to throw the blanket over the chestnut's back otherwise. Her arms didn't stretch far enough to pull together the straps on either side of his deep belly.

"If I was in Long Stable I could get the horses to make *levade* to me and then I could get under their bellies and still stand up and pull the straps together," she boasted. She loved the vocabulary of high-schooled horses.

Powell had his hands on Nomad's off rear fetlock. Obediently the gelding lifted.

"So, what happens then, after you've thrown the blanket over the war horse and he does *levade* so you can walk under him to fasten it?"

"I guess it slides down over his tail, before I can buckle," she confessed slowly. "But I did get the right blanket for Nomad. I matched the number on his harness collar with the number on the blanket. See, I've learned something in the last days," she declared.

"You never knew anything, so of course you've learned *something*," he said.

She bit her lip to keep quiet. Once again she'd neither

impressed Powell nor amused him. She had learned more than one thing, however. Powell was the real power on Three Trees. He trained the war horses. She was supposed to learn to do that too. Another thing she'd learned was that if she kept quiet, Powell often continued to talk and then she learned things that she wanted to know.

Powell buckled the straps on the horse blanket. "What are you thinking of, girl? Your supper? There's a lot for third shift duty to get done before we go in."

She was chagrined that the Stablemaster thought she might find her own meal more important that the horses'. "Oh no. I was thinking of how my mother said to do what I was told. But it's hard to know who to listen to sometimes—except here in the stables with you and the horses."

Powell wondered if she were learning the art of flattery from Thurlow. And there it was again, this listening to the horses. But he was touched by the forlorn note in her voice.

"Do you miss living with your mother and father at home?" he asked.

Her shudder was visible even under the layers of clothing. "I miss Stella, a little. I like it better here than there—now that I don't have to work in the kitchen. I wish I didn't have a father at all, or that our Baron was my father."

For a minute she saw how it would be if she were still on the farm. At the table she'd be cutting up something for supper while Stella drilled her in the catechism or listened to the hymn she'd set Glennys to memorize. Then she'd go out to the barn to feed the animals and her father would throw something at her—if he was there at all. She'd be dreaming of horses instead of living with them. Then she'd have to help put the babies to bed, then pray with her mother for a long time, asking Alam to help her be good. Then in bed, if her father was home, she'd hear him and Stella argue about how the farm should be worked—if her father wasn't too drunk to talk. In the morning her father would yell at all of them to be quiet and blame feeling poorly on the Aristos.

"Ye-ah," Powell said, without knowing the girl's memories. He'd been born and raised on Three Trees. He shrugged his shoulders inside his fur-lined leathers.

"It's going to be harder here than you think it is, that's what I think. You'll see when you ride with us into Dephi, when the Baron goes to do the King's Justice. You'd better be prepared to hear your congregation call you some ugly things.''

Her eyes opened wide, glowing like the flame in a lantern when the fireguard was opened. She remembered Tuescher's sermon that day when she and Stella carried stones. Just in time she cut off a scream of joy.

"I'm gonna ride a horse into Dephi? My pa and old Tuescher's gonna see it? When do we go?"

"Hold your horses in, girl. We've got to clear the rest of the County roads first."

"I'm going to ride into Dephi, I'm going to ride into Dephi on a horse," she sang softly to herself, remembering the final g like Thurlow told her to do several times every day.

"Don't be more trouble than you're worth," he said sharply. "You don't know how to ride. You'll be on Merrylegs, who you should have fed and curried by now. That old pony gave Stogar, Thurlow, and Hengst their first riding lessons, so he knows his business. And you should think about how it might go with your mother when the congregation sees you with Three Trees' people on a tax-assessing trip."

Powell had pulled off his half-gloves, to get more easily into the two valleys formed by the swallow in Nomad's near forefoot. He thought there might a stone sliver in there. Glennys looked at his big, wide fingers probing the center of the hoof. They looked like the Baron's.

"Our Baron will fix the bloody Lighters if they do anything to Mother. He said so when he took me away."

"Don't badspeak your pedigree," snapped Powell. "You're an Alaminite yourself."

"Anyway, Mother's different now. She's stronger and she's not carrying a baby in her belly for the first time in I don't know how long."

"Just remember, Glennys," said Powell, "the Aristos only think about what's good for them, not anybody else."

But Glennys was gone. He could see her lantern bobbing toward Merrylegs's manger.

Powell went on with work, checking the legs and cleaning the hooves of all the teams. A black mare called Sweetie had a swelling on one of her fetlocks. He told a groom to apply handsful of snow to the affected area.

"Don't wait for fourth shift duty. After supper come back and wrap a standing bandage on her with an ice pack if the swelling's not gone down."

Glennys hurried over the work on Merrylegs and came to watch the operation. Sweetie stood perfectly still, though her flesh quivered up to her shoulder when the men touched her. She whickered and pushed her huge head with its white nose against Powell's chest. He made much of the mare, telling her how brave and strong she was, how much they appreciated her work.

"She really likes him, doesn't she?" Glennys said to the boy holding the bucket of snow.

Powell said, "Sweetie's the gentlest animal on Three Trees. She's better than us. But all our teams are good-tempered. Otherwise how could we get such big animals to work all day breaking down the snow, going back over it again and again with scrapers and packers, hey, lady?" He rubbed Sweetie's neck affectionately. "These horses work harder than anyone here. And have you fed all the ponies yet, Glennys?"

When Powell finished his rounds he came to check over Glennys's work. "Stablemaster," she asked, "do you like the work horses better than the war horses?"

"The war stallions and the King's racers go away," he said. "The work horses, all three sexes—mare, stallion, gelding—live on Three Trees all their lives, like you and me. They work hard for the other horses and for us, not just for the glory and the prestige of their Aristo masters. The cold-bloods are entitled to as much respect as the hotbloods."

Glennys heard what he said but its meaning was unclear. She repeated the words to herself.

Just then a grey pony went for Glennys's arm with his teeth. She slammed his jaw quickly with her elbow and yelped in pain. Her clothes were so thick that no flesh was torn, but there would be an ugly bruise.

"That's a mean little piece," said Powell. "He's not supposed to be in the loose box with the others. He should be tied up in a stall by himself."

The grey squealed and nipped the shoulder of a pretty bay gelding. "Remember, you've got to keep your wits about you all the time with horses. Even a nice one will try to take a chunk out of you on occasion if he thinks he can get away with it.''

While Powell grabbed the grey's jaw and ears, Glennys put a halter on him. The Stablemaster checked the knot when she tied the line.

He'd gotten her through all of her third shift duties. "Enough out of you for tonight. Get on up to the House. And remember to wash yourself and change clothes before coming in to the dining hall. Go up the back stairs from the kitchen and there should be warm water in your room. Can you remember to do that?''

Glennys rolled her eyes like a horse with too many trainers. "There's a lot to know about horses besides riding, isn't there? When do you think I'll know it all?''

"Never," he answered bluntly.

Glennys looked up at him, listening.

"I've been learning—and doing—since I was much younger than you are now," he said.

"Then you must know just about everything," she answered. "Like the Baron does. And I'm gonna know too." In her secret heart she didn't think she'd ever be old like Powell, but she'd know about horses, oh yes, she'd know. She gave each of the ponies a final noserub, not forgetting the grey either, and headed out. But first she went to Long Stable.

She knew Three Trees' barn was the biggest building in Soudaka because it was even larger than Reverend Tuescher's new one. The snow crunched under her feet and great clouds flew from her breath. It was very dark. She was proud that Powell trusted her with a lantern of her own. The stableboys from Old Nolan weren't allowed lanterns out of sight of the grooms. She recognized Hengst's steps behind her, hurrying to catch up. This was better than going up to Stella's house by herself from the barn.

Hengst pretended he'd caught her doing something wrong. "I saw you. You sneaked into Deadly's box. What did you give him?''

"Some of my potatoes from noon dinner.''

"I guess that's all right then. Potatoes shouldn't hurt him. He's probably had worse things to eat on campaign.''

Glennys swung her lantern in great arcs that bisected those

coming from Hengst's. "What would you know about what Deadly eats? He doesn't even like you."

There wasn't any malice in it. They were playing like yearlings. Hengst threw a hard-packed ball of snow against a garden wall just to hear the whack when it smashed apart. "Jump-off," he said. "Are you going to take a bath? It's such a waste of time. We get clean and then go out in the morning and smell like shit all over again."

"Ye-ah," said Glennys, imitating Powell. "I know. Sometimes Thurlow acts just like my mother."

"Dad's having a meeting in the Library office after supper. Do you want to hide with me under the stairs in the front hall? Then after the meeting starts we might be able to hear something. We'll play spies."

After they took off their outer work clothes in the cellar she said, "After supper, under the stairs, all right?" They shook hands on it.

"Don't tell Thurlow," Hengst warned. "She'll try and stop us because she didn't think of it first."

After supper Glennys played spy. She had to go where others didn't see her. She took the long way around through the upstairs gallery. All the little rooms that opened off the passage and the cross corridor had blankets neatly fastened in the door frames to conserve heat, since there were no doors. They were empty now, except for a lieutenant using a chamber pot or a dog left in his room by his master. A tall, narrow-snouted sight hound, bred for a warmer climate, looked up from its curl of spine. Its fine-bred nose lifted from under its plumed tail and he whined. She made a smacking noise at it and the dog curled tighter in its master's blankets.

The front stairs were the clue to the Big House, she thought. Downstairs, the front hall steps were broad, curved, and carpeted up to the landing. Above it the staircase concealed the rest of the steps. Those were straight, narrow, and bare. She could use them to go up and down as she pleased. Outsiders only saw the first five carpeted steps. The stairs reminded her of Stella's embroidery, with the pattern of horses on the back. She liked to stand on the landing and look down into the front hall and back behind her into the staircase. It was like being in two worlds at once, and you had to live in the Big House to know both of them. The elegant carpet and graceful curves didn't reach all the way to the top. She didn't notice how worn the blue and gold pile rug was.

Hengst had arrived at the bottom step first. He was shuffling a pack of cards. Rampalli's voice in the Library office could be heard clearly through the open door.

"Muran, the ballet was *not* invented in Nolan. It first was thought of in Tourienne, before Nolan made that country and my Langano part of Dominion. And I say that the ballet has conquered Nolan. What do you see at Queen's Opera Theater—and opera was invented by my Langano, not even the Nolanese can deny that—but ballet, ballet, ballet? You even use terms borrowed from the ballet to name your war horse maneuvers."

Muran said, "I've always heard that ballet wanted to imitate the precision and power of the war horse."

Glennys yawned.

Hengst tried to open the door beneath the stairs quietly. The closet was dark and stuffy, full of fur coats, sheepskin wraps, fleece-lined boots, and wool caps.

"Some of this is old. It belonged to my mother and grandmother. But a lot of it's Thurlow's," he whispered.

From the darkness of the closet came a harsh whisper. "You fools! Be careful! Spurs are on the floor and they clank!"

Thurlow was inside, throned on the hide of a Northern bear killed by some former Baron of Three Trees. She left the door open a crack and watched the company's seniors drifting towards the Library. They had to go through the drawing room from the dining hall, past the stairs, before going into the office.

Glennys whispered, "Now what?"

"Now we're going to spy on my father," answered Thurlow.

Glennys was sleepy. It was warm in the closet. She'd forked a lot of hay, carried a lot of water, curried a lot of ponies, and shoveled a lot of muck that was just on the other side of being frozen solid. At supper she'd eaten a lot of meat and drunk most of a pint of mulled ale.

Suddenly she pulled out of her doze. "That's one of Prochnow's boys from the Coach Inn. What's he doing here with the Baron?" She felt betrayed. She was the only Alaminite special enough to be on Three Trees. She remembered the things the Prochnows yelled when their rods struck Stella's legs after she'd fallen.

"They're busy now. Let's go out on the steps where we can hear better," Thurlow ordered.

The Baron was reading names from the County tax rolls. At certain names the Prochnow boy would say something. ". . . yes . . . he talks with Reverend Tuescher every day . . . yes . . . yes . . . he brings messages from Durl congregation for our Reverend."

Occasionally Muran's voice asked them to go more slowly while a group of names was read off. "I can't write that fast," he said.

"How did your father get Prochnow to come here?" Glennys asked.

Thurlow rubbed her thumb and index finger together. "Gold, you silly, gold."

Glennys was shocked. "Nobody would take gold to tattle on the congregations."

Thurlow hissed, "Maybe Prochnow is angry with the Reverend. Maybe he wants the money to get away from his dad. *You* should understand about that, I should think. Or maybe he's just a greedy pig."

Sometimes the Baron would tell Muran not to include somebody. "I remember Fensker from my boyhood. Remember, Powell? He's got to be eighty, if he's a day. . . . Littke lost an arm in the last campaign. We can't use him."

The names from the Bohn clan were read off. Muran said quietly, "They've always taken good care of the School."

"I believe you, Schoolmaster. But there's one of those boys who is really gifted at the forge and we need another blacksmith. Write him down, Muran. Don't worry, we won't put him in irons. One Bohn comes on every campaign and does well and brings back what he's learned—just like Stella's family did in my father's time."

Some of the kitchen people came up the back passageway, carrying glasses and decanters of brandy. Hengst sighed. "I want some of that."

They heard the men moving around now that refreshments had arrived. Hengst crawled on his belly like a caterpillar across the passageway.

"My reconnaissance expedition has learned that they're

looking at maps," he whispered. "And the Senior Colonel's choosing which men should go out with the teams to clear the roads and who's going to the farms and the public houses. Wildan is going on with my dad to visit the Old Men out there in the Badlands who watch the free-pastured horses. I wish I could go with Dad and Wildan."

They heard the Baron's rumble. "That's it then, Muran. Make copies for the Colonels. Put a note at the top that they're to double-check the wool and produce so the Lighters don't stick us with inferior goods."

"I've started making the copies now, Baron," the Schoolmaster said.

"Prochnow, you've done a fine job and we appreciate it. Here's your pay. Powell will find a place to store you while we're gone. You'll enjoy Three Trees' hospitality until Justice Day's come and gone."

Prochnow's voice squeaked. "But my pa, he expects me back. He thinks I've gone to see my sister, the one just made Tuescher's fourth wife."

"Take him out of here," ordered the Baron.

Powell emerged from the Library office into the hall. Two lieutenants followed him, with young Prochnow between them. Prochnow looked bewildered. He was clutching a small leather pouch.

Thurlow was mending a pair of gloves. Hengst was dealing Glennys a hand of cards. Powell said three words. "Go to bed."

Glennys was glad to go. This hadn't been interesting except when Hengst had squirmed on his belly to get closer to the Library. She'd liked watching that.

Hengst said, "Good night, sir."

Thurlow straightened her skirts and swayed in front of the men to the drawing room. She rattled a ring of keys. "I'm going to see that the hall is clean and the kitchen is in order. Then, if you men are finished, maybe I can see my father."

After the Baron sent the rest of his men out of the Library, he had a loud quarter of an hour with his daughter, chasing her out when Powell returned. The two men talked about why Powell hadn't liked what had gone on that evening. Then the Baron changed the subject to the business of Three Trees.

"How's your apprentice working out?" asked the Baron.

"She's greener than grass and she's overeager. She says that the war horses and the racers can 'hear' her. And she can 'hear' them."

The Baron refilled his glass. "Is that so?"

# SEVEN

Glennys woke screaming. Deadly had to get out of Long Stable! She dragged in a ragged gasp of air.

In the pause between waking and breathing she realized she was on her feet, standing up in the kitchen. She knew the Baron and Powell and the men and the teams had been gone for twelve days.

The oxen bellered a long, continuous call of fear. Above the oxen, higher pitched, she heard the mules, all braying madly. A horse's shriek of mortal agony cut through the din.

The horse who was hurt wasn't Deadly, but Deadly was going to hurt himself if he didn't get out. It had been Deadly's bellows of rage inside her head that had sent her running barefoot through the dark House in her sleep, down the back stairs into the kitchen.

She screamed with Deadly and wrestled with the door. She had to get out! The cellar way was too long. Deadly screamed again and so did she. She couldn't stop.

Cook pushed her aside and threw open the heavy kitchen door. Above the garden wall they saw flames shooting out of the hayloft in the barn. Thick rolls of smoke, the kind that came from burning packs of hay, crawled around the roof like fat worms.

Hengst vaulted over the garden wall, yelling, "Get the men out of the barracks and over to the big windmill. I'm going for the animals."

Now Deadly's voice was outside and inside her head. It hurt so much between her ears that she crouched in the snow, her hands pressed against her temples. Deadly would kill himself if he didn't get out. She tumbled over piles of snow scraped out of the compound, breaking through the lines of people converging on the burning barn. She ran to Deadly.

She jerked the latch on the side door of Long Stable and he burst out. She was knocked to the planks laid over the ice at the threshold. Deadly leaped over the drifts and ran straight across the pasture toward the northeast. The few horses left behind by the men who had gone out into the County with Powell were stamping in their stalls. None of them had the frenzy that possessed Deadly.

"Come back!" she screamed. But she had no voice left. Her throat was as burned out by her sleep screams as if she'd eaten fire.

The high shriek from the hurt horse had never stopped. She blundered toward the barn. The ground streamed wet from melting snow and buckets of water. A sheet of ice, refrozen out of noontime melt, slid down the side of the barn. The avalanche turned into clouds of scalding steam as it fell into the flames. Ox-sleds full of snow had been dragged over and dumped against the walls. Pails of snow and water were being hoisted to men on the roof. The steady Soudaka wind carried currents of embers across the yard.

"The hay ricks! Somebody go to the hay ricks!" the gardener puffed, as she waddled to the barn, carrying two buckets of water. Though Glennys had seen Mabley, the woman burned by the Dephi congregation, only a few times, the gardener looked like her as the flames lit up her sweating face. But the hay ricks were safe under heavy canvas and a blanket of ice.

"Thurlow! Jump to your right!" yelled Rampalli.

Thurlow jumped. A vane from the top of the big windmill, the one closest to the barn, plummeted to the ground where she'd been a moment before. Damaged in the blizzard, its gerry-rigged repair hadn't held. Even though the wind was steady, it didn't pump water fast enough. Three Trees saved only a part of its barn.

The most horrible sound, the shriek of the horse in pain, stopped. A dark pool spread under a huge shape on the ground. It was Sweetie. The smell of burned hair and flesh was rank. Cook stood by the body, butcher knife dripping into the blood. Sweetie's belly had been burned to the entrails. She was covered with voided excrement and the inflammation on her fetlock had burned to the bone. She'd been kept home while most of her mates cleared the roads of Soudaka.

Glennys and Hengst wept together over Sweetie's body. "Deadly's gone," she rasped, nose running. "I let him out because he was gonna kill himself. It's my fault."

Hengst said, "Somebody was careless and we're all going to catch it when they get back. The barn, Powell's favorite horse, and now Dad's stallion."

Glennys quit sniffling and tried to stand up straight. The punishment for losing Deadly would be awful. She hoped she could take it. There was no anger in her to keep her safe from that.

"Lady Eve! Just look at Glennys's feet. And look at our hands!" Thurlow's hands were cracked and bleeding. Runnels of soot tracked over her wet clothes. Her uncovered hair was grey with ashes. She was a ghost of what she might be forty years from now.

"In St. Lucien we call healers out of the Fortune Houses if we're sick or hurt. But out here I guess it's up to us. I need bandages, and salves, and—herbs. Glennys, your mother knows what to do, doesn't she? You said my mother's herb book has your mother's handwriting in it." Thurlow's voice trailed off as she looked at the barn and all the people standing there.

"We've got to shelter the livestock," said Hengst. "You and Cook can get us something to eat and drink, and send for Stella."

A stallion's call of triumph carried over Three Trees. Against the horizon they saw Deadly's bulk rearing high. He pivoted on his hindquarters, threw down his head to his forelegs like a colt at play. He was far away but sharply defined against the penumbra of the sunrise. He was so beautiful, and Glennys wanted him so much. He charged over the pasture, elevating effortlessly over the snowbreaks. He cantered over the compound and drew up out of reach of the humans banded together. His neck arched; he shook his head. His mane, grown out like a high crest of feathers, wobbled. He nickered then, head lowered, ears pricked forward, front legs wide apart.

Glennys mouthed his name because she couldn't talk. He

trotted over and dropped his nose into her hand. It was covered with bloody slime. He wrinkled back his lips, showing big teeth traced in blood. Shreds of flesh were stuck in his jaws. His legs and hooves were muddy with blood, brains, and bits of bone. He expected praise.

"Where's the Prochnow boy?" asked Muran. "Powell had him locked into the harness room in the barn."

Prochnow's name was like a charm that the Three Trees staff repeated over and over again.

"I think," said Hengst, "that what's left of Prochnow is out there." He waved toward the pasture.

Thurlow said slowly, "Someone's got to clean up Deadly. I think that's you, Horsegirl." Under the smut Thurlow's face was white. She bent over and vomited.

Deadly knelt and Glennys heaved herself over his withers, her numbed fingers hardly able to grasp his mane. Strings of bloody saliva from his jaws flew back against her legs.

The cross timbers of Long Stable's side door were scarred with long gashes. The aisles were covered with debris from broken sacks of corn and dismembered butts of straw. The gate to Deadly's box had been broken into firewood.

She couldn't forget Sweetie's body, charred to the bone while she was still alive, and how the gardener resembled Mrs. Mabley. She thought of the burning her mother had refused to have her witness last summer. She saw the sow who had eaten her own farrow and how her mother had butchered it and how they had all eaten of the meat. She remembered her childish dreams of horses, never imagining this grisly grooming ahead of her. Thurlow had gotten sick. She hadn't. She wouldn't.

Her mother's embroidery with the pattern of horses on the back, the front stairs in the Big House, Deadly. Everything seemed to have more than one face.

She worked over Deadly, who had killed a man, because she was the one he allowed to touch him. But others had to tell her what to do because she didn't know what salves and medicines to put on the places where he'd hurt himself.

The stablehands and grooms whispered, questioning the others who were moving some of the rescued stock into Long Stable. Powell wouldn't have allowed so much noise in here.

The regimental remounts squealed, charged with nervous energy, with nowhere to use it.

"All the blankets, tack, and harness," moaned a groom. "The Lighter bastard got his revenge against the Baron for locking him up. Powell was right. He knew something like this would happen."

Prochnow had torched the barn. There was no other answer.

The Prochnow boy had more than two faces, Glennys thought. He'd betrayed his own and then he'd betrayed Three Trees. He'd tortured a helpless, gentle horse, like the Alaminites had burned the old woman, like they'd hurt Stella, like they'd hurt her.

But Prochnow had been locked up by the Baron's orders. She wouldn't think about that.

Deadly's teeth snapped an inch from her eye.

"Watch yourself, Horsegirl. You're not paying mind to what you're doing," warned the head groom.

She tried to take his advice but her mind pelted along another path. Unlike every hamlet and farm in Soudaka, Three Trees didn't have a fire bell. If they'd had one to ring, no one would have come. She'd been thinking that Three Trees was large and crowded. But now, measured against the County, it seemed small and lonely.

She finished Deadly's grooming at mid-morning. The stallion was edgy, sending challenges to his stablemates. Glennys was tired and sore. Her feet were like lumps of ice, even though Thurlow had sent out her boots and clothes. She'd had nothing to eat since last night. Her head was hurting like it had when Deadly's screams inside of it had sent her to the kitchen door. Now, when he trumpeted, her head hurt even worse.

"I can't handle him anymore," she signed to the head groom.

"We can't tie him up either," he returned. Deadly never was tied. Even during campaign he was hobbled, not put on a picket line. And now there was no gate to his box.

The grooms had a conference and decided to put him in the stallion shed. It usually stood empty except during breeding seasons. Now it had the oxen in it. A light, wet snow sifted over them as they followed Glennys and Deadly to the shed.

She was miserable and stupid when she climbed out of the cellar into the kitchen. Cook was complaining.

"Things were just back to normal, and now this happens! I'm going to have to feed the hired carpenters when the barn's rebuilt, and there's enough to do just keeping our own fed and laundered."

He watched Glennys stumble across his soot-tracked floor. "Horsegirl, get yourself into the dining hall and eat something, right now!"

She looked back at him dumbly, and sneezed. Everything from her chest on up hurt.

Cook moaned, "She's going to have influenza." He glowered darkly at his staff. "We'll all get it."

Then, more cheerfully, he said, "You know, Horsegirl, since you were smart enough to let the Baron's stallion loose to kill that Lighter, none of us will be blamed for the fire. Now go and eat so you don't get sick!"

The dining hall looked like something between a dispensary and a commissary with a harnessmaker's workbench thrown in for good measure. Glennys felt as though she never wanted to see an open fire again, but her chilled bones were drawn to the blaze behind the giant fender. A woman was standing there, stirring drops out of a bottle into a pot that released aromatic steam. She turned around.

"Glennys? You've grown at least an inch." Stella kissed her daughter's dirty face. "Becky and Debbie, come and greet Sissy."

Her sisters acted as though Glennys were a stranger. She hardly recognized them, or her mother, either. She'd never imagined them in these rooms.

She pointed to her throat and shook her head no. A cookgirl brought over a mug of hot spiced brandy. A groom said, "The Horsegirl can't talk. She tore out her throat raising the alarm."

Muran fussed about her, sitting her on a bench just far enough from the fire so she felt safe, but close enough so she'd thaw out.

"So, Glennys, I hear you're a heroine," remarked her mother. "Waking the House in time for Hengst to rescue the stock, freeing Fulk's horse and all. When you were home, nothing but a shaking could get you out of your bed once someone got you into it."

It was a blessing she couldn't talk. Glennys thought. She'd told Powell that her mother had changed. So Stella had, but some things about her would never be different.

They thought the rousing was of her own will. It had been Deadly in her head that had done it. Didn't they know that her windowless room in the winter-shuttered House didn't let her hear anything from outside? She listened to the busy chatter around her.

Among the animals that had perished was the vicious grey pony. He'd been tied up too. Half the chickens had crushed and suffocated each other in the coop because they'd been frightened out of their birdbrains by the noise. Most of the mules broke out as soon as Hengst had thrown open the doors. Two hitches of oxen had been saved.

Out of what she heard she decided it was Hengst who was the hero. He'd gotten sacks over the heads of the three draft horses and ridden one out, leading the others, while fire ate away their stalls. She tried to think how he'd done that. He was only three inches taller than she was.

She hadn't known what to do. She'd only screeched until someone had come and done something. There had been a pressure in her head and she'd done what it said. And now her mother came over to warn her against getting full of herself. She didn't need to hear that. She knew it better than Stella did.

Glennys ate what was given her, chewing it like a cow with her cud. Hengst, looking like a fabulous blackamoor, pranced into the dining hall. Thurlow brought him a slab of toast spread with butter and honey before she helped Stella pull off Glennys's boots. Glennys would have screamed if it were possible when the warm air hit her frostbitten feet.

"Not as bad as it might be," assessed Stella. "She'll be fine in a day or two. No toes will be lost, not even a nail. All my daughters are strong and healthy."

Muran said suddenly, "I have to go to Dephi today and reopen the school."

Hengst said, "Schoolmaster, we need you here to write up a report for my father." His mouth was thickly smeared with a salve that now was mixed with butter and honey. There were blisters all around his lips. The hair on one side of his head was burned off. His right arm and hand were wrapped in a bandage that was already filthy. He'd been picking through the debris of the barn under the falling snow. He could walk just fine, thought Glennys. He'd been smart enough to put on his boots before running outside. Not like her.

"I think Prochnow jumped Davy and that's how he got loose," Hengst announced. "Nobody's seen him today. He was a new boy here. There's a body cooked to a crisp on the barn floor. It's small enough. It could be Davy's."

Even giving out news like that didn't halt Hengst's swagger around the dining hall. He reminded Glennys of Deadly after the stallion had come back. Hengst was proud of himself, satisfied with his performance of the night.

She limped through the door into the drawing room and stopped. There was no fire in the room but there was the smell of smoke. The body of Torvill, a groom, was laid out.

"He breathed too much smoke," said Stella. "I tried to ease his dying. He rests in Alam's light now."

Torvill didn't believe in Alam, Glennys thought. And neither do I.

As she helped Glennys up the stairs to her room, Stella declared, "I always liked these stairs best of everything in this House."

Glennys was resentful that Stella had known the Big House first.

# EIGHT

"No. Don't ask again. A governess is another name for a gossip whose job is your wardrobe. That's a luxury Three Trees can't support."

Glennys, sitting on the front stairs, heard papers rustle. Thurlow wouldn't give up yet.

"All right then, look at the accounts if nothing else will

satisfy you! During the present month of Darkcold the first line of expenses are those for St. Lucien's Eve festivities. Compensation to Davy's family and Torvill's for their deaths. Personal expenses. Regimental expenses that have to come out of my private purse—that line will be carried across every month that this campaign lasts and it's going to be the longest one Nolan's seen in my generation. Here's what will have to be carried for the months ahead—rebuilding the barn, replacing stock, tack, and equipment. The yearly bonuses of each of Three Trees' staff. And none of this reflects the expenses from Powell's stable books.

"Over on accounts receivable, what do you see to carry Three Trees through until the fall when Powell sells the Badlands' crop of four-year-olds? Nothing but my share of Alaminite taxes, and most of that will be in kind, not cash."

Thurlow wasn't convinced. "Where's the money that you're getting from Leon's exchequer, Father?"

"That's for campaign expenses. It isn't Three Trees' business at all. Or yours." He was getting very angry.

Thurlow always saw the Baron first. Glennys sat with her fingers crossed. She'd made a wish on the first star tonight when she'd come in from third duty. She'd wished that Thurlow wouldn't get him so angry that he'd cancel his appointment with his Horsegirl.

Thurlow countered with the argument Glennys had heard often in the last two days.

"It's all an excuse. I saw the correspondence. You never planned to pay a wage for a governess. How am I to be equipped for a place when I leave here? I'll look like a carriage horse put in the traces for the first time."

The Baron tried patience. "If you and Hengst are as smart as both of you have boasted since the fire, what's to keep you from learning what you need from Muran and Rampalli? By the time Hengst's of age for the Equine Academy, Rampalli will have him prepared with the sword and courtesy. Powell will have your brother trained on Three Trees' own stock, the highest bred war horses in Nolan. The Academy costs dearly, and so will the officer's commission, and his fitting out afterwards. But the expenses aren't begrudged, whatever your mule-minded selfishness has decided. You see them listed and anticipated all through the next years."

Thurlow's voice was sharp with resentment. "What about me?"

The Baron told her, "You're an exceptionally pretty girl, Thurlow, and you're going to grow into a beautiful woman. You're already assured a marriage worthy of your blood. Waterford's family is like ours and they approve of your being here and getting the training they're interested in. You see the funds in this separate account? That account was established to pay for your wedding in the days when your mother was alive. I've never touched it."

Glennys heard something that could have been a small fist hitting a leather cushion. "Waterford's an old man—my half-uncle! He was your blood brother's father! And he sits in a house just like this one, half garrison and half horsestable, on the western march of Nolan! Please, let me go back to Aunt Abigail in St. Lucien while you're out of Nolan. I've got to have a chance to have some life of my own before I end up sitting around with old people who dream about the old days that they can't even remember!"

Glennys had heard the Baron's counterargument before.

"If I left you in St. Lucien with my scribbling sister-in-law as guardian, the next thing I'd hear is that you'd done just what she did. You'd have run off with some come-lately family's younger son, one who can't tell a horse's forehand from its hindend and who thinks ballistics has replaced the cavalry charge."

Thurlow would try beguilement now. She'd flutter her long lashes like the wings of a tiny, vulnerable bird. That always made Glennys do whatever Thurlow wanted.

"I think, Sir," Thurlow paused, "that I could handle the young lords."

"You've just proven otherwise to me. Don't spill honey and expect *me* to lick it up from you. Fooling with young uncuts is no doubt just what you'd like. I know our blood! You'll stay on Three Trees and become a woman worthy of your Old Nolanese pedigree, mated with one of your own kind when your season comes, my dear."

Glennys heard an interesting chink.

"Do you want it? It's your quarterly allowance. The Post Stage runs between Old Nolan and Dephi, you know, even in winter. You can send for whatever you like."

"Will the Schoolmaster pay me my allowance every quarter after he's taught me to sew a fine seam?" Thurlow asked.

"Don't be scornful about Muran, Thurlow. Like Rampalli, his qualities are excellent. I wouldn't have anything less than the best around my children—which you'll understand when you have children of your own. If you and Hengst grow up ignorant, it won't be Muran's fault. He's the one who will remind Powell when your monies are due, and, on my say-so, he can hold the monies back if you and Hengst don't work," the Baron warned.

Glennys heard a squawk.

The Baron said, "Take advantage of Muran. Like the Dancemaster, he's poor, but he's got bottom. He won't be here forever. He'll get a better position when he goes back to Old Nolan than he'd find without the experience and recommendation of doing my work as well as the Dowager Queen's. I've marked him and, even these days, in Old Nolan my blood has respect. He's ambitious and smart. He's a good Nolanese who'll serve our purposes well." The Baron added thoughtfully, "Even as we serve his."

"May I have my money now, Father?"

The hairs on Glennys's arms prickled when she heard the Baron say, "Yes. You may take your money after you've kissed me."

A rustle of skirts followed the long silence.

"Here then. Send Glennys to me."

Thurlow stalked out of the Library office. A patch of red glowed across her cheekbones, the rest of her face paler than usual. Gold coins glinted between her tightly closed fingers.

She glared at Glennys. "He's all yours, Horsegirl. Enjoy yourself!"

Glennys had been waiting for the Baron's notice and now she dreaded it. She'd hoped that if she ever got to be alone with him again, it would be like the St. Lucien's Eve when he'd judged her. She'd passed the test and he'd protected her. But, she thought sadly, St. Lucien's Eve only came once a year.

She gathered her courage. She knocked on the door to the bear's den even though it was open.

"Come in. Shut the door behind you."

The Baron wasn't behind his desk but stretched out on the

horsehair lounge. His boots rested on a footstool close to the fireplace fender. He liked hearths better than stoves.

His face had lost flesh while he'd been out in the County. Except where his thighs bulged fatly with riding muscles against suede trousers, he looked frail. His eyes glowed against the color in his windburned face.

He hooked an ankle around the leg of a soft chair and pulled it in front of him. "Sit here where I can see your pretty hair." He ran his hand through the strands brushed smooth and shining over her shoulders. He felt her body quiver.

Fulk regarded her silently for some time. He twirled the cut-crystal snifter of Tourienne cognac between his thick fingers. She liked seeing his big hands move delicately.

"I want to thank you properly for letting Deadly out the night of the fire. You saved my horse—and you saved me a lot of trouble. I didn't have to hunt down Prochnow, which otherwise I'd have had to do. If the news has spread that a Lighter fired Three Trees' barn, so has the news that my war stallion executed the arsonist on the spot. I think you're a piece of good luck and I'm proud of you and what you did."

With an effort of will Glennys pulled her eyes away from the firelight dancing in the grooves of the crystal in the Baron's fingers. "It wasn't me, sir. It was Deadly. He made me do it. It's false praise and I can't be proud."

She was focused again on the sparkling rainbows in the snifter. Her pupils contracted and expanded in rhythm with the colors wheeling around the glass.

"I wonder why he was locked up—Prochnow, I mean, not Deadly," she said dreamily. "He helped you. If he was free there wouldn't have been a burning. He'd still be alive."

Her limbs were soft and relaxed. She tried to sit up straight. "I nattered. Mother says I never stop nattering. I don't want to think about that night."

Her eyes were mesmerized by the swirling lights. "It's like stars," she said. "Like the stars shining on St. Lucien's Eve when I rode behind you on Deadly."

The Baron's tones were conversational. "The Prochnow boy was an Alaminite. We had to keep him safe from Tuescher so we locked him in the harness room. He didn't know the codes of a Horseman, the honor of a warrior. That's why he perished by the jaw and hoof. If he'd been like you, true to me, he'd be alive. It was a criminal execution, not a murder. Torvill and Davy died because of Prochnow. Deadly protected Three Trees. He's true to the codes of a war stallion, and to me, your Baron. I protect you and your mother from your father, from Tuescher, from Alaminites.''

She roused. "He burned Sweetie alive like the congregation burned the dog lady, Mrs. Mabley, last summer. I'm glad he's dead.''

Fulk was still, like a cat watching unaware prey. He waited to see what happened. This was a small diversion from his concerns, but it was pleasant. It helped soften the rage he felt after hearing that Prochnow had turned his coat twice. He should have hypnotized the boy. He had a high regard for his own judgment of character and it had failed. He didn't have to hypnotize Glennys but he liked doing it. It pleased him that Lighters would call this witchcraft.

"Prochnow hated you, Glennys, like your father hates you, like Tuescher hates you and your mother. He was an enemy, like your father and Tuescher are enemies. Nolan keeps you safe. I keep you safe. Deadly keeps you safe.''

Glennys's eyes were half closed. Her arms fell open. Her hair was over one shoulder, a soft nest of gold tangled against the curve of her neck. She was as pliant to his will as the night he and Deadly had changed her life. It was a source of pride to Fulk that he didn't have to rely on a diamond or a snifter of cognac to make a woman docile. The gift had nearly died out among the old bloodlines but he'd received it intact.

Glennys nestled deeply into her chair. "He's big and strong. I want him to belong to me.''

Fulk's eyes narrowed. He wondered if she meant Deadly or himself. The gift of hypnotism was spoken of rarely and only among the elder males of the old blood after a long day of working or drinking together. Duke Albany maintained that hypnotism had made a balance between the Stallion Queens and the men of their tribes. Albany said that the Eidel Kings could work it on man and woman alike. Albany declared that hypnotism was another term for the gift of seduction.

Fulk thought of his other concerns while watching Glennys slip more deeply into her trance. *What the Eidel Kings possess, they know how to keep.* The Alaminites' hatred was a check and balance to the old blood of Fulk's line. Give the march between Old Nolan and isolationist Alaminites to someone like him and both the throne and Nolan were served. The people in these flat lands were subservient to Fulk, but because they hated horses, they'd never make an alliance with him and challenge the Eidels. The Lighters were useful to Fulk and their hatred of horses made him despise them. He'd never be tempted to make an alliance with them. It was a balance that gave him his own territory. He didn't have to be a lap dog in the palace, a merchant mule in the City, or a minister in the King's Cabinet. As long as Leon kept guns and cannon out of Nolan's Domains, Fulk's territory was safe. It was the best world he could imagine. This girl could be useful for keeping his world the way it always had been.

"Glennys, tell me how you woke up the night the barn burned down."

Her hands flailed, her body twisted in the chair. "I have to get out," her voice choked. "I had to . . ." The rest was a mumble.

He asked the question again.

"It hurts. I wake up in the kitchen. The mules and Sweetie hurt. I hear Deadly screaming. I have to scream. I'm in the kitchen and Deadly is screaming."

That wasn't the right way to ask the question. He shifted his weight and leaned toward the girl. "Did you know Deadly wanted to get out before you could hear him?"

A human voice couldn't make the sound that Glennys was trying to force out of her chest. "I have to get out!"

The Baron put down his snifter. He didn't know the words. There must have been words once, before the old bloodlines learned how to write.

"He can't have it! It's mine!" The scream was horrible, gurgling around words. Fulk picked her up and held her against his chest.

"It's all right," he said. He walked the floor, holding her close.

He sat down, stroking her body. "You've been good, it's all right. You're good." It didn't matter what he said, as long as he stroked her, whispered approval.

He poured some cognac, put the snifter to her lips. "Breathe deep, now drink." She drank it all.

Glennys was drowsy. She hoped she hadn't fallen asleep. She was warm against the Baron. He smelled of leather, sweat, spirits, and Deadly. She rubbed her head on his chest, pressed as close to him as she could. She was asleep and this was a dream. She was the only one who knew.

Fulk heard that low, throaty laugh he'd heard many times before. She rolled her head under his throat. Her tongue made an exploratory lick. Her teeth nipped his skin. "Father can't see me here. I'm the biggest, fastest horse in the Saquave and nobody can see me."

One of her arms crept around his neck. She'd grown some since he'd taken her out of the Lighter barn. His fingers traced her collarbone. They lingered at the hollow of her throat. His arm tightened around her shoulders. Her nipples would feel hard as oats in his fingers. She squirmed on his lap.

The Baron got up. He put Glennys in her chair. She was eleven years old, too ignorant to breed. When he came back from the Sace-Cothberg campaign her hips and buttocks would be thick with muscle from riding. The rest of her would have caught up with the growth in her breasts. There were women here among the itinerant help hired while his men were with him this winter. They were skilled and willing. Powell would go loco if his Baron bred his eleven-year-old apprentice.

The Baron snapped a finger against the snifter and it chimed sweetly. Glennys smiled and shook her hair in place with a gesture he'd always liked, whether in a whore or in a lady of the blood.

"You're good luck for Three Trees," he said. "It was charming to spend a part of my evening with you."

He kissed her fingers and sent her to bed. He sat in front of the fire, holding a book open on his lap that he didn't read. It was *the Hystorie Booke; which is to say a true and real and brief Description of the Beginnings Causes Origins and Derivations of the Central Nolan Dominion.*

The next night Thurlow came into Glennys's room while the Horsegirl bathed. "Here," Thurlow said, thrusting garments at her. "These things are for you. Our Baron's such an old skinflint that he's giving you riding leathers that he wore when he was a mere suckling. If the boots are too big, he says, wear extra stockings.''

Glennys was delighted. She said, ''Everything's got the Three Trees' gold emblem on it. These boots are just like the ones Hengst has. I'll wear them when we go to Dephi.''

''No doubt,'' said Thurlow dryly, ''that's exactly what you're supposed to do.''

# NINE

The evening before Justice Day Glennys didn't feel good. She watched Hengst come into the dining hall. If he walked any closer to Wildan, she thought, Hengst would step on the aide's heels.

Hengst pulled his stool into place next to hers. ''How come you didn't come and watch when Cook cut up our wild boar? He was a giant. You could have heard him shriek all the way back at the Coach Inn when we got him cornered against the rock pile in Tuescher's field.''

''Butchering pigs is kitchen work,'' she said shortly. She had an urge to slap the boy. ''I've seen it before.''

During second duty she'd helped turn out the war horses from stable to paddock and she'd gotten stepped on. Her big toe was throbbing, three times larger than it should be. Merrylegs had thrown her and then kicked her. Everyone had laughed. Powell had scolded her for giving too much corn to the three-year-olds that the Baron had brought from the Badlands. The only good thing about today had been working three-year-old Tornado on a lunge line. The young stallion's call-name was Torrie. He was Deadly's get, and he was her special care. After she learned her basic riding skills on Merrylegs, Torrie was going to be her mount. She couldn't see why she had to wait. Tornado liked her. Merrylegs, that short old pony, hated her.

After the supper things were cleared away and the ale jugs

replenished, Hengst had talked some more about the pig hunt. Fulk had sent his younger men out to kill the wild boar running around Dephi as relief from tallying the sleds of taxes in kind coming in from the congregations. From the way Hengst went on, thought Glennys sourly, you'd think he'd personally killed the boar. But he hadn't. Wildan had made the killing thrust, as she'd heard many times already.

"Even now in Darkcold," Hengst boasted, "he was fat. He was as bold and clever as a beast from the old days. It was a good hunt, wasn't it, Wildan?"

Glennys moved her stool closer to Thurlow's. She wished Hengst would stop talking. "You don't know anything about pigs, Hengst. He was fat because he's smart about raiding chicken coops and digging out the garbage pits around the farms. He ain't gonna be thin again until Marche."

"Pigs don't eat meat," he thrust back at her.

"Stupid. Yes they do. Pigs eat everything, just like you, greedy-guts," Glennys said rudely.

"What do you want to fight for? You've been acting like Thurlow all day. You're just jealous because you couldn't be there."

"I am not jealous about killing a stupid pig. I've killed some myself," she snapped. It was a lie. She'd only helped. "I hate blood."

Thurlow put her arm around Glennys and whispered in her ear. Hengst saw Glennys whisper back. He tried to read their faces and find out what they were talking about. He couldn't. Thurlow would leave him out of things but Glennys had never been mean to him before.

The two girls excused themselves.

"Where are you going?"

Thurlow said, "I'm taking Glennys to my room and then I'll make her something special to drink. The recipe's in Grandmother's book and boys can't have any."

Hengst sat and tried to puzzle out why his ally would desert him for the company of his sister.

Wildan grinned behind his ale mug. He leaned over and splashed a head on the boy's ale. "No brooding, Hengst. There's days when the boys should be separated from the girls. Don't take it personally."

Hengst settled in to listen to the men talk. This was better than being with girls. He'd miss this more than anything after Justice Day. He looked around the hall. He wondered which of them he'd be like when he was their age and finished at the Equine Academy in St. Lucien. He wanted to grow up like Wildan. Wildan had guts and he was smart. He wasn't mean like Acker, reckless like Gordon, or low like the dark-eyed Burton.

Soudaka County was the first hard duty Fulk's younger men had pulled so far. Unlike the testing courses they'd had at the Academy, this was real. The Baron and Powell had pushed them from sunrise to sunset, working them in the saddle the whole time, without a day off. Fulk had to complete the Crown's business and his own before the big storms buried Soudaka in the coming month of Rue. He had to sail from St. Lucien at the end of Marche's alternating freezes and thaws. Marche was like that in Soudaka, Hengst reminded himself, but not in St. Lucien. Marche was a month of rain for the southern port capital. And in St. Lucien the men supported themselves, or their families did, if they didn't mess and bunk at Headquarters. Here all the burden was on Three Trees. Powell was eager for Fulk's men to be gone.

Acker wore his long blonde hair in two tails. He chewed the end of one of them. "I never saw anything as desolate as the Devil's Lake congregation. And here I'd thought Dephi was the end of the world! I got fishbones stuck in my craw yet. My Savage did a bloody fine job though, on the ice and the snow. He's out of Three Trees' stud, like all the horses on my picket," he boasted.

Politely, his companions drank to his horse, whose birth, breeding, and early training had come out of their Baron's country.

Burton said, "Who got some tail while out in the County?" He glanced around the table. No one met his eyes. Everyone knew better than to brag about what happened in congregational Soudaka, because everyone knew that nothing did.

Burton looked gloomy. "You'd of thought at least one farmer's daughter would have lifted her skirts to say thank ye kindly boys for digging me out of the snow," he complained. "But not a one did. Ungrateful Lighter bitches."

Muran was more offended by their ignorance than by Burton's crudeness. The Baron was meticulous about clearing away the first blizzard so the Alaminites had no excuse to miss Justice Day in Dephi. After he got his cash and kind he'd leave the other congregations to dig out as best they could. Three Trees would only clear the part of the coach road that ran into Dephi. There'd be no communication with Old Nolan for his more distant colleagues during the next weeks of winter. It could have been me snowed in out there, he thought as he pushed back his curls and took another pull from his mug. But it would never be him, out in the middle of nowhere until the day he died. He wasn't like the other Schoolmasters, sorry weaklings that they were. He worked harder. He looked for opportunities to better himself. There was always a way to make the best of your luck if you were smart. He'd learned all he could about Soudaka while still at the Seven Universities. He'd found a groom who'd worked at Three Trees—for triple Old Nolan's wages—and requested the Dephi School. The others hadn't even bothered to learn where Soudaka County was.

Acker had picked up the complaint. "Did you see even one of those Lighters you'd let into your bed? There's a few tolerable ones around Dephi, like the Bohns have got, but out there? Nothing. No smiles, no talking. Just black wool and hatchet faces.''

Muran said, ''The Lighters marry their girlchildren off before they're full-grown and start them having babies before they learn how to flirt. It's their way, just like it's their way to have more than one wife if the man can afford it.''

"I wonder," said Wildan, "is it because the Lighters have to give so much to the Reverends that it leaves nothing for the ladies to buy pretties?"

Acker said, "Every mule-damned road here goes to a Reverend's gopher-hole kirk. All of them are just like the women here, bloody cold and bloody ugly!''

Acker shook out the last drops in his jug and lunged for the one Glennys and Thurlow had left untouched. He said, "Our Baron should geld them all after they've had one son. Soudaka belongs to him and the Crown. He could do it.''

Acker chortled at the image of gelded Alaminites. He pulled a knife from his boot and began to carve a smutty tattoo in the board. Wildan was on his feet like a cat and leaning over Acker's shoulder. He took the knife out of Acker's hand. The room went silent as Wildan said, "You're talking like a raider now, not like the Baron's man in his country. This is Nolan too. And you aren't allowed to damage the Baron's property."

Everyone at the board was watching, waiting to see if Acker would answer with a challenge.

Ignoring Acker and Wildan, Gordon began to talk. He stroked the long Gordon tail and drawled, "Sure would have hated this duty more if the Lighters had gotten hold of some crossbows or that other stuff that's crawlin' into the Outremere Domains. I've heard say that's what we should be prepared for, in Sace-Cothberg." He pulled over Muran's ale jug and filled his own mug without even offering the Schoolmaster a head. "There's a drop or two left in there, teacher," he said.

Gordon was a bloodline descendant from the legendary General Gordon. Every cadet and soldier swore by the old General. He was the first one to prove that Nolan could sail across the sea with her horses and dominate the lands over there.

Wildan sat down in his own place again. Gordon continued. "What's the honor in bringing down a man with a cannon or a musket? There's no hand-to-hand, no cavalry charge. They're soft over the water, that's what it is. And they always have been. They live without horse's honor or horse's luck. One Nolan warrior and a horse in light armor has always been able to handle any twenty of them."

The ale mugs beat on the boards.

"Drink to that! Ye-ah, drink to that!"

Muran was insulted but he kept his contempt to himself. They were young, bright, and strong—and never tested. They were privileged boys who'd been protected all their lives. They didn't have the imagination to see that Sace-Cothberg wouldn't be a jubilee, but a war. Their blind confidence strengthened his belief that Nolan's future depended on men like him, educated to something besides swords and horses— modern men who worked to develop the qualities of their intellect. Nolan was their country too. Since Hengst's education outside of horses and swords was in his hands, he could teach the younger generation that.

Wildan poured ale for Muran out of his own jug as he

began to talk. "I finally saw what Soudaka's got that makes the Baron so determined to keep the County. The Badlands. The Baron and I rode over it all to see his free-ranged studs and mares. There's no people there except the ones that the Baron calls the Old Men, the ones who live in sod houses and watch over the horses. We were mounted on horses that were bred, born, and raised in that country. Even at night, they never missed a step or fell into a gully or stepped into a hole. Remember too, that all the broken places were smoothed out from snow cover. The look of the land is like the morning of the world before everything was fixed into its place and shape. There's trees bent and twisted from the wind and the weather. Sometimes you'd see smoke. That's from underground coal that caught fire a long time ago and just smolders away down there all by itself, whether it rains or snows. You can laugh at me if you want but I've got to say—I felt bigger and stronger than anything in the world out there."

Burton said, "That's because you went to the Kings' Coal Mines first. I bet you and the Baron spent most of the night with the King's Daughters in the Mine Pleasure House!"

Wildan made a gesture of disdain. "A new batch of King's Daughters was there all right," he grinned. "But that wasn't the reason. In the Badlands I felt like I had enough air to breathe. We Waterfords don't have anything that big and empty in our County."

"Nothing that cold either," said Gordon.

Muran understood why Hengst had developed such a strong case of hero-worship for Wildan. He hoped this last Waterford son would survive the Sace-Cothberg war.

The comfortable kitchen clatter erupted into exclamations and squeals. One of the maids ran into the dining hall. "Come outside, come outside and look at the sky!"

Cook came into the dining hall to unbolt the winter shutters that sealed the garden doors. Hengst heard Thurlow and Glennys run down the front stairs and out the front doors of the Big House to join the Baron and Rampalli on the porch.

The sky was full of luminous colored smoke. A weightless curtain of silk seemed to hang straight down. It was banded in white, green, and rose. The bands rippled in surges from east to west, creating deep folds of light and color. Diaphanous rays of crimson sparkled in the north. Banners of pale light converged at the apex of the display.

"We call this the Northern Lights," explained the Baron softly. "You've never seen them before, Thurlow," he said. "But I'll bet Glennys has." He touched her hair.

Glennys and Thurlow had their arms around each other against the cold. The Baron had one of his arms around the same woman he'd taken from Acker on St. Lucien's Eve. She had clouds of red hair like Jerold and Milton Tuescher. Glennys hated red hair. She wished that itinerant hired girl would go back to wherever it was she'd come from.

The men moved back and forth, between the gardens, the porch, and the stable compound. The streamers were so transparent and delicate that the lights looked different wherever you stood.

Muran didn't feel strain in his neck muscles or the cold as he gazed above him. How could a man write about this for remembrance's sake? How could he describe truly this tremulous evanescence that appealed directly to his organ of imagination? Such a vision made self-pity unthinkable. It took a man out of himself and allowed him to believe in himself at the same time. It made a kinship with everyone who was outside of the Big House, standing entranced by the spectacle in the sky.

The lights were fading and the people realized how cold they were. Cook ordered the dining hall shut and cleaned. He refused to give the Baron's men any more ale. "Justice Day tomorrow. You've got to be clearheaded. It won't be a picnic."

Muran said to Wildan, "I'd like to hear more about the Badlands."

"I want to hear more too," declared Hengst.

Wildan had the most charming smile, Muran thought, of anyone he'd ever met.

Wildan said, "If you can find us something to warm our guts I think the Schoolmaster and I would be willing to share a glass of it with you before you head to bed. We can go into the Library office. Your father won't be using it any more tonight—nor Powell either, I think." He nodded in the direction of another itinerant kitchen maid who was heading for Powell's bedroom, next to the Library.

The Northern Lights had faded and, now that they were in

the Library, so had Muran's sense of kinship with the soldiers. He removed a leather-bound volume, *Dreams of an Old War Horse,* from the lounge so Wildan could make himself comfortable. Pages fell out of the binding. The Schoolmaster picked them up carefully and replaced them in the book.

Wildan said politely, "This room's much like my father's Library. Like our Baron, my father also prefers fireplaces to stoves."

Hengst came in and things felt more comfortable. The boy wiped away the dust from a bottle that had a label in the language of Tourienne. "From Grandfather's time," Hengst announced with satisfaction. After taking out the cork, he pulled cushions off the divan against the wall and piled them on the floor between the lounge and the fire. Hengst's smooth skin glowed in the firelight.

Rampalli might have been looking for a warm, private place to play his flute, but seeing the Library was already occupied he took his instrument from his mouth.

They all asked Wildan questions about the Old Men and the Badlands. It didn't matter what he said. What mattered was that they weren't alone in the cold and the dark. What mattered was that there was companionship and warmth and something good to drink.

A cry leaped out of the Master Bedroom and ran through the corridors and rooms of the Big House. It was the sound of a woman taken out of her daytime self, into the long, deep passages of the night, where she wasn't alone.

Hengst pretended, like the others, that he hadn't listened to what they'd all just heard in the stillness of the Big House gone to bed. Rampalli began to play a slow, sleepy tune. Another cry, less sharp than the first but just as sweet, came through the wall that separated Powell's bedroom from the Library office. Wildan watched Hengst push himself up, wrapping his arms around his legs. It wasn't the first time that Wildan had noticed that Hengst's eyelashes were as long as his sister's.

The Library was quiet, except for coals snapping on the hearth. The winds slapped the Big House with gloved hands. In the final silence, after the final glass, Wildan and Hengst went off to bed. Rampalli too went off to his tiny room at the end of the downstairs corridor that he shared with Muran.

The Schoolmaster was alone in the Library when Cook made his last round of the House. "Sleep, Master. You have to ride to Dephi tomorrow too. Then this business will be over and we'll have Three Trees to ourselves again."

# TEN

Many hours later, long after Alam's winter coat of many colors had floated over Soudaka's night sky, the Elder Jervis hurried over the path that connected Tuescher's farm to the garden behind the kirk.

In Reverend Tuescher's great-grandfather's time as Bishop there had been a revelation. The Coals of the Lord from all over the County were to plant box elder trees and crickwillow as windbreaks on the northern edge of Dephi to protect it from the duststorms that had followed three years of drought. A further revelation extended the shelterbelt around the Tuescher farmyard and gardens, leaving a path between the trees. The path was wide enough to accommodate a hitch of oxen and a wagon so that tithes could be brought from the kirk to the Reverend's farmhouse for safekeeping.

Jervis was glad to catch sight of the kirk garden. The covered hot dishes he was bringing from Tuescher's wives were making his hands uncomfortably warm—just like his Reverend made everything uncomfortable. He walked quickly past the eternal fire that burned in the center of the kirk garden. His feet and nose were cold. He was afraid he'd drop the dishes.

Inside the kirk, in the pulpit room, Elder Beal wished Jervis would get back with Tuescher's breakfast. He didn't like being alone with Soudaka's Bishop these days. He hadn't liked it since the Coals of the Lord had burned the witch.

The pulpit room, unlike the rest of the stone kirk, had been built of wood. The floor was covered by thick rag rugs braided by the women of Tuescher's family. The benches had both backrests and cushions. The cushion on which Beal's substantial body rested had a cover of cross stitchery on heavy linen. It had been donated, like many other things in the pulpit room, by his own first wife. He shoveled some more coals into the stove and sat back down on the cushion without looking at it. That particular cushion always made him remember the years in which he'd striven to achieve Deacon. Without the Deacon's office he'd couldn't be considered for an Elder's Hat.

Beal touched the Elder's Hat, the sign of his high office, and almost wished he didn't have it. He stole a look from the corner of his eye at his Reverend, the Great Bishop of Soudaka County. Reverend Tuescher was an unmoving lump, just as he'd been during the midnight hours. Except to indicate he wanted more Fire Ale, Tuescher might as well have been a granite boulder in one of his fields, Beal thought.

No one admired Tuescher's stony qualities more than he did. But the Reverend was too hard on his creatures these days. Flint that sparked the Fire of Alam was called for, not this dumbness of stone. Beal wanted to know what Alam had revealed by opening his coat of many colors last night, the night before Justice Day. Tuescher had remained silent. One thing had become clear, however. Many of the congregational men, both in Dephi and in the outlying parts of the County, thought the Light wanted them to attack the Baron.

There was a scratching at the pulpit room door, a sound like a very large rat would make. Elder Jervis, unaccustomed to women's work, made a clumsy thing of opening the door while juggling hot dishes. With Soudaka's Bishop waiting for Alam to reveal his will, any woman, no matter how deft in service, would be an abominable distraction inside the kirk. Jervis served Tuescher at his desk.

The desk had been constructed by Jervis's own cousin, before the cabinet-maker had become a Deacon. The napkins that used to be in the robing closet, the ones embroidered by Stella Heitkamp, weren't there anymore. It was another sign that she wasn't a member of the Dephi congregation in good standing.

Kolkiss had come squeaking to the Reverend that his oldest girl had gone off to apprentice to Three Trees' Stablemaster, just like he'd come squeaking about Stella's refusal to go to the witch's burning, just like he'd squeaked that his wife had lost herself after the last dead baby. Kolkiss never would redeem himself, thought Jervis. He could never be respected or advanced in the congregation after the way he had lost his father-in-law's cooperage. The Bohns had taken it over, like they'd taken over so much else.

Elder Jervis thought righteously of his first two wives and the obedience he'd exacted from them. No man could find favor in Alam's sight when he couldn't even keep his women in order.

Tuescher pushed his bench closer to the desk where his breakfast had been laid out by Jervis. The two Elders watched anxiously as he lifted the first mouthful to his face.

"Get out of here," Tuescher commanded. "The sight of the two of you gaping makes me lose my stomach."

Jervis and Beal escaped to the kirk basement where the jugs of Mule-Kick sent around from Three Trees last night had been stashed.

Jervis took a deep swallow of Mule-Kick, spilling the strong drink over his glossy, black beard. Like many of the brethren, he'd been nipping all through the cold night. "Long hours with our silent Bishop unsettles my belly as much as it does his," he complained.

Beal had taken his spirits sparingly. Unlike Jervis, he'd kept quiet the whole time last night's discussion had raged. The Coals of the Lord, from all the congregations, had been loud and determined. They wanted to fight against Nolan, not fight for her.

Before last night's prayer meeting Dephi congregation's wives had set out a big supper for their guests from the outlying congregations. There was lots of food left. Jervis rubbed grease from cold roast goose on his chest. He'd forgotten he wasn't in his work clothes.

The two Elders couldn't stay still. They paced the stone floor to keep their blood moving. A mouse scurried along the basement wallstones.

Jervis repeated what had been said many times last night. "The Baron's here with soldiers. That means there's another campaign for Nolan coming up. That's why they're here.

They're here to make us fight another heathen war! Attack them instead, that's what we should do!''

Beal lost to temptation. He accepted the half-full jug of Mule-Kick when his companion handed it over. Beal was cold, his belly unsettled. "Which way do you think the Reverend's going to jump? Will he advise the Coals of the Lord to do it?''

Jervis opened another jug. His eyes watered and he sneezed with tornado force. He wiped his running nose on the back of his hand. "Prochnow wants vengeance for his son. And I think it's out of Tuescher's hands and in Alam's. I looked over the shed where the muskets and crossbows were stored. It's empty. Ever since the survivors from the last campaign came back, our Bishop was always willing to have the young brethren practice with them. He likes guns. He says they carry Alam's Fire.''

Beal tested Jervis a bit. "If our Reverend gives no orders, neither Aristo nor Alaminite can legally hold him responsible for what happens." He neatly wiped his mustache and short-trimmed beard on a linen handkerchief.

Jervis saw the lay of the land with different eyes. He said, "Some of us still have the fire as hot as when we were Coals of the Lord. I've got two newborn sons at home. Your youngest has been in pantaloons for a long time already.''

Beal wondered where he was going to get land enough for his five sons so they could achieve the same life he had— several wives and the tribute of Alam's favor of many children. Jervis didn't seem to worry about that, even though his farm had less acreage than Beal's.

Jervis declared, "It was a revelation that the last conscription brought back guns and crossbows. It was as much a revelation as Alam's coat of many colors in the sky last night.''

Beal said, "It was only bits and pieces of the conscription that came back at all. I understand how the young brethren feel.''

Beal rubbed a bit of goosegrease from his cuff. The Aristos had always extracted a large toll for Alaminite resistance. He didn't think this time would be any different, guns or not. His lifelong devotion and zeal had made him the head of a prosperous clan. He had the cares of his congregation in his hands. He wanted to keep it that way. But the Coals of the Lord, the pack of younger brethren that included two of his own sons, had no families or farms of their own. They wanted to fight—anything, all the time. It would be almost a relief to have them out of the County.

Jervis made a fist. The Mule-Kick had sent heat flowing down into his rough hands. "I remember what it was to be a Coal of the Lord. It would have been the sweetness of the honeycomb to strike for Alam against the Aristos. Our time has come. We've got to make a stand, no matter what happens, or else we're not men! We endure too much from the fornicators who grab our Lord's own."

Beal was tired of Jervis's dissembling. "You're not the only one who has more sons than land to give them. You believe that if they fight against the Baron they'll lose as we always do. Your oldest sons, angry against going off to fight the heathen, will forget there's no place for them here either. I won't fight against the Aristos. Neither will the Reverend and neither will you."

"I will too," declared Jervis, who opened another keg of Mule-Kick.

Beal sampled some of the new cask too.

They felt warm again, and therefore hungry. They lurched back toward the table holding platters of food. The mouse thought they were only another two pillars holding up the kirk. Drawn by the torn-up feast high above it, the mouse squeaked. Jervis's boot smashed down inches from where the mouse's long tail really was. Jervis burped and broke wind. He dropped to all fours, like his youngest sons. "Got to find that mouse. We can't have no mouse in Alam's house."

He sat up on his haunches when Tuescher's voice roared like Alam's tornado out of the pulpit room. "Take this slop away and put a jug of Mule-Kick into my hands!"

"That's what I wanted to hear," yelled Jervis as the two Elders raced up the basement stairs.

Most of the hot food was uneaten. Beal put the covers over it. No sense in wasting good food. If he was still in Dephi when this Justice Day was over he'd see that an unfortunate sister-cousin got these leavings from the Reverend's meal. He made the Circle of Light in front of his chest to seal the vow.

He filled Tuescher's chalice to the brim with Mule-Kick.

The Reverend said, "What better to fire revelations about Aristos than their own stuff brewed on Three Trees? Both of you drink up with me." Tuescher drained his chalice and shoved it under Beal's nose.

"More. I am ready to receive revelation. What be like the town and my people?"

Beal touched his beard and his lips. He spoke carefully, a master since childhood at telling Tuescher what he wanted to know without saying what he didn't want to hear.

"The Coals of the Lord emptied the arsenal since last night."

Tuescher's rawboned body jerked in the bench behind his desk. "They believe that Alam helps those who help themselves, I see."

Jervis broke in. He never could stand to be left out of anything, even as a boy, Beal thought. And unlike his, Jervis's words were slurred. He never could match Tuescher drink for drink like Beal could.

Jervis was excited, saying what he'd not told Beal. "Your first wife told me that your third daughter-in-law told her that the Coals of the Lord helped themselves to the arsenal. All the rest, outlying congregational Elders and Reverends, are behind closed shutters. They pray without ceasing that Alam grants their Reverend and their Bishop a revelation to take on the fornicating Aristos."

The ancient clock bonged the morning hour. Beal parted the heavy curtains over the diamond-shaped pieces of glass that made the window. Through the wavery lines of glass he looked into the garden in the back of the kirk. "Alam's Light is throwing shadows from the east garden wall. Soon Nolan's men will display themselves before our women and children in their disgusting fornication pantaloons."

Tuescher's laugh scraped like a pick on granite. "I've seen you, Beal, in pants that open up in the front myself."

Beal was surprised that he was slightly fuddled. "Only in my own house, among my own women, Reverend. In the sight of other men's wives and daughters I wear decent clothes that button up the side," he said with dignity.

Jervis thought that though he and Beal were as close to Tuescher's councils as a hen to her egg, the Reverend liked to see them squirm like a worm in the hen's beak. If he were a

Reverend and a Bishop, he wouldn't treat his cronies like this. Lord forgive him, Jervis thought. The Mule-Kick had started to work in him after all. He saw Beal leaning against the pulpit room wall. He had a seemly expression of solemnness on his face.

Tuescher drank again from his chalice. For the first time since returning to the pulpit room from the meeting last night, he stood up. He pissed long and strong into the slop jar in the corner. He hawked and spit after.

"Yes," he said, fumbling with the buttons on the side of his trousers. "My people don't abate their prayers."

The volume of his voice expanded. It filled the pulpit room. "I feel the heat of my people beseeching Alam. His fire grows hot in my heart from the warmth of their prayers."

Beal thought his eyes played a trick on him. He thought he saw Tuescher reeling as he reached for the jug of Mule-Kick and his Bishop's Hat at the same time.

The pulpit room was hot. So was Tuescher. The slop jar in the corner was a strong stink. The air vibrated, breaking into lines of hot and cold. Tuescher breathed air in cold and breathed it out hot. "Alam! Alam! You're close! You are close to me!" Tuescher implored. "Show me what I must see!"

Reverend Tuescher tore open his coat. He leaped high in the air. He sank from his leap to a bench. He bent over the Bishop's Hat in his hands. The Seeking Stone, sewed into a pouch in the Hat's crown, sagged heavily between his thighs. He plunged his face into the Hat, up to his ears. Heat rose off him like vapors from a slough during the noons of high summer.

Beal's and Jervis's eyelids quivered. The lesser seeking stones owned by every patriarch showed where to find water and things that were lost. The Great Stone sewn into the Bishop's Hat revealed Alam's will. The excitement from being present while the Great Stone was used made the two Elders grope for the jug.

Tuescher threw back his head. His arms and his shoulders shook from Fire that worked in him. "Lord," he gasped. He rocked on the bench. "Your servant is here and fills with your Light and your Heat. Give it to me, Lord, give it to me! Give it to me!"

Tuescher snarled like a bear, barked like a wild dog, squeaked like a gopher. He thrust his face back down between his knees, into the Bishop's Hat. He bucked to his feet, head up, eyes staring wide. All of them turned to the east wall. It flickered blue, yellow, and red nimbi, like the highest-grade coals in the stove.

"Horsewhore, I see you. Stella's dark spawn. Dark without the Light of Alam in you. Full of filthy horse love. Aristo pet. Like your mother, you rub around them like a dog rubs herself in crap." Tuescher's teeth snapped like a trap on a rabbit's paw.

The heat drained away until the room was only warm. "Alam has shown me what he's shown me," Tuescher panted. "The Aristos come. Tell the young brethren that Alam's blessing is with them. What they do is the first step that will take us from this place of Nolan that corrupts the soul. We will go to the clean, empty mountains of the Southwest. There Alam wishes us to establish the Kingdom of Alam on Mittania. There will be no Aristos, no Horselovers, no Kings of Nolan. Go out and give my people Alam's revelation."

Jervis kneeled on the floor. "Blessed be Alam's stones." Jervis found that getting up from the floor was more difficult than getting down. Without waiting to see if Beal was with him, he lunged out the pulpit room door.

Tuescher examined Beal with eyes both serene and sly. "And you? Don't your knees bend on this morning of revelation?"

Beal was no longer the least bit fuddled from the Mule-Kick or lack of sleep. He shook his head. He did feel drained and found it astonishing that Tuescher was so calm and upright after what he'd just been through. "It's all clear to me, just as if I'd gone face to face with the Seeking Stone myself." Beal shook his head again. "Praise Alam, I didn't have to go through that ordeal, we have you for that. I've never seen before what it takes out of a man to see what the Lord illuminates."

"What is it you see, Beal?" asked the Reverend.

Beal was elevated, floating in revelatory light. "Attack the Aristos on Justice Day. The congregations will suffer the true Aristo Justice, which we've forgotten can be put on us any-time at Aristo pleasure. The consequences will be one more goad for exodus to the Promised Land. No Aristos, no Kings. Only the Lord's Chosen People. In the Promised Land there will be no pollution from witches like old Mabley, the worldly like the Bohns, or the heretics like Stella. It will be the Great Gatherin.''

Tuescher looked at the man he'd known since they'd both had cornstarch on their bottoms. He'd never seen Beal so full of Alam's Light.

"I couldn't have said it better myself," said Tuescher. "But remember, Alam has to use frail men. Don't forget that there's a tunnel that leads from the kirk basement here in Dephi to—someplace else. I need smart and willing hands to go with me, to chart out the land, to do the work necessary before we can lead our sons to the Kingdom of Light."

# ELEVEN

Like the humblest congregational farmer, the Baron had to take the weather into account in whatever plans he made. After the first blizzard, Darkcold's temperatures were bitter but the skies were generally clear. Then came the month of Rue and snowstorms that followed each other like wolves after deer. If the Baron wanted a ceremonial Justice Day it had to take place before Darkcold was finished.

On Justice Day Glennys woke up early, thinking about her moves. She had wanted to be the first person awake, but almost everyone else had stumbled in the dark to their work early too. As long as she was where she was supposed to be and doing what she was supposed to be doing she was invisible. She wanted it that way.

There hadn't been a public payout of taxes since before the Baron's last campaign. It was an opportunity for Dephi to have another big market day this year before Rue shut the County up in snow and ice. Glennys couldn't wait to ride in front of the members of Tuescher's congregations and be seen by all eyes on horseback with the Baron's people.

Glennys lounged on Torrie's back. Everything was so good here on Three Trees. The Baron protected her. He thought she was good luck. He gave her Torrie. She wanted to be like the Baron in every way.

She yawned and laid her head against Tornado's neck. She let her arms dangle, pretending there weren't any bones inside the flesh. She worked hard at patience. It was still too soon to put a saddle on Torrie. Someone might come in and notice before it was too late to get her on that bloody pony.

She loved the fur inside her riding leathers and the way they creaked. After all this time the Baron's scent was still in the fur. She liked the Baron's smell.

Everyone was supposed to have their horses outside so Rampalli could put the Baron's people into a seemly column. Glennys could hear him cursing the cold for putting his fifes out of tune.

She'd been sly. Several times during the week she'd asked where she was supposed to be. It was smart that she'd asked often because Rampalli had changed his mind more than once. But he'd not fret over her as he did about the men who lingered over the hot breakfast ale. She was too excited to eat. She'd get something at Cook's stand in Dephi's market later. She muttered soothing promises into Torrie's ears. He was restless because he could hear and smell his stallmates outside. He wanted to be with them.

She heard Powell grumble to the Head Groom at the other end of Long Stable. She'd heard the complaint before. "This parade is a waste of time. There was no bloody reason Fulk couldn't have collected cash and conscription while they were out in the County. If he'd done it like that they'd be out of here by now and Three Trees could be doing its proper work of training war horses."

Soon after Powell's grumbles had faded away, Thurlow came in the side door. In her white furs she picked delicately through Long Stable's center aisle. She was on tiptoe, holding her split skirts above her ankles.

Glennys giggled. "It doesn't do you any good to walk in stable muck like a ballerina. The fur boots get covered with horseshit just the same."

"I thought this was where you were," Thurlow said with satisfaction. "My father's going to start soon. You'd better get out there with Merrylegs."

Glennys had enjoyed the hours in Thurlow's bedroom last night. The tea she'd made took away Glennys's cramps. After the Northern Lights had faded Thurlow had told her about the man she was to marry and what her life had been like in St. Lucien. Glennys thought they were friends. She said, "You must understand that I can't ride into Dephi on a pony." For good measure, Glennys tried to flutter her eyelashes like Thurlow did.

"What's the matter with your eyes, Glennys? Got dirt in them? No? Get on your pony and come out into the yard."

That stung. "You aren't my Stablemaster or my Baron either. I don't have to do what you say."

Thurlow rubbed her cheek against her furred shoulder. "Maybe," she purred, "I'm like my father. Maybe I like to tell girls what to do. Especially one like you, that he says trains so well."

Glennys decided that Thurlow was as elemental as the weather. The only thing you could know for certain about her was that sometimes she was nice and sometimes she wasn't. But the stable and its matters weren't Thurlow's business. "Get on your own horse, Miss Thurlow. I'll be there when I'm ready. You're talking too loud. Tornado's getting edgy. He's not run today, only worked on a lunge line. Powell'd send you outside."

"By Gordon's Balls!" Thurlow swore, just to see what would happen.

Tornado's head came up and he snorted. His ears twitched between the fur-wrapped girl outside his stall and the voice, weight, and warmth on his back that had taken the place of his Badlands mates. One hoof raked the straw. Glennys squeezed her thighs and calves against his ribs. She hitched forward toward his withers. He took a couple of steps ahead. She hadn't tied him.

Thurlow didn't back down. She used the same voice that a mother uses on a small child. "You cannot take a fresh three-year-old stallion, one that hasn't been handled since last fall, into Dephi among a lot of people. He's clumsy on his first snowshoes. He's sweating now. You can't ride. You're not really going to be so stupid as to try what you're thinking about.''

Glennys liked looking down at Thurlow from Tornado's back. "I can make Tornado do whatever I want. If you keep making us jumpy, we're gonna scream. Either go away or go get Powell, but leave us alone.''

"I don't need Powell. I don't believe you've got the bottom to try it,'' Thurlow said speculatively. "But I bet Hengst will put money on it that you will. We'll be waiting.'' Thurlow left.

Glennys had no time to wonder about bets. She took Tornado to a mounting block. Getting the saddle on his back was hard work for someone her size. She was running with sweat before she succeeded. He took the bit sweetly and she slipped him a piece of bread soaked in honey. His slobber cleaned off her sticky fingers.

It was a tricky business leading him out of Long Stable. He knew he was going to join the other horses. She kept his head down, her hand over his nostrils, determined he shouldn't call out to his brethren. She had to stop often to keep steady. When they halted she had to convince them both that they were doing just what they wanted to do.

On his back she collected the reins and encouraged Torrie's forward desire. She allowed him a high, happy whinny. He informed the other horses that he was coming. Smoky, his stallmate, gave back a cheerful welcome.

Powell's voice cracked like a whip to Glennys's ears. "Just what do you think you're about, Horsegirl? You know better than this.''

"Good boy, Torrie," she murmured. "Keep walking to Smoky. Don't buck, please don't buck. Don't trot, don't reach for the bit, not yet. I can't feel the reins because my fingers are so cold but I know you're there and you know I'm here. I'd rather be on you without a saddle too, but we have to have one to be like the others. You're big and beautiful and on you I'm tall and good. You're not going to stumble and I'm not going to fall. Then we'd be failures and we'd have to stay home alone. You're not like that nasty pony, you're so much better and so much taller." It didn't matter what she said as long as she kept him believing the sound of her voice.

Deadly stood under the Baron. The big black stallion's ears

pitched forward. That voice belonged to him just like the voice of the man on his back. Torrie pranced across Deadly's position. Torrie wrinkled back his lips like he'd done as a foal in the Badlands, telling Deadly that he was only small, that he couldn't challenge the dominant stallion.

The Baron liked seeing the girl's small figure mounted on the charger. There was a queer fitness about a horse born to carry a man to war who was also pleased to carry a little girl. A war horse needed a trainer who could teach him to perform on command. A war horse couldn't learn to think for himself if his trainer didn't have the spirit for it.

She was supposed to ride next to Muran. Thurlow and Hengst would hold either end of their line. Powell moved faster on foot and outflanked Glennys and Torrie before they got to their place.

Glennys was proud when she leaned back and brought Tornado to a halt right in front of Powell. This was very important. She inhaled the smell of herself and horse, leather and the Baron. She pitched her voice to carry to the Baron, but low enough not to startle the horses.

"It will look stupid to have a pony in with all the horses. If I can't ride into Reverend Tuescher's town on a horse, I shouldn't go at all."

Powell reached for Torrie's bridle. "Stablemaster, please, don't shame me. You told me I shouldn't take another man's bridle while the rider's still got the reins in his own hands. I've got the reins."

The Stablemaster stopped in mid-reach and looked at the clumsy collection of reins in Glennys's bare fingers. He talked over his shoulder. "Fulk, this isn't a pleasure ride. Tornado's too valuable to gamble with this way."

The Baron tongued his toothpick to the other side of his mouth. "Sure it is. Sure it's a pleasure ride." He stood in his stirrups and stretched. "Looks like the Horsegirl's going to try for her spurs even though she got thrown and kicked yesterday. You and I weren't much older ourselves when we got ours."

"Some horses suffered for it too, as I recall," Powell responded.

The Baron pulled the brim of his hat further over his eyes. "It's like being a doctor. You've got to kill your patients before you start to learn anything."

Deadly farted and Tornado broke wind right after. Laughter finished the discussion.

Glennys and Torrie walked past Thurlow and Muran. This was the most difficult maneuver, the one she'd woken up thinking about. They had to insert themselves into the line without disturbing the others. She backed Torrie in between Hengst's Smoky and Muran's mare, Battle Ax.

Hengst put out his fur-gloved hand to Thurlow. "I win, you lose,' he said. A foolish smile spread over Glennys's face.

Fulk laughed. To Powell, who had mounted his own horse and moved next to him, he said, "It's nice to have a fresh one around the old place."

"Spoken like a father who leaves the work of training to someone else," Powell shot back.

"Head out," ordered the Baron. "No music, Rampalli, until the last milestone, where a unit of my men will be waiting." Then, looking back at Glennys, he said, "And you'd better hang on with everything you've got."

The only transfiguring moments Glennys had ever received inside a kirk had been when the congregational voice raised in choral harmony and hosanna chorus. Now she sang hosannas under her breath. This was as close to the transport of her own herds, dreamed out of the skies of Soudaka, as she'd ever come. This wasn't like her dreams but it was real. She sent a beneficent smile around Muran's body over to Thurlow.

Thurlow blew back a kiss. "The day isn't over yet," she said. One of her legs was hooked over a sidesaddle. She was as beautiful against the snow as her schooled white filly named Will Tell, or Willi for short.

Bannerets and pennons winged over the last milestone to Dephi. As Powell unwrapped Three Trees' flag and thrust it into his stirrup boot, he said, "We didn't meet a single person coming in from the farms."

The Baron said, "They're already drinking and eating and praying. This is a big event for Dephi."

It was at this milestone that Tuescher had struck Stella when she'd fallen to the road. Tornado bucked and Glennys's teeth bit through her tongue. She swallowed the blood. She wouldn't spit on the ground where her mother had been punished. She looked away from the milestone and up to the flag of the Eidel Kings. It was quartered in blue, yellow, green, and red.

Muran, too, remembered that scene. His shoulders expanded out of their hunch inside his fur cape as he handed her a handkerchief. "Glennys, wipe the blood off your mouth."

Rampalli and the music corps ran over the signals they'd drilled. He listened critically to the saddle drums. Wildan, Fulk, and Powell conferred with Colonel Rastall. The Colonel was scowling. His big nose swept from side to side, trying to smell the wind.

"The town's fuller of Alaminites than a pig shed's full of shit. The market's doing a fast business. The Coach Inn's well-guarded front and back. We'll escort the Lighters in according to the order you've made on the tax rolls. When you've collected the cash tax, send the farmers you want out the back door for their cup of King's Health. We'll put them into the stable. There's nowhere else since the garrison wasn't ever rebuilt."

The Baron said, "When the Lighters burned the garrison Grandfather burned Dephi. They remember that! Don't stint on the drink in town. As soon as our column arrives at the Coach you can beat the buggers out of their kennels if they don't want to come on their own. Get them drinking Three Trees' courtesy cups. A Lighter will take as much as a mule if he can get it."

The Colonel nodded. "We sent around casks of Cook's Mule-Kick all over town last night too." His expression lightened. "The town's clean as your mother's titty—pardon me, Fulk. But no broken staves means they got drunk and they'll need something more to cure today's pain."

His nose lifted out of his mustache and shivered like a snake's tongue testing the breeze. "It'd be easier if we could treat them like foreigners. This place doesn't feel like Nolan. I never could stand these god-believing places."

He raised his voice. "Schoolmaster, we've had your bloody colleagues on our hands. They've been up at the Coach for two days, won't stay in the Schoolhouse. They've been drinking up the Queen's Bounty before you've handed it out. But they're Nolanese so we made Prochnow give 'em credit. My opinion is that they couldn't learn a dog to eat vomit."

The Baron slapped the Colonel's shoulder. "Soldiers and

civilians don't mix any better for you than Nolan and Alam, hey?''

"I don't get pleasure out of taxes, Baron. I want to get to Sace-Cothberg and have action."

Glennys and Tornado stomped their feet. They wanted to get moving away from this milestone. She felt even now there were eyes on her that waited for her to fall.

# TWELVE

Glennys had imagined that all of Dephi's congregation would gather along the one cobbled thoroughfare and watch her ride proudly with Nolan's horse soldiers. But the few people standing out on the street were coal traders and cloth merchants. Their cheers were thin and far between. Instead of impressive horsemanship, Glennys displayed her ignorance and her horse was humiliated. She knew even less than Torrie what the others had mastered during years of practice and training.

The horses advanced into Dephi at an extended trot. For a second, their forelegs paused high in the air. On the downbeat of the drums, their forelegs dropped. Torrie didn't know how to do that. Smoky and Battle Ax neighed at Torrie and it wasn't a playful warning. They were at work and he wasn't doing his part. They laid back their ears and showed big teeth. Battle Ax bit Torrie's neck when he stumbled into her withers and made her lose time. The old mare and the middle-aged gelding moved in close to Torrie and tried to hold him in line with their shoulders, even though he couldn't follow the steps. Neither Hengst nor Muran had any skill at this, but their horses did.

Glennys's seat was not proud or correct. She scrambled just to stay on Torrie's back and keep his head up and pointed in the right direction. He wanted to veer to the side and stop. Her numb fingers clung to his mane and she sat on the reins.

The other riders bent to their horses' ears, signalling the well-known language of toes, heels, calves, thighs, and balance. Dephi echoed to the war cry of Nolan's horses, answered by the stallions under the Baron's men stationed at the Coach Inn. Torrie squealed in frustration. He didn't know what to do.

The Baron's men put their horses into *courbette,* a prancing leap in which the horses' forelegs advanced equally at once. They raised themselves on their hind legs and jumped three times. The wind instruments were silent. The drums were alone, giving the beat. The horses executed the *piaffe,* a collected trot on the spot, marking time but not moving forward.

At the kirk, Glennys and Torrie were hopelessly out of line. Men swore at them. Their horses wanted to kick the intruder who had penetrated their guard.

Torrie was as anxious as Glennys was to get back between Smoky and Battle Ax. They were older and more experienced than he, but one was his stallmate and familiar, and neither one was a dominant war stallion. Glennys was completely ashamed. She hid her red face in Torrie's mane. It was her fault and she babbled apologies to him. She'd never hear the last of this from Thurlow—if the Baron and Powell even allowed her to remain on Three Trees.

She had to get control of herself so she could get control of Torrie. The Coach Inn, their final destination and the end of this nightmare, was still far up the street.

Eggs were precious during winter, but the air was full of them. The right side of her leathers dripped yellow from broken yolks. Torrie's mane was full of broken shells and yolk. It was going to be a long grooming to get it properly clean. The thought of how much extra work that would be began to make her angry. She stopped babbling at Torrie. The guilty scarlet subsided.

"Horsewhore! Aristo's horsewhore!" Glennys knew the voice. That was Milton, Tuescher's son, the plague of her school days.

She stood in her stirrups and yelled at the rooftops. She could feel Torrie become more confident. "Lighter bully! Come down here, Milton, I dare you!"

She saw her Baron look back over his shoulder at her when

Torrie's neigh rang out with a note of challenge. The Baron winked.

Muran grabbed her shoulder. "Sit in your saddle and shut up! You already have more trouble on your hands than you can handle."

Then shit hit the street.

A pail of nightsoil splashed over the quarters of Powell's stallion. He squealed but remained in line. Ox flop dripped down Nolan's flag. Colonel Rastall shouted, "That wasn't here this morning when I rode out of town." Glennys didn't know what the Colonel meant.

She saw Elder Jervis running up the street. He was shouting like Colonel Rastall, but she couldn't understand what he said. The Baron was bellowing to Rampalli. Wildan was blowing a signal to the column from a trumpet baldricked on his shoulder. Muran was yelling in her ear.

"The pot-guts! Why didn't I come in and see to it myself?" He cursed the blockaded school.

Smoke belched from the stovepipes but the school's roof was invisible under deep banks of snow. All the snow scraped out of Dephi had been collected and contemptuously dumped over and around the school.

"If my colleagues had been where they belong this wouldn't have happened. They don't deserve the Queen's Bounty!"

Muran was leaning over Torrie's withers, and Battle Ax didn't like that. She began to punish Torrie in earnest. Torrie wasn't going to put up with it anymore.

He reared, bucked, and plunged through the horses in front of him. He was getting away. Horse and girl rammed between the Baron and Wildan. Torrie ran flat out over the ground that separated them from Queen's School.

Glennys's whole body relaxed into the rhythm of Torrie's alternating gather and release. This was easy, not like fighting with her ignorance back in the line. She thought she was getting in control again.

Something whizzed past Torrie's shoulder, followed by a whole swarm.

They were headed for the bank of snow that spilled across the street from the schoolyard. They wouldn't get hurt running into snow.

Behind her she heard the Baron's voice, "Muran, get my children away from here."

The snow loomed in front of them. She felt Torrie's muscles collect under her. They made a tremendous leap and landed on the top. It collapsed under them. They skidded in the slush on the other side in a nest of armed Alaminites.

Crossbows released a host of quarrels. Pig stickers jabbed at Tornado from all around them, ripping his flesh. The quilted leather over Glennys's shoulder partially turned the blow from an ox flail. She hung on, fingers frozen in Torrie's mane.

Down the street, horses trumpeted and turned in *pesade*. Moving, but still in place, the riders assessed the field and collected their weapons.

Rampalli blew *renvers*. The riders became targets that moved in profile. At the sound of *repolon* the horses switched to the sideways gait that turned around the center, which was Fulk.

The air broke. It smelled as though a granite boulder had been split by lightning. Glennys and Torrie were on the other side of the ambush. It wasn't a question of controlling her horse. She was *in* him. His voice was a growl. His neck snaked low and long. His knees flexed. He stalked his prey in a half-crouching run that was as fleet as a wolf's. The enemy was in front of them. Torrie threw himself forward. His forehand rose, hiding his rider from the man. A fist struck their faces and thunder tore their ears.

The Baron's men turned in formation and charged.

Torrie went down and took his target with him. Glennys flew free of the saddle just before Torrie hit the slush. He was crying but something had happened to her ears and she could only hear him inside her head, and that hurt worse than the other way. She put her hand on a rock in the pile there for Alaminite slingshots.

There was no time for the Alaminites to reload. Snow had dampened the powder. Cold winds, one after another, flew over her head while Alaminites scattered and ran in all directions. The Baron's men at the Coach Inn and those that had followed after her and Torrie leaped back and forth over her fallen horse and the body sprawled under Torrie's neck.

The men were at ease in their saddles, and enjoyed riding

down Alaminites. They slapped and struck with their swords. They dropped nets over them. It would have been something worth watching, but Tornado was blind. His chest was mangled and his front legs were broken. His body had protected hers from the flintlock's discharge. That was what a war horse was supposed to do. He wasn't dead.

"Cook!" she screamed. "Please, Cook, come here, I need you!" She could hear herself now. She paid no attention when Acker took away the man who'd brought them down.

Glennys found a long knife that lay under the hand of an Alaminite who looked little older than Thurlow. His head was partly separated from his shoulders by a swordcut. His hand was crunched into the snow by a hoof shod in heavy, ridged snowplate. He was dead, but Torrie wasn't.

A horse's windpipe is a wide, thick, tough cord. Cook pushed her out of the way. He straddled Torrie's neck, pushing away the egg-pasted mane. In three strokes it was done.

"The Coach Inn is safe. You go there now, Glennys. There's still a man's work for me to do here."

He gave her a push up the street. Behind the schoolhouse, in the open field around Dephi, she saw the Baron's men running down fleeing Alaminites. The shiver and crack of doors beaten open was heard all over town. Alaminites were stupid. She'd always known they were stupid. And she'd been as stupid as they were.

Young Gordon galloped past her. "You got the luck of my ancestors, Horsegirl." She felt all wrong. By the time she reached the Coach she could hear women screaming and children weeping in terror.

The horse that the Baron had entrusted to her was dead. High, thick clouds were moving over the sky, spoiling the pristine blue, just as the snow back down the street had been made rotten with blood. But the air smelled neither of blood nor snow, only of winter that was going to stay for a long time.

Wildan's charger was led past her to the Coach. She tried not to look at the square-headed bolt that was lodged in Wildan's ribs. Bright red blood had flooded over his chest, the color that comes from torn lungs that pump one last time.

"This is war. This is what war looks like." Her old habit of talking out loud had returned.

Young Gordon handled Wildan's body gently. "This isn't war. This was a stupid brawl. A bloody shame that Wildan's luck ran out in a bloody stupid brawl. He was the best of us. *Your* luck is as strong as my ancestor's balls, Horsegirl."

"Why do you say that?" Glennys asked, having no notion of what he was saying, just wanting someone to talk to her.

"You're alive and he's dead." He softened a little. "Your horse taking off like that because he was young and untrained like you. That set off the ambush before it did us big damage. The Alam suckers couldn't hold their fire. Your horse scared the Mule-Kick right out of them. They shot off their bows and firearms before they should have. Or else they got excited because their friends were throwing shit at us and they didn't want to be left out. That's what I mean about it not being war. They didn't discipline themselves or work together."

Glennys followed Gordon up to the door of the Coach, but was reluctant to go inside. "Do you know where Hengst and Thurlow are?"

Gordon shrugged. "The Baron told Rampalli and Muran to get them out of Dephi."

She'd heard the order. The Baron had been worried about his children. Nobody worried about her. If she hadn't gotten Torrie killed she'd have someone to be with.

Some of Stella's words came to mind. "When your stomach turns sour the only cure for it is good, hard work." What was going on around her wasn't her work. She heard some of the soldiers cursing the Schoolmasters who refused to get out of the Coach. She'd take Wildan's horse to the stable and groom it good. She wanted to feel the horse's flesh under her hands. It was warm, smooth, firm. It was alive.

She was turned away from the stable. It wasn't a place for horses now. It was a place to keep Alaminite prisoners. "Acker's in charge of bringing in the first of them and they're coming along right while I talk to you," said one of the grooms who worked for the St. Lucien Post Stage Company. "I'll take that horse and find out where to put him, girlie. You go find yourself some nice, warm place."

She hopped to the top of the fence to get out of the way. Acker liked his work. He had a horsewhip. It must have belonged to the Post Stage Company because the lash was long enough to reach the front pair of the three teams of horses that ran in the Company harness. Acker wasn't really flogging anyone, just "tickling" them. That's what Reverend Tuescher and Elder Jervis called the whacks and thumps laid on their charges during catechism class. They were just tickling them to keep them lively and paying attention.

Kegs of Mule-Kick, but no water, were put in with the prisoners. All the aches and pains in Glennys's body felt worse while she listened to Acker jeer at the Alaminites.

"You, girl!"

Now he was going after her. "What do you want?" She despised this man who liked to kick someone who was down.

"You know who lives in these parts. Was Tuescher or Reverend Neary, Reverend Durl, Elder Beal, any of them in this bunch?"

Acker was as stupid as an Alaminite, she thought. "Of course not. The big men don't have anything to do with the Coals of the Lord. Only Deacons talk to them. The only one I saw was Elder Jervis and that was a long time ago. He was running. The Reverends and the Elders wouldn't have been at the school."

"Pretend you know an awful lot and tell it with an awfully proud tongue, I'm thinking, for a rider who lost her horse," jibed Acker.

"I think you talk awfully tall for a junior whose stallion tried to take Deadly after the Sword Dance," she taunted.

"If you don't know where Tuescher or any of the leaders are, pot it, slut. *Lighter* slut. That's all a Horsegirl is, a slut like all the King's Daughters." Acker's Savage reared and made a full *pirouette*, and dashed out of the Coach yard.

She had nothing to do so she had to remember. Sitting behind Tornado's neck while he faced their enemy before the kill had felt good. She'd never tell anybody about it but she had liked it. It had been something like what she'd felt when the Baron had picked her up in his arms on St. Lucien's Eve. But this time she'd been the one on top.

She pushed her hair back, pulling some yolk out of the strands closest to her eyes. She'd lost her headgear. She squirmed, remembering her disastrous ride into Dephi. Every time before, if she'd gotten into trouble, she'd tried to stay out of the way of those who dealt out punishment, hoping they'd get distracted by other things if she wasn't around to remind them. Stella always said pride and anger were deadly sins. If the Baron gave her absolution, maybe Powell would forgive her too. She had to do something, give the Baron something.

Glennys felt as though she'd been working hard all day. She was ravenous. She didn't think she'd get anything to eat today. She didn't deserve to eat when she'd killed Torrie.

She was alone with nothing to do. Since she'd come to Three Trees there was always someone with her, except when she slept. She climbed off the fence because her bottom was getting sore sitting on that wooden rail. She felt sticky inside her leathers. She pulled her shortcoat open at the neck and turned her moist face into the warm breeze that smelled damp and sweet. There was a slow drip of melting snow off the roof of the Inn.

Snook Wind! It thawed out the County in a short, false spring at the close of Darkcold every year. It could last as long as five days or be as short as twelve hours. But when it had spent itself, the ice froze everything tight-shut for weeks. Teased by the warming air, a horsefly buzzed around her head. "What little fly tunnel did you crawl out of?" she puzzled, shaking her head to shoo away the insect attracted by the moisture on her skin.

Tunnels were under all of this country, she thought, swinging by her arms on the fence. A tiny line of light crept through a knothole in one of the fence rails and traced a white path through the shadow thrown on the ground on the other side. It was a backwards tunnel. It was sort of how you saw things in a mirror. A tunnel is dark, but in the dark, a tunnel would be light. She knew where Reverend Tuescher and the other Alaminite leaders had gone. There was a tunnel out of the kirk basement.

She squinted her eyes at the fence shadow. When she was very young, not six, she was too young for kirk school but old enough for catechism class. There was a recess because Zebulin Monty never had his memory-work right and Tuescher took him down the basement to flog him and she saw because she was there. It was winter and she had to relieve herself and the pots were kept in a little room in the basement in winter. She was trapped.

Zeb had got it hot from Tuescher all right, and he sent the

crying boy back upstairs and she wondered why Milton and Jerold never caught it. They never learned anything. She was embarrassed to have the Reverend know she had to pee and she stayed behind the curtain. She always felt there was something about Reverend Tuescher that wasn't natural. He seemed both larger than life and not real to her little girl eyes. He was spooky, that was what it was.

While she waited for Tuescher to go away, part of the north wall just opened. There stood Elder Beal. Tuescher scolded him for using the tunnel. He yelled at Elder Beal just like he yelled at Zeb. The tunnel was supposed to be used only if there was terrible trouble, like with Aristos. Then the Reverend's sharp eyes spied the trembling curtains and he pulled them open. She was sure he'd beat her too, but he hadn't.

They had to have gone into that tunnel. She had to tell the Baron right away.

Fulk was raging. "Filthy, freaking Soudaka weather! It's going to come down like a demon hammer when the Snook quits. There's no other way. You got to go out there, farm by farm, congregation by congregation. Take every piece of brass, silver, and gold you find. Take anything else that looks valuable. Take every man between sixteen and sixty, as long as he's got two arms and can walk on two legs. You've got six days."

"Six days, Baron," replied Colonel Rastall, "if you include today."

"Count this Snook-fart day! This is Soudaka. It's either the weather or the Alaminites or both, but life's miserable."

"What about supplies, remounts?"

"Your weapons are enough. Take a change of horseshoes because you're going to have to change from snowplates to regulation campaign and back again before you're through. Remounts? *Of course remounts!* Live off the County. They asked for it. No skimming on the cash. Gelding for whoever puts one brass penny in his own pouch. Because it isn't you, it's me Eidel's going for if there's embezzlement of Nolanese funds from Nolanese citizens. Understand?"

"Fulk, you can't take everything!" Powell cried. "The women and children have to live through the winter and be left enough to plant in the spring. If you ruin them completely, how is Three Trees going to carry on without their contributions?''

"Shut up, Powell. Rastall's been at his business for a long time. He knows how much you can squeeze and still leave enough for the weeds to pop back up next year. It's the miracle of life," he said. His smile was brutal.

Glennys was desperate to get his attention, but she couldn't get into the chamber behind the Coach Inn's public room where he was. But she could hear him.

"The great-balled Great Bishop of the Alaminites? Why hasn't he been brought to me? Where are his conspirators? Where's your balls? You ride stallions and you can't find a fornicating man-god loving Reverend?"

Colonel Rastall left the others to face the Baron's wrath. He called his aides and lieutenants. "Come, my boys. We go to pillage Soudaka County and we've got less than six days. When your ass breaks from the saddle and your eyes fall out of your head, remember Wildan."

Glennys threw herself against him. Off his horse, the Colonel wasn't impressive. His game leg, injured by a horse falling on him in some long-ago battle, gave out under him. Instead of pushing her away, he grabbed her shoulder for support. It gave her a moment to babble out her conviction.

"I'll take you back to the Baron. But I hope you know what you're talking about. Guards, let the girl in."

Fulk took one look at her and ordered her to be gone. "Get out. I haven't time to fool with you."

She stuttered, her tongue tripping itself. "I know-know-know where Tuescher and the others went."

Fulk sat back in his chair. He put his hand over his chin and lips. He regarded her with eyes as hot as those of a hawk scouting a rabbit. After a moment he said, "I bet you do. Why didn't anyone think to ask you in the first place?"

She prudently said nothing, except about the tunnel.

Fulk said, "Children are to be seen and not heard. It's Gordon's Luck that this one saw as well as was seen. Send our Gordon on this one. Not Acker. He's too hot. And, child, you go with them to show them where it is—keep them from getting scared in a kirk."

The Aristos didn't find Tuescher and the other leaders in

the tunnel or at the end. But they did find lots of jugs of Mule-Kick, sacks of grain, and other provisions.

"Smart," said Gordon. "The only smart thing I've seen a Lighter do. End the tunnel in the wellhouse instead of his home, which we'd immediately have occupied."

He and the detail searched over the flat, white land behind Tuescher's farmstead. The Reverends and the other leaders of the Alaminites were out there somewhere. It didn't seem possible that they couldn't be seen. There was nothing to hide behind.

"They're on foot, too," said Gordon.

"On snowshoe and ski," Glennys corrected. "But the Snook Wind will spoil the snow real soon now. The top layers'll melt and thaw, and then freeze again after noon. It's gonna be crackle crust tomorrow, real hard going."

"Hard on a horse's legs and hooves too," Gordon said gloomily, thinking of what was ahead of him.

The Aristo detail had to satisfy itself by smashing the wellhouse. When the ground thawed in spring Powell would plow the tunnel into the ground.

Glennys was thrown up behind Cook to go home to Three Trees. Behind them they heard the Aristos riding out into the County. Burton had made a marching chorus to commemorate his first tour of duty.

> *The horse's dick is big and thick*
> *And he will help us kick the butts*
> *Of all the Lighters and their sluts.*

"Do you know who the man was that you and Tornado took down, Glennys?" asked Powell, who rode next to them.

She forced herself to look her Stablemaster in the face. It was starting, all the reminders of how badly she'd behaved.

"It was your father. You might like to know that he was stunned, not killed. The recoil from the flintlock he used knocked him over at the same time Torrie hit him."

Glennys had believed that Powell was going to say something else. "I always thought he wanted me to be dead," she said.

Cook started to talk. "I hope we have good weather this summer. It's going to be a hard year, what with the

Aristos scouring the County clean. If the Lighters don't get good crops, we might as well put boards over the kitchen door."

But Glennys had been hearing gloomy predictions about weather and crops all her life. No matter what, the people of Soudaka County would keep working.

# THIRTEEN

Glennys pretended she was studying. She really was doing nothing at all. It was another indication that spring was on its way.

The last of the King's Guard that had been billeted at Three Trees in the wake of the Gunpowder Ambush had returned to Old Nolan. Their mission to find Reverend Tuescher and the others high in the Alaminite hierarchy had been a failure. All the King's Guard had found was a rumor that their quarry had left Soudaka County.

With the Guard's departure Glennys's extra duty of feeding their horses, mucking out their stalls, and exercising the remounts was over. Then Powell and the horsehandlers took the young stallions out to the Badlands. There, he'd inspect the mares who were in foal and then bring back to Three Trees another batch of young stallions for elementary training. He'd also bring in the crop of four-year-olds that would be sold in the fall. For a few days Three Trees' furious activity was in a lull, suspended in the rains that made the ground unfit for horse training or exercise, poised between winter and spring.

The battered chair in which she sat leafing lazily through her notebook creaked as she twisted and stretched. The old horseblanket slid off her knees to the cluttered floor when she got up to look out of the rain-dimpled window of the stable office. It wasn't raining now.

Glennys swung the window open wide and leaned out to

look at the new thermometer, which had come all the way across the sea from Tourienne. It had a small platform all to itself. The red-dyed alcohol had risen steadily in the fine glass tube as the Marche rains and thaws broke up the snow and ice. The red line hovered close to the forty mark on the graph.

The Baron and Deadly were always in her thoughts. Today, she knew, they would sail from St. Lucien to the land of Sace-Cothberg in Outremere. One of the interesting things she'd learned this winter was that St. Lucien, though Nolan's capital, had been founded and named by coal merchants from Tourienne a long time ago, before the Aristos had ridden into the land. Though she'd been learning new things every day, it didn't make up for the absence of the Baron and Deadly. Deadly had a way of wrinkling up his black lips when he said hello, then curling his tongue around her wrist. It was as though extra life passed into her then, the same as when the Baron stroked her hair.

Glennys ran her hand over the braids behind her neck. She'd understood that the Baron loved long hair when she watched him reluctantly clip off Deadly's luxuriant mane into the neat campaign ridge. He'd talked to her about war horses while the clipper-blades flashed in the lantern light.

"A war horse is an extension of his rider and gives his life for his rider," the Baron had told her. "Their exercises aren't taught only for ceremony or attack, but are defensive as well. When the horse raises his forehand above ground in the *levade*, not only can he come down with great impact upon the enemy, but he's shielding his rider. He'll take the enemy's cut and thrust on his own chest and belly."

Tornado's death had taught her that perfectly. Though the Baron had relieved a portion of her guilt that last night before his departure, some of it remained. She felt not quite worthy of the horses and Powell. She was supposed to be like the Stablemaster—skilled, loving, and careful with these horses, so that they could die for someone. It was hard not to feel sad about it. Her sadness made it easier for her to obey Powell's order not to talk about hearing the horses.

She picked up her notebook from the chair. Her name was on the cover. The shelves on the wall had line after line of notebooks. Some had Powell's name on them. Others, falling to pieces, ink faded, leaves crumbled, had been made by stablemasters and apprentices who had long since crumbled away to dust themselves.

This was Glennys's first book. As the pages progressed, the handwriting changed into smaller, finer lines. She had to do a lot more writing on Three Trees than she'd done at Queen's School. These were Powell's lessons, but Muran was the one who taught her to outline and abstract, and to make both the ideas and the penmanship clear.

> *The training period is long. The first two years cover only the usual elementary training, except that the highest degree of exactness is required. In the third year the horse graduates from the Lower School to High School, and in the third and fourth years come daily riding and work sessions for varying periods depending on the qualities of the horse.*

> *Never let a horse stop a day's training with a sense of defeat. If he is going well, release him early in the flush of achievement.*

Part of the notebook was vocabulary lists, which she'd done over several times because new knowledge mastered demanded new organization.

> placenta *is the afterbirth which must be pushed out by the mare shortly after the foal is dropped.*

> summer sores *come from eggs deposited in wounds on the horse by flies.*

> sweet itch *is an inflamed, itchy thickening and scabbing of the skin on the rump and/or withers which become bare of hair and weepy in the flesh when the horse scratches against anything he can find.*

Everything she wrote in her notebook could be found in the other notebooks. But this was a memory drill. Part of her work with Powell was learning what was in these other volumes and folios. Though some were the notebooks of previous stablemasters, pertaining to specific horses long dead, there were also the pedigree records of the Fulk stud. This heritage was an Aristo's most precious possession. It couldn't be faked or imitated. It was contained in flesh and blood horses and reached back to the days when the Aristos gave up their nomadic ways and began writing their records instead of relying on oral memory.

There were also classic works on breeding, training, horsemanship, and medicine. There were volumes about stable management, which meant learning to keep accounts and knowing enough mathematics to calculate the amount of feed needed by the various breeds on a stud farm. It also meant assessing the skills of those who worked for you, and organizing the work by day, week, and season.

She was supposed to become accomplished in all these areas during the next five years. Then her apprenticeship would be completed and she'd receive her license from the Horseskillers Association, on Powell's recommendation and signature. She couldn't see that far ahead, and Powell always reminded her that five years from now she'd still be green as spring grass. Whenever others praised her work, he'd say "Tornado," and she'd want to sink into the ground.

But she loved the work. She put out of her mind that Three Trees' effort was creating superb creatures whose destiny was death on a battlefield far from the land that bred them. It was exciting to help a horse learn his own abilities. It was gratifying to teach him to perform on demand. The important thing for a trainer to know, Powell stressed, is that a horse can't be taught something that his nature hasn't equipped him to do.

She saw the thermometer's red line resting firmly at forty degrees. When she'd gotten up this morning it had trembled just at the frost line. She felt that winter was finished even though there would be at least another storm or two. She was restless. She didn't want to go back up to the House and join Thurlow and Hengst in a dance lesson from Rampalli. She didn't care that many of the terms for ballet were the same as those for schooling war stallions. Ballet wasn't something she was equipped to perform, she thought, either by nature or at someone else's command. But Thurlow and Rampalli both insisted she and Hengst dance. Bowed legs and the habitual awkwardness of the rider on the ground were prevented by dancing, they said.

She liked old Rampalli, but solitude was precious to her. Muran, Powell, and the stables left her little free time or privacy. And whenever she was alone, the Dancemaster would seek her out. He'd make her dance, sing, or listen to him lecture about the properties of various blades, various dances, various courtesies and, always, ravings about the Ballet, Empress of Dance.

For Thurlow it was different. Ballet came easily and naturally to her, like anything else that had to do with making herself lovely. Glennys would rather watch Thurlow dance than try to do it herself. But Thurlow needed someone to work with her, and this was one of the areas in which Thurlow, for reasons Glennys couldn't quite explain, had the right to tell her what to do.

Glennys hung out of the window, trying to sniff up the vagrant promise of green grass and mild air deep into her winter-shriveled lungs. She could hear the thumps and bumps of the men removing the charred timbers from the barn's foundation. Then hands ran up and down her spine under the long wool sweater she wore, and without turning around she said, "I was just thinking about you, Thurlow."

"I was thinking of you, too, otherwise why would I be here? Why don't you study in the Library office in the House? Then I wouldn't have to run out here when I wanted to talk to you."

Glennys said, "Up there I'd have to wash and change my clothes."

"You're such a serious little Horsegirl, Glenn. What's your hurry to know everything? Powell's going to live forever, so you won't be Stablemistress until you're very, very, very old."

Glennys shrugged. "I'm not so little anymore. I'm going to be taller than you by this time next year."

The older girl wasn't in furs or lace or silk. She wore a split skirt and an oiled leather rain cape designed to cover a horse's haunches, shoulders, and chest, as well as the rider's legs. The hood hung behind her neck and the bottom was rolled up to her ankles.

"Let me guess what you wanted to talk to me about," teased Glennys. "You want to go out, don't you?"

"Only Lady Eve knows how I want to get out of here. Muran's droning on in the Library with Hengst, about the nature of man as opposed to the nature of the horse. Are they the same? Are they different then? Can you teach a man to behave contrary to his nature? I think Muran's as bored by antique philosophy as I am. The nature of the horse interests him not at all and I think he's too interested in the nature of man." Thurlow pulled some of her curls over one eye, which gave her an admirable appearance of rakishness. "You can teach a man anything, if you do it right."

Bluntly Glennys said, "I wouldn't be so sure of that. Have the Alaminites ever learned not to go up against somebody stronger than them?"

Thurlow yanked on her hair. "Don't you start it too, Glenn. I can't stand it. I never want to hear about that stupid Gunpowder Ambush again. Now that the King's Guards are out of here, I forbid it. If anyone had listened to me in the first place none of it would have happened. I wouldn't have gotten my furs ruined and Wildan would still be alive." She smoothed down her ruffled hair. "It's a pity. He was a beautiful man. If his hair had been darker, if he'd been richer and not a younger son, I'd have made him carry me off."

Sensibly Glennys didn't respond to that. She asked, "Do you want to try riding in the north pasture? It's not so boggy there since it wasn't grazed last summer. The grass is still thick."

Thurlow said, "I want to go to Dephi. I need to order some things from St. Lucien at the Coach." Her voice wheedled now. "Will you saddle my horse, Glenn? I'll be the one to tell Rampalli that we're going to miss his lesson."

Glennys hadn't been off Three Trees since Justice Day. Since she'd been good through Rue and Marche, Powell now allowed her to take Merrylegs and ride by herself.

"I'll saddle you something if you don't ride Willi. She's as dainty about getting muddy as you are about your petticoats. When she's dirty she's in a bad temper and bites whoever has to clean her up. And somehow, that person's never Miss Thurlow." Glennys spoke from experience.

"That's one of the few advantages of being my father's daughter in this horrid County," said Thurlow in her haughty manner.

Glennys saddled a black pony named Cinder for Thurlow, and, with a sigh, Merrylegs for herself. She put a knee to his blown up belly. Then she did it again. The old boy was clever. He'd make a big show about expelling the air he was holding when you fastened the girths, but keep most of it back. He'd fooled her that way more than once and she and the saddle had slipped under him. He was teaching her every bad trick a horse could devise to make life miserable. For good measure, she punched his belly with her knee one more time. The glint in his eye made her suspicious. A pony with a sense of humor, who also thought he knew more than you did, had to be dealt with carefully.

"Just my luck," Glennys muttered. "Everyone here, even the ponies, tries to teach me lessons."

Merrylegs whinnied.

"Sounds like a horse laugh to me," said Hengst, leading a saddled-up Smoky into the stable.

Hengst hadn't spent much time with Glennys since Justice Day. He worked long hours with Rampalli in daily sword lessons. His wrists weren't as strong as he thought they should be and he walked around with ten-pound dumbbells all the time. He took off his sword only while eating or receiving instruction from Muran. Glennys had understood that Wildan's death had changed him, just like Tornado's death had changed her. They both had put childish things behind them.

This afternoon he looked more his old self, except that like her, he'd grown taller. He hummed one of Wildan's favorite drinking choruses as the three of them rode through the sticky clay mud that made up this section of the approach road to Three Trees.

> Give me head, give me head
> Give me head on my ale,
> And I'll give head to you.

"I need an adventure," said Hengst. "Things are dull around here."

"I bet they've learned not to be interested in adventures," observed Thurlow, gesturing at the people who worked in the field on their near side.

Looking like dolls made out of mud, women and children

worked with hoes, picks, and shovels that were too large for them. They were opening the drainage ditches around the field. Others filled in the depressions of standing water or leveled off the frost-heave elevations which spilled moisture before it penetrated below the ground. These were the first of the tasks it took to get a field ready for planting.

One woman, who was breaking up clods close to the Coach Road, lifted her head. She looked at them with eyes brilliantly blue in her mud-streaked face before she bent down again and beat the earth. Her blows were harder after she saw them.

It was man's work. Even Glennys father had hired someone to help him with it, instead of using his wife and daughter. It was too hard for women and children—unless there was no one else to do it. Stella had been given money out of Three Trees' accounts to hire someone to work her fields. But she'd decided to leave them fallow and expand the sheep flock instead. There wasn't anyone to hire to do field work.

It was only Merrylegs under her, Glennys thought, not a grand war horse, but there was a difference between her and those who walked. She was glad to be the one riding, but the eyes of the woman who'd looked at them stayed with her. Though she knew everyone who lived around Dephi, there was no way she could tell which of Ehlers's wives it was under the bulky clothes and the mud who broke up cold lumps of earth.

There was a better stretch of Coach Road ahead and they put their mounts to a canter, leaving the toiling Alaminites swiftly behind. Even Merrylegs went with a will.

These days the oldest Prochnow wife ran the Coach Inn. It had been her son who'd fired Three Trees' barn and been executed by Deadly. The Prochnow wives' husband and four oldest sons had been seized by the Baron's conscription.

The Inn's public room was quiet. The one King's Guard who'd remained after the others had gone back to Old Nolan, a couple of coal traders, and a pedlar sat drinking. The Guard cheerfully was telling the story of the Gunpowder Ambush to the others, without regard to Mrs. Prochnow's angry, set face.

"The Baron's men rode through the County, just ahead of the Rue blizzards. It was a great trick and it worked very well. At every congregation they rang the fire bells, and waited inside the kirk with their horses. When the Lighters came running to save their kirk, the Baron's men rounded 'em up like stupid sheep.''

"I live in Drake," said one of the coal traders. "How come I never heard about this? We're not far from the Soudaka County line."

"Fulk wanted to keep it quiet, I suppose. It did make him look as though he'd been caught with his trousers down. He pulled 'em up again in a hurry though. He and his men can ride the guts out of anybody. He kept it down to a little incident in the hinterlands, nothing to make a ballad out of. Now if there'd been a massacree all over Northern Nolan, it would have been a different story. But there wasn't a chance of that." The Guard spoke with the jovial contempt of a civil service soldier who never sees war.

The pedlar, his pack leaning against the stool next to him, looked morose. He cheered somewhat when Hengst, followed by Glennys, came over. Hengst carried a big pitcher of ale. He sat down at the pedlar's trestle. "What news, packman?" Hengst asked, pouring him a bumper.

"Only filthy Soudaka weather," he said.

The pedlar's manners were bad, Glennys thought.

He lifted the ale and saluted Hengst. "You belong to Baron Fulk, so you must be the younger son—the one who won't run the place unless Stogar has something happen to him in Sace-Cothberg. The lovely girl over there must be your sister."

"Ye-ah. That's my sister," said Hengst, ignoring the man's jibe. "She's leaving orders for the Post Stage Company about silk and satin from St. Lucien."

The pedlar looked cunning. "I'll charge a smaller fee to take the order into Old Nolan than she'd have to pay the Company," he said.

"But the Company will do it faster. You've only got your two legs and they've got a straight road and six horses. You've got a heavy pack and twisty line to wherever you're going. You'll stop at every house along the way and show off what you've got in your pack—and drink up your customer's ale, no doubt."

"Don't suppose you want to see what's in my pack, young Master?"

Hengst drawled, "You don't sound very confident, pack-man. Business poor?"

Glennys heard a new sound in Hengst's voice, which re-sembled Thurlow's in her most unpleasant moods. The pedlar wasn't an Aristo of either the old or new bloodlines. But he certainly was a Nolanese, not an Alaminite. He walked, she thought. He was a Nolanese who didn't have a horse. Until then she'd assumed all Nolanese had horses.

"There's no business!" the packman exploded. "I always time myself to get here before the markets and Gatherins start again after winter. No one's been anywhere or spent anything in weeks. People get married in the spring and even Lighters let their brides wear ribbons."

Glennys thought the way he said "Lighter" made the word sound as ugly as Acker made it.

"Sons are born, winter or not, and Lighter pas want some-thing special on the pillow for the Showing in the kirk. But this year all the men are gone. There's no cash money, hardly any kind to barter with, and how would I carry kind anyhow? I have to leave that for the rich pony pedlars in the fall," he complained.

There had to be something wrong with this man, Glennys thought, if he didn't have a pony or a mule. Everyone in Old Nolan was rich. Even the traveling hands that Three Trees hired had their own horses. Only Alaminites did without even ponies, and that was because they were stupid and believed they shouldn't have them.

From across the room Thurlow's voice, cool and smooth as cream, called, "Glenn, dear, come here. I want you."

She got up, eager to leave Hengst's toying with the pedlar in whom, she could tell, he wasn't the least bit interested.

What Thurlow wanted was lace. She was too poor, she said, to afford the lace out of St. Lucien. Glennys wondered how Thurlow could consider herself poor. Her quarterly al-lowance was more cash money than some Soudaka families saw all year.

Mrs. Prochnow said, "The women in the Bohn clan are excellent lace-makers. Much of their work is bought regularly at the market here and sold in St. Lucien." Mrs. Prochnow gave Glennys a look that made her feel uncomfortable.

"Ask Stella's daughter there, if you don't believe an

Alaminite woman. The congregation thinks the Bohn women do quite as good work with needle and thread as Stella Heitkamp. The Bohns and Stella have a deal in common, including some very good friends.'' That meant the congregation didn't approve of how lightly the Bohns got off. Only one son had been taken by Fulk. Mrs. Prochnow spat in front of Glennys's riding boots. ''The Bohns and Stella share plenty.''

Thurlow seemed oblivious to Mrs. Prochnow's hostility. The woman looked hard and invulnerable, from her iron-grey braids to her muddy pattens.

Thurlow took out a half silver forient and offered it as a tip for the information. She didn't pass it over graciously and unobtrusively. If Mrs. Prochnow wanted the coin she'd have to reach out her arm and take it from Thurlow's fingers.

She took it. ''Stella's girl can show you the way. A girl that knocked down her own father with a horse for the King's army must be smart enough to find her way to the Bohn house. My own girls can't spare the time to show you the way. They've got to clean up the filth in the rooms where the King's Guard sleeps for free.''

Many of the houses they rode past were missing panes of glass in the windows. Rags had been stuffed efficiently into the holes. A very young Alaminite boy, wearing shoes too big for him, kicked a hole digger and hammer spread out on burlap in the mud behind his house. He looked helplessly at the sagging fence around the chicken run, where two lonely hens scratched in the mud while he scratched his head. The public watering trough for the oxen leaked a steady trickle of water into the dirty street. All this told a story of a congregation without the men who ruled it and kept it in repair.

The kirk, however, was as neat, tight, and whole as it always had been. Three women came out of the front doors as Thurlow and Glennys rode their ponies past. The women stood close together on the steps and watched them. They tied their scarves tight and pulled the fronts down over their eyes. Two of them made the circle sign of the Light of Heaven, but the other put up her fingers in the gesture to ward off evil. ''Father betrayer!'' she cried.

''Hard times,'' the others muttered. ''Alam help us through

these hard times where horses parade shamelessly before the house of the Lord.''

Glennys thought about the cold, stone floor in the house of the Lord and how it felt against her sore legs with her mother's body in her arms last year. She wished Fulk's men had burned the roof off the kirk. Her mouth filled with saliva and she spit like she'd seen the Baron do, over the neck of her horse, and then, like him, rose in her stirrups to stretch her legs, flaunting her horsemanship in front of the kirk. Then she remembered Torrie and that it was her pride that had gotten him killed. She squirmed for a deep seat in the saddle, which Merrylegs approved by stepping out smartly and making the mud fly at the women.

What did she care about their hard times? It was always hard times in Soudaka County, one way or another.

''Go up to the door, Glenn, and knock. Tell them that Baron Fulk's daughter wants to see their lace,'' Thurlow instructed. ''No, say to them Baron Fulk's daughter would like to see their lace if it's convenient. But it better be convenient because I've got hard cash to spend and I am the Baron's daughter.''

Glennys didn't want to do this. She didn't think it was fair that Thurlow ordered her to do it either. She hadn't seen any of these people in a long time. She didn't know the Bohns well enough to talk to them.

She knotted the reins on the gate first. Knowing Merrylegs, he'd bolt back to Three Trees without her if she didn't. The Bohn clan's house, yard, and fence showed the usual winter wear and tear, but not the appearance of neglect that many other buildings in Dephi did. She glimpsed Elder Bohn himself around the back of the house with two of his sons. His good behavior toward Muran had saved him from Fulk's wrath. He'd lost only one son and paid a big fine for ''damages.'' They must have been working in their fields outside of Dephi. Tuescher had never liked Elder Bohn, she had heard her father say. But he was too upright to be denied an Eldership. Prosperity like his proved that he was in Alam's favor.

A sister of Bohn's second wife opened the door to the girls, her hands wrapped in her apron against the damp cold. She led them to the big room at the front of the house where the women worked every day.

The lace-makers were by the window where the light was best. By each of them burned expensive spermaceti candles, which told, louder than words, that lace was the basis of Elder Bohn's fortune. The more wives he acquired, the more lace they could make. The more lace he sold, the more wives he could afford.

The long table in the center of the room was surrounded by females, old and young, cutting, snipping, and clipping. The younger girls sang a hymn softly while hemming coarse pantaloons and shirts.

The woman who was working the hardest looked up at Glennys and said, "Good afternoon, daughter. You're in good time to lend a hand. We're altering the work clothes of our departed men so the less fortunate sisters and their children can wear them in their fields." Stella's smile was steady and clear, as though she really couldn't imagine that Glennys didn't want more than anything else to join the girls sewing.

This was rotten luck for certain, thought Glennys. Her mother never used to go visiting like this. What was going on?

Thurlow rescued her. Thurlow's character responded immediately to fine sewing and skilled seamstresses. She started asking questions of the lace-makers.

"It goes like this," said Sister Susannah. "You make a design on thick paper backed with cloth with an outlining thread. Your needle loops, plaits, and twists interlacing linen threads over the pattern. No, never allow the needle to penetrate the backing. When the length is finished, take a sharp, very sharp knife, and cut the stitching thread from the backing, and lift off the lace. Wrap the finished lace in soft cloth and begin again."

Glennys only knew a little about lace-making. Her mother made more money at embroidery, which she could do alone.

Thurlow gave the women respectful attention and unfeigned admiration, which they seldom received. Praise went against the Alaminite grain, because performance of duty was its own reward. But evidently they liked Thurlow's praise, and soon they were singing and talking as they had been before the girls from Three Trees arrived. If they'd been hostile at the beginning, they'd hidden it well.

Glennys yawned and felt a proper fool, completely out of her element. She wasn't dressed to be among ladies. But Thurlow looked right at home. Some Alaminite women, like these, made lovely, feminine things, but they seldom wore them, except on occasions like their wedding day or their funeral.

Glennys took the shirt her mother handed over and pretended to sew, waiting for Thurlow to get tired of this new amusement of charming Lighter lace-makers.

Susannah asked, "Miss Thurlow, have you ever seen the fine work that Sister Stella does? She allowed us to buy from her a cover for the Show Pillow." She turned to Stella. "I've always thought we took advantage of your generosity. You nearly gave it to us, and we know that the laborer is worthy of his hire even though the winter's troubles had so disrupted our labors that we weren't prepared when little Darwin was born in Rue."

The other women held their breath at Susannah's artless reminder of the Ambush and conscription in front of Fulk's daughter. But Susannah kept talking, enjoying her opportunity to see someone who would actually wear what she'd worn out her hands and eyes making. She took a thick, fringed piece of embroidery out of a press, shaking it out over her arm. The design suggested shoots of young wheat and corn in pale green and gold. Tiny blue flowers the exact shade of blooming flax were exquisitely worked in each corner. Glennys recognized it at once. It had been made before either Deborah or Rebecca had been born.

"I'd love a cloak like that, to wear to the Opera," said Thurlow.

Susannah was amazed. "It's a cover for a Show Pillow. It's only for kirking newborn boys."

"Yes, of course. Pardon me." Thurlow's cheeks went red. Glennys knew that very little embarrassed Thurlow. But she'd been working hard to get these ladies to like her and was angry she'd slipped. Now they'd ask a higher price for their lace.

"Tell me more about kirking and all that. I really don't know much about Alam," Thurlow said.

Glennys was disgusted. Thurlow cared as much about Alam as she did about the nature of man versus horse.

Hesitantly Susannah said, "Taking your newborn son to the kirk is to show him to the Lord, to knit him into the covenant Alam makes with his people."

The others continued to work but occasionally added something. But gradually it was Stella's voice that became dominant. "The covenant with Alam is that you give your life to him because he gave life to you. Your life is a tool for the purpose of Alam's intention, like a spade is a tool for the purpose of digging your garden. The covenant is not concerned with the laws of Kings but exists by faith in Alam's ultimate purpose.

"Alam is within each of us, in each of our own hearts. As Alam is within, each of us is a congregation in herself. You don't need a Seeking Stone for Alam's Light to be revealed. His Light is revealed in the hearts of those whose faith in his love is whole and complete."

Through her boredom Glennys became aware that this wasn't quite what she'd heard for years from the Elders and Reverend Tuescher.

"Complete faith demonstrates itself. You waste not and thus you want not. You are diligent in your duty for the duty's sake. You abhor sloth, which is the devil's delight. You are united with your family as your family is in unity with the congregation, and the congregation is united with Alam."

Glennys bit her lips. Stella's own family had ever been one of disunion. She'd never been wholly united with the congregation either.

"Complete faith is demonstrated by good works, which is shown today by this little congregation gathered together in this room to assist the less fortunate sisters of our congregation."

Glennys hated sermons. She'd hoped she was free from them forever now that she was a Horsegirl.

"You have respect for *all* the members of your family. Your family includes all who live with you, even to a lesser degree, the animals, the earth, and the fruits thereof, the very things that make the life Alam's given to you possible. The greater your respect for your family, the better your family will bear fruit."

The women in the workroom listened attentively. Unlike Glennys, they found sermons interesting and instructive. When

Stella had said that each of them was a congregation in herself, some looked puzzled. Some appeared apprehensive. One or two of the eldest, who had the most gentle and peaceful faces, like Susannah, nodded. The small sermon was brought to a conclusion by the introduction of bread thinly buttered, and pitchers of weak beer. After politely putting the sour stuff to her lips and crumbling the bread, Thurlow laid out some money and received several cards of exquisite lace in return. It took several minutes of polite bargaining on both sides. Susannah was gentle, but like the other Bohn wives, she valued her work for what it was worth, while Thurlow's ability to extract the greatest value for the smallest price matched that of an Alaminite.

Slogging along on their ponies outside Dephi, Thurlow asked, "Well, what did you think about that?"

"I wish I had stayed home and done Rampalli's ballet lesson, that's what I thought. Don't try to make me do that again. You want to see them, go by yourself. I hope Mother doesn't say what she said today again, either. If Tuescher hears about it he's going to call her a witch when he comes back."

"Glenn, you don't have to worry about Tuescher or the Coals of the Lord. They're all on their way to get killed in Outremere."

"I'd worry less if I knew where old Tuescher's got to, though," Glennys said. "I know he's not with them and he's looking at all of us with that great Seeking Stone that's sewed up in his Bishop's Hat. That wasn't in the kirk either when it was searched. My mother's talking heresy. I've heard enough about that from the kirk pulpit to recognize it when I hear it. They train you for it in catechism class. Listening to your own heart instead of the Reverend's revelations is heretical. That's how my mother got into trouble last year."

At the milestone they heard hooves pounding up behind them. When Hengst pulled Smoky up to walk next to the girls they saw he had a black eye, a split sleeve, and a big grin.

"You've been in a fight," said Thurlow.

"Ye-ah. I won. He said I wore my sword because my private equipment was too short to be a real man. He was a big snotsucker, bigger than me. But Smoky and my sword taught him a lesson. I whacked his hinder good with the flat of the blade after I called Smoky to me. I think his name was Milton.''

They rode faster. It was starting to get colder and it was raining. By evening the rain had turned into a snowstorm.

# FOURTEEN

During the next two springs and summers the temperatures were cooler than usual. Soudaka County received more rainfall, as though to make up for the drought of the summer when the Mabley woman was burned. The weather wasn't good for grain crops but there were bumper harvests of strawberries and raspberries. The apple and plum trees yielded bushels of fruit. Alaminite women, as well as Cook, put up long shelves of preserves in crockery jars. But in the spring of Glennys's fourteenth year the rains fell without stopping. The fields didn't dry out enough and the seed grain rotted in the earth. Summer came hot and wet. Before one thunderstorm passed, another one rumbled on the horizon. In the midsummer, brown water rushed high as a horse's shoulder under the willows on the banks of Shoatkill Crick. A person didn't need a revelation or weather luck to predict there would be no Harvest Gatherin this fall.

Even away from a barnyard and in the rain there were so many flies and mosquitos Glennys could see them. Thunder groaned. She pulled the clammy hood of her raincape over her head again. The rain had slacked off towards mid-morning, leaving her no excuse not to see Stella. Glennys was late turning over the wages for her last quarter's work. But before facing Stella, Glennys had taken a look at her mother's fields. They were full of standing water.

"Up and at 'em, Dodger, old boy." This summer Glennys rode a six-year-old chestnut stallion out of King Leon's stud. "You're going to be the best thing the Aristos ever saw going on a mud track, aren't you, fella?"

Dodger cantered over the bad ground, his neck in a cheerful curve. He whinnied gaily and, without breaking stride, gathered himself lightly and jumped over the drainage ditch that emptied into the Shoatkill. His hooves connected with the ground without slipping in the mud. Dodger was a grubber horse, one of those who liked being dirty and enjoyed mud and rain. As long as he got enough to eat, he didn't mind anything. But what Dodger considered a meal made other horses look like they were on a training diet.

This fall Dodger would run the Grand Nolan Point-to-Point for the first time. The King's groomsman, who had delivered the stallion to Three Trees, had instructed them carefully as to Dodger's character. When his feed was cut back during conditioning he'd train with a will because he'd learned that he got to eat after his workouts. If he didn't work, they didn't feed him. And Dodger liked to eat even more than he liked to jump. Though Dodger was a bit young and inexperienced for the grueling, cruel Grand Nolan, the groomsman had already bet five gold forients on him to be in first place. The King was counting on Dodger to win as well. The King always expected his colors would come in first, but this year the Eidel prestige needed the prize.

The groomsman was gossipy and determined to impress the hinterland hicks with his knowledge of important world events. Nolan's forces in Sace-Cothberg were doing about as well as the farmers in Soudaka this summer. Fulk and the other old-line Aristos fought valiantly, but their abilities were blocked by explosive, projectile armaments wherever they turned. Instead of fighting with grand cavalry charges, a large part of their might was penned inside the capital city of Nemour. They were besieged in the city they had taken over a year ago.

Dodger's early conditioning here in Soudaka's mud and rain would give him an added edge against his competition in the Grand Nolan. Therefore Soudaka's weather was good luck for King Leon, for the good luck that came with Dodger's win would certainly rebound upon the King's army in Sace-Cothberg.

When a person's life was wholly bound by horse-breeding, racing, and war, the forces of chance meant everything. Glennys had imbibed the Aristo beliefs effortlessly, but she thought that whatever good luck Leon got out of Soudaka, there wasn't any for Three Trees. Where grass and hay had come up this year, it was pale and limp. There was no nourishment in the stalks. This past winter Three Trees had run out of its own feed and what it had received from the congregations. Powell spent valuable time buying feed in Old Nolan at high cost. The delivery charges to the border County had been extortionate. Three Trees was behind schedule training this year's crop of four-year-olds. Most of them were going to be shipped across the sea into Outremere for delivery as remounts for Fulk's men instead of being put up for auction at the autumn horse fair in Gordonsfield.

Powell and Muran spent many winter evenings going over the account books and the letters from the Baron. Fulk's demands were frequent and imperative, as well as brief. "Send me 5,000 forients. Give me twenty stallions."

The King's groomsman said, "Feed Dodger and the others as much as they want." Muran and Powell composed a letter to the closest bank in the city of Drake and asked for a loan.

That was one of the reasons Glennys's quarterly payment was late. Another was that Powell had used her for the first time in the Badlands. They'd taken as many horses as they could spare from the operation of Three Trees back out there so they could free range. It was drier in the Badlands and the grass was good. But Leon's horses had to stay, along with the war stallions in training, where they got intensive attention. Dodger was used as her riding horse because that was one way to get something out of him for his board. Besides, he and Glennys liked each other. His rakish, easygoing ways were an interesting change from the Three Trees war stud, whose breeding was designed for aggression and defense.

When Glennys tried to ride Dodger past the hen house, he balked and shied away. That was out of his character entirely. Feeling there was a confrontation waiting for her inside the house, Glennys wasn't in the mood to persuade or force her horse to do what he didn't want to do. She gave in and took the long way around to the barn. It was still raining, though not heavily. Maybe the weather had just about rained itself out. But the air hung miserably hot and still. The wind stayed up with the thunderclouds.

Glennys carried the hoof-cleaning tools with her these days

as constantly as Hengst wore his sword. She tended to Dodger's hooves and the mud guards on his pasterns before going in, even though Stella knew her daughter had come. A surprising addition to the farm, a dog named Geezer, had barked at her arrival.

"Better do it now, Dodger. By the time I come back out I'll just want to get out of here."

His barrel was oversized. There was plenty of room in there for his tremendous lungs to do their work, which gave him extra staying power, which counted more in point-to-point races than speed. She loosened his girths and tied him securely so he wouldn't eat her mother's stock of animal feed.

Six-year-old Deborah, leading Rebecca, came into the barn. "The tomatoes," Deborah announced solemnly, "have all drowned."

"Are you my sister Glennys?" asked Rebecca, as she did every time she saw someone on a horse. She asked the same question of Thurlow, whom she saw more often. Thurlow rode over to pick up the sewing work Stella did for her and got help with the work she did by herself. High water, or none at all, Thurlow's trousseau had to be made. Glennys thought that Thurlow enjoyed having consistently friendly relations with Stella when Glennys couldn't manage it.

"Yes," said Glennys. "I'm your sister. This here's Dodger. You want to rub his nose? He'd like that."

She dug in a pocket and found a few kernels of corn. "Put this in your hand and hold it flat like this. He'll lick it off your hand and it will feel good when he breathes on your fingers and licks the palm with his tongue. It's kind of like tickling, but much nicer. Don't squeal when that happens. It might scare him." Glennys gave the warning from habit. Nothing startled old Dodger, but on the other hand, he'd never balked or shied at something as common as a henhouse before either.

But, as she did every time, Becky screamed when Dodger's nose touched her hand, and she started to cry. Glennys picked her up. She couldn't understand her sister's apprehension about horses. Greedy as Dodger was, he was a gentleman and never bit the hand that fed him, though he would bite his manger or the bucket when he thought the rations stingy. Oversized barrel or not, his blood showed. When he got put down to racing weight, his veins and ribs would be prominent, and he'd be beautiful.

"My mother wrote a hymn. Do you want to hear it?" asked Debbie. "She sings it when folks die."

Debbie sat down on the harrow, which hadn't been used since Glennys had gone away. Her sister pretended to hold someone's hand. Her head was bent and her eyes closed.

> Though life be a winter of worry and sorrow
> And death be the longest of nights
> Though we walk with our burden of darkness and shadow
> We'll shine with our joy in the Light.

> In the Light,
> In the Light,
> We'll meet once again in the Light.

> In the Light,
> In the Light,
> We'll meet once again in the Light.

When she'd finished all the verses, she stood up, and put her hand in the pocket of her apron. She pretended to take something out and give it to another pretend person.

"What did you give, Debbie?" asked Glennys.

"Pennies. You give pennies to people when somebody dies. And pies. That's what a mother does. A mother cooks and sews and washes clothes and makes gardens and gives money. She listens to Alam in her heart, which is most important. Alam's in my heart too, though I'm too little to hear him yet. But I will when I'm bigger."

Glennys rolled her eyes. When she was Debbie's age she'd played pretend all the time, right up to the night she went to Three Trees. But her games weren't like that. Hers were all about horses and running free over some trackless, unknown country, alone and wild. She shifted Becky on her hip. "Let's find Mother." They ran for the house in the rain, Geezer barking and dashing around them.

"No, Geezer," said Debbie. "You have to stay outside and keep the foxes from the chickens and the lambs."

Glennys's farsighted eyes saw the sheep while she struggled to take off her riding boots on the door stoop. The sheep were in a huddle around the feed troughs, pulling at the straggly grass that remained in their fold. They looked less thrifty than the last time she'd seen them. Well, so did most of the stock in the County. She'd get Hengst to help her smuggle a little feed from Three Trees to Stella before Powell came back from the Badlands.

As soon as her sisters slipped off their pattens they went to their room to brush their hair. Glennys's hair was in a tight ballerina's knot that Thurlow and Rampalli had spent a lot of effort persuading her to learn. The damp tendrils on her neck felt natural now. She hung up the big cape and kissed her mother on both cheeks in the Aristo manner. She was taller than Stella now. Stella touched Glennys's fingertips briefly before turning back to the kettles of comfrey and raspberry cough syrup that cooked on the hearth. An old queen cat, who had in her youth been a champion rat hunter, dozed in arthritic age by the fireplace. Like the dog outside, a cat in the house spoke eloquently of a kind of change not to have been imagined if the County had its young men and Reverend Tuescher.

Glennys bent to stroke the old black-and-white cat. She'd never dare mention her father to her mother, but if he'd been here, the cat wouldn't have been. They'd never said a word to each other about what had happened that Justice Day. It was something that had grown out of that night when she'd held her mother in her arms in the kirk and her father hadn't come.

"Alam showed me that you'd be here today, that's why you've found me at home. I should be at the Ehlers's farm again. Two of their little boys are down with this sickness. Their grandfather died of it two days ago. You must have brought me money since that's the only time I see you these days." That was how Stella was, changing from one subject to another with no warning, like an untrained horse changing lead.

The kitchen was as hot and steamy as outdoors, but Glennys picked up the cat before sitting down at the table. The cat took the place of what couldn't be spoken.

Stella cleared her throat. Softly she said, "The laborer is worthy of his hire. That old cat's worked hard all her life. If I didn't keep her in here, she'd die having another litter of kittens. Old or not, the toms will jump her. She's going to pass when fall comes in, but Alam understands that she's earned a peaceful death.''

Glennys handed over a thin roll of silver forients, her wages. A larger roll of forients was from Thurlow, payment for the tiny flowers of seed pearls sewn on a head net for her trousseau.

''I'm sorry I'm late with the money, Mother, but I was in the Badlands with Powell. Thurlow's staying home because of the sickness—and the weather. Muran's back in Old Nolan at his Seven Universities for the summer, so there wasn't anyone to send. The financial side of things is hard going these days, as I don't have to tell you. And Powell's got so many things to take care of.''

''My agreement,'' Stella said, ''is hard and fast with the Baron himself about your labor. Powell's problems have nothing to do with my papers on you. I need that money for the congregation now and in the hard winter that's coming.'' She touched the forients with her spoon. ''That will make the difference between eating and not eating for some people, Glennys. Don't forget that.''

Stella added Mule-Kick in which mint leaves had steeped to a batch of the raspberry cough syrup that cooled on the side of the hearth. ''At first we thought this coughing sickness was influenza that had come from all the wet air. But it's like nothing I've seen before. The coughing tears a body's chest and throat apart, the sweats come. If you can keep the coughing under control, the body quiet, there's a chance for life. But when the black fluid starts to come from the nose and anus, it means death. The very old and the very young always die. They catch it more easily too.''

Glennys liked seeing her mother this way, strong and calculating what she could do to defeat the sickness. In Soudaka you depended upon yourself and your neighbors for treatment. In the last years Stella's neighbors had gotten into the habit of calling on her for help when sickness was severe.

''Alam brings good out of evil, Glennys. You're his instrument now and that helps make up for the sins you've committed. Your wages, like Thurlow's payments, are a sign of Alam's forgiveness for things you and I shouldn't have done. We've hurt the congregations, but we also help them.''

It took every bit of stable discipline that Glennys had mastered in the last years to keep from shouting. "Mother," she said calmly, "I'm happy if you're happy that I'm doing something to help suffering people. I work very hard in return for the money you receive. But I am not Alam's tool. It's the luck and it's the training. That's all. There is no big man with a beard up behind the sun or in my heart that decides what I do."

A tiny, frozen smile thinned Stella's lips. She covered one ear with the hand not holding the spoon. But Stella suddenly turned from the fireplace and faced her daughter as though she wanted to strike her with the big wooden spoon.

"I never thought I'd hear a daughter of mine, even you, talk in such a sinful way. A heathen, an Aristo who didn't have the chance to know better, talks like that, but you were brought up differently."

"But I am your daughter and, like you, I can think for myself. You've been thinking differently from what the Reverends have told you to think all your life, haven't you? And since the men were taken away, haven't you been giving sermons, telling other women in the congregation how you think, praying with them, even talking from the pulpit in the kirk? I am your daughter and the breeding always tells in the end, so if you don't like what I am, still, you're a part of it and made it that way." Glennys knew she'd gone too far. Her mother's eyes were glistening with tears. She'd set her lips even tighter so they wouldn't tremble.

Glennys put the cat back on her pad by the fireplace. "Please, Mother, let's just agree not to speak of what we can't agree on."

Glennys began to tell of her journey into the Badlands and how much she enjoyed it out there. She talked of Dodger and why she rode the King's horse instead of a young war stallion. Three Trees' horses, to make a good appearance, couldn't be worked as hard as in the good years because it was hard times. Glennys was placating. She said their troubles with feed and ground were just like those of the farms in the congregation. They had to balance the cost of grain with the number of hired trainers. They had to balance the cost of feed and labor against the cost of upkeep for the King's horses.

Stella wasn't interested or impressed. In the middle of Glennys's outpourings she called Debbie and Becky to the kitchen for catechism drill. She made Glennys ask the questions about the nature of Alam's will while she began boiling mush-meal. When the drill was over Stella sent the girls to the henhouse for the eggs. Glennys stood up ready to go back to work at Three Trees.

The rain had stopped. It was getting close to feeding time for the four-year-olds. She might be able to exercise them in hand with the long reins later in the afternoon. When she forced on her boots she saw a thread of grey, the first, in Stella's hair. The gold color was darker, not so bright. Glennys kissed her again, even though it was hard for Stella to accept embraces that came easily from Glennys, who used her entire body to get a horse to understand her.

Stella said, "This coughing sickness is bad, Glennys. Every day or two more go down to it. I'm worried about the women now. They don't have the strength they did three years ago. These hard times are only getting harder."

Glennys ventured to say, "At least they aren't having babies to eat away at their strength."

"Shame on you, Glennys. What do you know of such things at your age?"

"Mother, we breed horses on Three Trees. I've helped stallions cover mares. I helped deliver foals this spring for the first time. It was wonderful."

Stella's cheeks were bright pink. "You aren't running after all those men you work with, are you?"

"Of course not," she said shortly. What was a horsehandler or a trainer next to the Baron? But that was one of the things that would never be spoken of, not just to Stella, but to anyone. What did she want with Alam or anyone else when Fulk's presence on Deadly's back as she'd seen him in the Sword Dance was in her heart forever?

"Well, daughter, you take care to stay away from anyplace where there's coughing sickness and hope it doesn't come to Three Trees."

"Yes, Mother, I will," said Glennys.

"Mother, Mother!" Deborah cried from the chickenhouse. She was very frightened. Stella hoisted her skirts, slipped on her pattens in one swift movement and ran across the yard.

They found one of the hens lying on her side, dead in her nest. Matter oozed out of the little breathing holes in her beak and from under her tail feathers. The other chickens had pecked at her until they'd torn out most of her feathers. They'd broken the eggs over which she'd been brooding and the naked chick embryos were torn to pieces. That's what happened, Glennys knew, when a member of the poultry yard got sick or hurt—or was different. The others rushed to destroy it.

Stella made the Circle of Light. "Alam help us. I think the sickness has spread to our animals."

"I'll get the spade and bury this mess, Mother. But first I'd better get some quicklime to put in the hole," Glennys said.

"Yes, be a good girl, Glennys, and help me for a change. I must put your sisters into a hot lye soap bath right away. At least, Alam be thanked, there's plenty of water."

Of course there was plenty of water. That was the problem.

Glennys took the bath too. If the sickness had spread to the poultry, the horses might also get it. She cursed her luck for riding King Leon's prize racer to the farm. No one knew why, but there was a connection between cleanliness and sickness. She couldn't take any chances.

Dodger made the distance between the farm and Three Trees in record time. She didn't give him any feed, much to Dodger's amazement. Instead, he got an enema, a long and messy business. In case there was anal irritation from the enema she inserted an ointment of a half ounce of glycerine, an ounce of spermaceti, and three drachmas of powdered camphor. She'd tied his tail up in a bag so it wouldn't be in the way. She freed it now so he could swat flies with it.

His nostrils were clear. There wasn't a rasp in his breathing. Dodger looked at her with misery when she left him alone in the empty brood mare stable. She buried the gloves that went up to her shoulders and washed her arms. Glennys swabbed the stallion's nostrils with Hacbutt Remedy as a preventative against pneumenitis. The stablehands did the same with all the other horses, ponies, and mules.

Maybe there wasn't any danger, but precautions weren't going to hurt. Dodger had refused to go near the henhouse and she was happier than she could express that she'd let him have his way. The stables and barn thrummed with anxiety and activity.

By the fading midsummer sunset she examined the sleepy chickens, turkeys, and geese going to bed in Cook's poultry sheds.

"What are you doing, Horsegirl?" asked Cook. Glennys was shaking her hands in the air. "Are you a new kind of scarecrow? If so, you've succeeded in scaring me. You look worse than I've ever seen you."

Her hair had come down. She was wet and dirty and she smelled like horseshit. "My hands itch from the sulphur solution I washed them in. I visited Stella today and one of her hens died. She's afraid the sickness is coming to the animals too. I was riding Dodger."

"If so," he said, "rotten luck indeed. What are we going to do?"

"First I've got to get rid of these clothes and take another lye soap bath. I wish Powell was here, but he's not due back for another ten days. By then it could be too late. I think we've got to take the King's horses to the Badlands, even though we're already shorthanded here."

Cook said, "If the sickness is coming to the animals in Soudaka, by taking the home stock to the Badlands you could be spreading it to the healthy ones out there. But maybe it's just hen sickness. They're worse than horses for getting sick."

"Black stuff came out of the hen's beak, Cook, just like out of the noses of the people who've died. My sisters discovered it. If something happens to them, I'm afraid of what will happen to my mother."

"Aren't you more afraid that Stella will catch it?" asked Cook.

Slowly, riding a hunch, Glennys said, "I think her luck is that those around her fail, but she has to carry on. I don't worry about her body. It's her heart. I think she has a different heart than most of us. I don't understand what she swears to or what she believes. She sure can't understand me."

Cook's response was a considered one. "Do any of us understand each other who are mixed up with Fulk's family and aren't Nolanese ourselves? But you and Powell have it easy. You swear by the horse and that's where your loyalties are. As long as you perform above and beyond your duties for the horses, as far as the two of you are concerned, everything and everybody else can go hang."

He stomped off toward the House to order a scalding tub fixed in the summer cookhouse. He brushed away the mosquitos that surrounded him like smoke.

Powell always said Glennys would feel green as grass when all the responsibility for Three Trees' horses was hers in the future. Glennys felt responsible today, and the grass wasn't green, but a sickly, sallow yellow.

She laid it out in the House that evening. Powell wasn't here. The Baron wasn't here. Not even Muran was here. Thurlow wouldn't be bothered to discuss the problem. She was as cranky as a baby with colic from the weather. Rampalli urged Glennys to use her own judgment. The stablehands, hired help who came and went, said she should smell for her luck. She was apprentice-Stablemistress of Three Trees.

She tossed and turned in her narrow bed. That was her past, present, and future—Stablemistress of Three Trees. Hengst had agreed with her. He thought she should take Leon's horses to the Badlands. He'd go too.

The first thing in the morning Glennys raced to the stables. Dodger, lonely and confused and very hungry, begged as clearly as speaking for company, for his corn and beans and hay. He promised he would be good.

Dodger, the mares in foal, and the thoroughbred stallions all seemed thrifty enough, though nervous. The stables hummed with flies, midges, gnats, mosquitos. The horses' tails flailed their flanks continuously. Their skin twitched, their legs stamped. Their heads tossed and they blew through their nostrils to clear them of the pests that swarmed to feed on their flesh, blood, and excreta. The smooth membrane of several stallions' nostrils had cracked from the constant snorting. The thin breaks were particularly attractive, like their swollen eyes, to the flies and mosquitos.

In these wet months the stables and the barn couldn't be kept properly clean. The stink from the running muck heaps outside was overpowering this morning. It wasn't raining and the cloudy sunrise promised a hot, overcast day. The air was thick and sticky. It felt as nasty on Glennys's skin as it smelled to her nose.

Glennys was startled by a rat that jumped out of the grain bin where she was sifting the horses' rations. Before it disappeared in a shadowy corner she saw it was a long brown one,

the kind that usually lived all year around by the banks of the
Shoatkill, not in the farmyard. Up in the barn's hayloft the
hunter cats twined around her legs. They had lined up last
night's kill neatly by the loft ladder: some of the usual small
grey mice, some short grey rats, and eight long, brown rats.

She grabbed a bit of breakfast from the kitchen and took it
to the Stable office. Her memory prickled from a notebook
entry she'd recopied last winter from Fulk's grandfather's
time. She looked for it.

> *A proper breeding farm for horses must be pros-*
> *perous and generous with property. It is preferred*
> *that the lands not all lay side by side, but be*
> *separated by extensive acres devoted to agricul-*
> *ture. Then, if sickness visits one part of your coun-*
> *try, your good fortune will be preserved in the*
> *breeding stock on another estate.*

She read the dead writer's description of a bloody black
flux that killed all the horses on Three Trees in a few days
with horrid coughs and incontinence from nostrils and anus.
The first member of Three Trees to get sick was a stableboy
fresh from Old Nolan. That had been a hot, wet summer full
of vermin too.

The lesson was clear. That year's crop of four-year-old
stallions had been lost. The mares, the younger horses, and
the stallions in the Badlands mostly survived.

Glennys felt smart and brave for the first time since Tornado had been killed. She was excited. She'd lay odds that
the Baron felt like this all the time. That was why men liked
to be leaders. That was why stallions battled to prove which
was top horse, why they raced to prove which one was fastest
and first. She rubbed the palms of her hands together under
her chin. She pursed her lips and narrowed her eyes. That's
what Powell did when he made decisions—and so did the Baron.

Hengst opened the Stable office door a crack and slipped
through, keeping out a mist of flies. "Well, what's it going to
be, Stablemistress?" he asked.

"I'm going to send a groom ahead to tell Powell we're
coming and why. We'll keep the King's horses pastured west
of the Mines for a few days to make sure they're not sick. We

can't take our own four-year-olds because there aren't enough of us. Two of our hands left this morning. They're tired of the weather and afraid of getting sick.'' The words came out squeaky and high. She bounced in the ancient chair and said the words again. This time her tones were deep and full.

While Hengst watched she wrote the letter to Powell. She'd ask Cook to send for her sisters. She thought Stella might allow it. The sickness was most deadly for the young and the old, and her mother's hands were already full nursing around the congregation. Hengst was coming. She needed a couple of other horsehandlers because she knew better than to try and take all these horses and supplies—and Thurlow too—across the County by herself. If she didn't have other hands with her Powell would know she'd used her gift of hearing horses and having them hear her, of getting them to do what she wanted.

''Get my children to safety!'' the Baron had ordered first thing in the Gunpowder Ambush. Thurlow was as important a piece of breeding stock for the old bloodline Aristos as Three Trees' mares. Thurlow invoked her function as constantly as horses swished their tails, both as a matter of pride and of complaint. It was Glennys's duty to see the Baron's get was taken out of danger. She hadn't forgotten Tornado's death, but her confidence that she was riding a good streak of luck was strong. Despite Cook's complaint, she could think of people as well as horses, she thought.

The day was filthy. The air hung hot and wet, as visible over Three Trees as a dirty blanket. They set out smudge pots around the livestock and the stables. The thick black smoke, out of low-grade coal, tar, and damp straw, was fuggy. The noxious smell and the dense airs warded off some of the flying vermin. The horses and the other animals got some much-needed relief from the plague of flies and mosquitos. They turned the horses loose as much as possible in the stables so they could go head and tail to slap flies off each other. A horse without a pal got less relief than the others.

Cook took a pony and cart into Dephi to pick up ground flour at the mill and to leave orders at the Coach for more kerosene and whale oil. For once Mrs. Prochnow had been almost friendly. Stella was nursing their four-year-old boy. Two children in Dephi had died of the sickness last night, as well as Elder Beal's mother. Stella was glad to allow Cook to take Deborah and Rebecca with him back to Three Trees. She'd killed all her poultry that morning when she found seven dead hens. Some oxen had died at Tuescher's farm with the telltale black exudations from the anus. Milton had told them that when sent by his mother to inquire of the Prochnow boy. He was the man of the house. Jerold and Ezekial, his older brothers, had been taken by Fulk.

Cook took the same precaution that Glennys had taken. He had smudge pots going around the House. By the end of the day the flies had multiplied their numbers at least twice. Supper was miserable and tasteless. All the doors and windows were as tightly shut as in winter, the dining hall was close and hot, and everyone sweated through their clothes. Even Thurlow.

The Baron's daughter picked at the food on her plate, then pushed it away. She demanded cold wine, not this filthy ale. "Cook, couldn't you have roasted a chicken and cooled it in the well instead of serving us this old salty bacon and peas?"

"I can't serve us chicken until we know the poultry is healthy, Miss Thurlow. I told you that." Cook was close to losing his temper.

"Hengst will shoot you a pheasant," Glennys soothed. "There's lots of them in the Badlands and they're just the right game for the bow and arrow Stogar sent him this winter."

"Hengst can shoot what he wants but I'm not going to be there to eat it. Sleep on the ground and depend for my meals on messes provided by my brother? Because a Horsegirl decided I should? I don't think so, Glenn. I don't think so."

Sweat dripped through Glennys's eyebrows into her eyes. Her skin itched and burned. She smelled from animal cocky, smudge pots, and mouldy corn. The elation she'd felt in the morning had faded into bad temper. There was still so much to do before they could leave.

"All any of you are thinking about are those horses. Nobody cares about me at all!" Thurlow cried.

"You're a stupid bitch, Thurlow. This is for your sake, you prize-blood filly! It's nicer out in the Badlands than here. If you don't pack your own clothes and get on your horse when it's time to leave I'll tie you naked on Willi myself and let you be eaten alive by mosquitos," Glennys threatened.

Sometimes, if your boot kicked Thurlow at the right time, she'd kiss it—if she didn't slap you instead. Glennys was getting skillful at calculating how and when to kick the older girl. "You'll look so pathetic tied on Willi, your white skin running blood from swollen mosquitos, someone will take pity on you and rescue you from me."

Rampalli's tenor voice provided a diversion. "No one's said anything to the contrary, so I assume I'm invited on this expedition, yes? I can drive the team pulling our necessaries. I'll bring a fiddle and my harmonica. We'll collect new botanical specimens in the Badlands, maybe find something we can bring home from Swallow Lake for your aquarium." He bowed to Thurlow. "It will be refreshing to leave the fumes and fugg of Three Trees and see something new for a change. Glennys says it's drier across the County, so there will be fewer mosquitos and sucking gnats. It will be good for us over-civilized types, like a long picnic."

When Rampalli said something was for your own good it sounded different than when Glennys or anybody else said it. Glennys wanted to kick herself, though. Rampalli's intervention gently reminded her that the coughing sickness was especially dangerous for young and old people. He really was old, not just a grown-up like Stella or Muran. He was old like Reverend Tuescher was old.

The matter was settled. "The Horsegirl, Thurlow, Hengst, Rampalli, Stratton and Tykker. . . ." Cook counted off on his fingers as he headed for the kitchen and the pantries. There wasn't a lot of food stored there, not nearly as much as there should have been.

Glennys counted Dodger and the twenty-five other horses in the King's stable. There would be Willi and Smoky as well. Stratton and Tykker would take two of the four-year-old war stallions to ride for each of them. They'd have better footing than the thoroughbreds and at least four of this year's crop would survive. Four ponies would have to pull the four-wheeled flat rig carrying their food, bedding, clothing, and other necessaries.

It wasn't a good ratio of hands to horses. Six people and thirty-two horses plus four ponies. But Thurlow and Rampalli had to be subtracted from the labor, except for Rampalli's part-time driving of the rig. Hengst and Smoky made a separate equation. That left her and the two handlers to take care of thirty-one horses and the ponies. Maybe Hengst would help out, but she couldn't count on it. Now that he was older, Hengst wasn't as interested in horses as he used to be. Weapons and hunting were more to his liking.

Glennys figured pecks and bushels of grain and beans in equations that would keep war stallions up during heavy travel, mares in foal on a gestation diet and heavy work, stallions who had to maintain racing weight, and one racer-jumper with no diet restrictions. Then there were those of the ponies pulling a load that included their own feed. She substituted mules for the ponies, though she knew Thurlow would scream. But mules worked harder on less and could get along without grooming.

Powell and Muran could do this in their heads in less time than it took her to cross out another set of numbers on sweat-wrinkled paper and get answers that made no sense. She'd multiplied numbers that should have been divided. Odd-numbered fractions always gave her trouble. But, with Gordon's Luck, it should take them five days. By herself, riding a mud eater like Dodger or a war horse, she could do it in two. The five days would be long, but not too hard, if nothing unexpected happened along the way. And what could happen, other than getting stuck in the mud, or going mad from flies, or breaking an axle, or losing a wheel, or a horse breaking his leg? She wasn't going to dwell on what might happen. It was bad luck.

# FIFTEEN

The little band from Three Trees traveled like ghosts through haunted country. Humans and horses were wound about with linen shrouds to protect them from the bloodsuckers that swarmed in the air around them like evil spirits. The sky was a peculiar no-color: not blue, not grey, not yellow. It was a low-hanging veil through which the sun shone a pale shadow of himself.

The sloughs, which most summers were only spots of dark green, had grown and claimed fields and pastures. Long brown rats swam where water hadn't run in generations. So much still water made an aura of uncleanliness that rose up from Soudaka like mist. It disturbed the Nolanese as much as the Alaminites. People whispered that the King's experiments with cannon and gunpowder had made unnatural rain.

The travelers stayed on the Coach Road and kept a wide distance between themselves and any others they encountered. The horses of Three Trees gave the right of way to Alaminite hitches of sore-footed oxen, whose hooves were diseased from the wet. When they met up with sheep driven across the Road, they hung far back and didn't push heedlessly through the puddle of dirty grey wool backs.

Mostly they heard the creak of their own wagon boards, the spill of notes out of Rampalli's harmonica, the rusty wheezes of protesting mules, the pull and suck of their horses' hooves in the muddy potholes of the Road. Or they would hear the thunk and wump of an Alaminite lad's slingshot aimed at the brown rats. Otherwise, the country was hushed. The tense and anxious silence was the fear of workers with little work to do.

Sometime during the fourth day of their journey to the Badlands, the congregational farmsteads and hamlets were left behind. The ground was drier and more broken, the grass longer and healthier, the ox lanes and wagon tracks infrequent. The sun was strong and sucked up the wet. They jogged along the dusty ruts of Coal Mine Road and felt the good dry heat. The flying vermin dwindled down to the natural numbers to be found around a small herd of horses.

In mid-afternoon they took a breather. Glennys, Tykker, and Stratton removed the linen drapes from the horses. They rubbed sweaty backs and withers, and checked the horses' nostrils and hindquarters for symptoms of illness. The horses showed good condition, considering the rigors of the journey. Though only a few hours away from the flies, they'd already relaxed, forgetting that horse life could be miserable.

When Glennys took off Dodger's saddle she didn't hobble him, but let him run free. She looked around her, feeling the same sense of roominess she always got from the Badlands. Her shoulders spread just a little wider as she breathed. Dodger tore greedily at the grass at first, but soon he threw his head up and just stared into nothing. He had realized there was no weight of hard leather on his back. He threw himself down and rolled in the grass, giving his itchy, sweaty back a long, satisfying scratch. He shook himself all over like a big mop. With his mane and tail furling around him he ran in long, looping circles that mirrored those of the red-tailed hawk overhead.

Except for the whisper of the wind, and the tear and snap of the animals' teeth in the grass, it was quiet. "The air smells different here," observed Thurlow, "but I like it." Dodger thought the same. He was still, his head held high. His nose explored each trickle of wind. Lightly Glennys matched with Dodger for a brief time, smelling with his nostrils. She recognized clover flowers and grass pollen. She sneezed when Dodger sneezed. He'd inhaled the bitter smoke from the underground burning coal.

Glennys gratefully laid her sore body down on the warm ground. She wondered how the Baron and his men could ride for days and nights at a time and not turn into one dislocated skeleton, housed in one aching bruise. Their endurance wasn't equal to their ancestors'. They didn't ride over endless, unpopulated ground as in their nomadic past.

Thurlow looked much better than she did back at Three Trees, Glennys thought. Her face wasn't sour and her voice wasn't whiney. She looked wide awake for a change. She combed her hair vigorously.

Rampalli examined a little break in the ground. From it a thin plume of smoke rose up from the burning coal. Wild mustard grew right to the edge of the broken earth.

Stratton and Tykker rummaged among the supplies left on the back of the wagon. They started a small fire to heat water for a pot of bitterberry.

For the first time in days Glennys was able to forget herself. She drifted in the currents of air that connected her to Dodger. Responsibility made you feel important, she thought, but it also made you tired. They'd made it safely so far, though. They were almost at their destination. They'd only gotten stuck in the mud three times. And one of the wheels did come off. She wondered if Powell would meet them soon. She hoped so. All in all, Glennys thought she could be proud of herself. Somehow she knew that the stock back on Three Trees was sick now and somehow she knew that much of it wouldn't recover.

She allowed herself to slip into a half-doze, to indulge in what she'd always thought of as her solitary pleasure. She didn't need to see Dodger so her eyes closed. Now she *was* Dodger, taking low-bellied leaps through the grass, feeling good as Dodger felt good. He didn't need responsibility. He didn't think about what to do, he just did it and what he was doing now was feeling good. The part of herself still matched with her own awareness felt it was much easier to be a horse. Horses never had to examine a conscience.

Hengst had stalked a pheasant with his bow. He'd missed. He'd forgotten to allow for the bird's zigzagging run before flight.

Glennys was bounding over the grass again with Dodger's legs when Hengst's boot toe prodded her shoulder. "Say, Glennys, do you think it's a good idea to let the King's prize point-to-pointer go running off by himself like that?"

Glennys's arms were behind her head. She squinted one eye open at the boot. She shut it again. "Leave me alone, boy."

"Hey, Glennys. I mean it. He's awfully far away."

She sat up in a lazy curve. Dodger was a good distance from them. Riding his sensations as she'd been doing, half-asleep, she'd felt as though he were right next to her.

"Hengst, you know as well as I do that horses don't like to be alone for very long. He's just exploring new territory. Dodger's an uncut. He's sure to come back since there's mares among us. But to please you, Sir Hengst, I'll bring him in."

She put the weight of command upon Dodger's sensibility and he immediately came trotting back to the wagon. He dropped his head so she could take hold of the cheekstraps of his loosened bridle.

"You're always showing off, Glennys," Hengst said, still angry about the missed pheasant. "How did you do that? You didn't call him; you didn't even move."

Suddenly Glennys felt uneasy. She mumbled, "He's a real

smart horse." She hoped that if she behaved as though it were only a childish thing, no one else would notice. She should have had more sense. Keeping a command on thirty horses so they wouldn't fight, run, or stray while they traveled had made her careless.

Tykker slowly took the grass stem on which he'd been chewing out of his mouth and looked so hard at her that she felt naked. "I didn't know you were one of that kind, apprentice. I've heard about people like you from my Dad, and my Grandy. We're horsehandlers a long ways back ourselves, but I never saw it done with my own eyes before."

Rampalli, who had been half-asleep, baking his bones in the sun, became alert. "Whatever are you talking about, Hengst, Mr. Tykker? What did she do that was such a revelation?"

Glennys made herself very busy re-saddling Dodger and said nothing. She felt a fool for making a spectacle of herself.

Stratton took it upon himself to reply to the Dancemaster's question. "She called the stallion back to her without sound or signal, like an old-time Horsegirl. It used to be a commonplace thing among us horse skillers but it's just about died out in these times. The Kings didn't like it." Almost to himself, he continued. "The Kings made it against the law for Horsegirls to breed with any of the old-line blood Aristos. I can't tell you why. But I've paid attention to the tales of Horsegirls."

Stratton had more to say but he was interrupted. Hengst, who'd sat on a thistle, poked at Glennys to make himself feel better. "Tales of Horsegirls. Tails of Horsegirls. Hey Glennys, let me see your tail!"

Without thinking, more angry at Hengst than she'd ever been, Glennys dived under Dodger's belly and tackled the boy. He went down under her surprise attack and she sat on his back, holding his arms down with her calves, facing his ass.

"You want to see tail, Hengst, show us yours!"

She put her hand down his trousers, the hand that had imprisoned three grasshoppers. Her laughter poked at him while he danced on the grass.

Stratton, Tykker, and Rampalli ignored their horseplay. Stratton said, "Supposedly there's a Horsegirl at the beginning of our line somewhere, but I don't know if that's true.

Only the old Aristo bloods keep pedigree records of their matings."

Hengst used Rampalli as a hostage behind which he negotiated peace with Glennys. He held out his hand to her to shake. Without taking his attention from the horsehandler's conversation, Rampalli did something rapid and mysterious with his shoulders, arms, and hands. Now it was Hengst who stood in front.

Stratton said, "What we call Horsegirls in Nolan don't get respect. They're just King's Daughters like all the rest of the women who bargain their bed company for money. Horsegirls don't even rate as high as ballerinas or singers. You never hear of a Horsegirl getting a concubine's contract."

"Ah," crowed Rampalli, "you often hear that ballerinas and opera stars have received very lucrative contracts, and being King's Daughters, they don't pay taxes either. They do quite well."

Stratton wasn't interested in the theater. He called to Glennys, who was back working on Dodger's saddle. "Do you know how you got it?" His tongue stumbled, feeling for the word. "The Horse Sense? You're a Lighter girl, how did you come to have it? It's got to have been hidden in your blood over a lot of generations. Who'd a thought there'd be a genuine marvel in Soudaka County?"

Glennys didn't answer because she didn't know what to say. She was disgusted to have let others in on what had been her secret. On the other hand it was good to learn that what she could do had a name and that other people knew about it. She wasn't a monster, a freak of nature after all. She thought about all she knew about breeding.

Finally she said, "My mother's people converted and came to Soudaka from Old Nolan after the first Alaminites settled here. That's all I know."

The horsehandlers let the matter drop. But she was a lot more interesting to them than before. The lore had it that those with the Horse Sense were more lusty than other women. They eyed her speculatively, until a cloud of dust up the road claimed their attention.

Powell was riding to meet them, accompanied by the groom Glennys had sent ahead as a messenger. Glennys swung into the saddle, aches and pains forgotten. She put Dodger to the gallop and yelled at the top of her voice.

"Powell! You don't know how glad I am to see you. You're right. I'm green." She felt light and free, relieved from authority and responsibility.

Powell halted his big blue roan stallion and hooked his heel over the low pommel on his saddle. He waited for the girl to come to him. His quick, longsighted eyes gauged the condition of the horses she'd brought from Three Trees. He nodded with approval.

"If I made a mistake, I'm sorry," said Glennys. "But I didn't know what to do and this seemed like the best mistake I could make."

Powell leaned over and kissed Glennys's dusty cheeks in the Aristo manner. "Admit it, apprentice. You were just looking for an excuse to come back out here and get away from the muggy, buggy mess back home."

She looked at him carefully, and then laughed. "You're teasing me, Stablemaster. But I am glad to be out of it. At this rate we're gonna be looking forward to winter." She sobered quickly, however. "I'd have stayed on Three Trees if it had seemed right."

He appreciated the skill with which Glennys managed Dodger, who was top stallion on this trip. Those mares back there were his, and he made that clear to Powell's Stoner. Both Powell and Glennys kept the heads of their mounts low, running signals with their fingers and toes, keeping their stallions' attention distracted from each other. Neither horse had the opportunity to challenge for dominance.

Powell stroked her dirty hair with his big hand. "No, you did right. The sickness will most likely touch our home but I think—I hope—it will pass by most of our people. But it was right to bring the Baron's children out of it. And we'd hate to lose you too, apprentice."

"Me?" Glennys's eyes went wide. It had never occurred to her that she might get sick. "No. I'm like my mother. I don't get sick, I help those who do."

Powell shrugged. "You were in danger too—not yet fifteen."

"My bones from this ride make me believe I'm at least a hundred years old."

Tykker asked Rampalli, "Powell's apprentice isn't really that young, is she? She's got to be at least twenty."

Rampalli neither liked nor approved of Tykker's speculation. He whistled suddenly, sharp and high. The sound brought the horsehandler's hands to his ears and made his horse buck.

"If you talk about our Horsegirl, stablehand," said Rampalli, deliberately lowering Tykker's rank, "keep a decent tongue in your head."

Tykker was bewildered. "But you know as well as I do that a Horsegirl is a Whoregirl. Just one of the classes of King's Daughters."

"But out here she's Three Trees' Horsegirl and she's going to be Stablemistress. If you put a hand on her Powell will kill you—if I don't myself. I teach the sword as well as dance, in case you've forgotten. She's not a Whoregirl." Rampalli spit out the term. He hated it. "She's got people around her who protect her, just like any respectable woman anywhere."

Thurlow listened avidly. A lot of questions she'd amused herself with seemed close to having answers. "Maybe," she said sweetly, "if you tried to do something against Glennys's will, you could have all of Three Trees' stallions racing to pound your head to a pulp. Even if you gagged her."

Tykker didn't like that picture at all. He pulled his forelock. "Yes, Ma'am. Yes, Sir. I apologize for my bad manners."

But still, Tykker thought resentfully as he dropped behind the King's horses to ride drag, this was Lighter country, and conscripted men or not, it was nearly impossible to find female companionship, no matter how much you were willing to pay for it. He'd spent a lot of his working life on Three Trees. The horses were the best and the pay was better than anything he could get in Old Nolan. But as soon as he went back home all his earnings fast disappeared into the pockets of various Kings' Daughters. It would be convenient to have a few Horsegirls on Three Trees like the ones who worked the stable in St. Lucien.

He stole a look at Stratton and guessed his companion thought the same. Stratton was wondering why he'd only thought of Glennys before as an extension of Powell, as if she were a third arm or an extra leg for the Stablemaster. Once you've noticed someone's a full-grown woman, it's hard to forget it, he thought. She was ahead, riding point with Powell. He hummed a bit of an old song.

> *Horsegirl, horsegirl, ride on me*
> *Though my legs be only two*
> *Horsegirl, horsegirl, ride on me*
> *And then I'll ride on you.*

Tykker made a sign to his old friend Stratton. The sign indicated they were getting close to the King's Coal Mines. There was a Pleasure House there.


# SIXTEEN


Rampalli had thought the settlement around the King's Coal Mines was bleak and empty. But after Leon's horses proved healthy, and Powell sent them with Three Trees people out into the Badlands, the Dancemaster began to understand what empty really meant. It meant the land was without cultivation or shelter. The only tracks across it were breaks made by the ground's shifting or thin trails made by delicate paws, claws, and hooves. Without man's signature on it the land appeared endless, and Rampalli had never seen anything like it in his long life.

He felt as though they'd journeyed, not only out of congregational Soudaka, but backwards in time. The way of life out here was close to the grass and sky. Horsehair tents were the only barrier between them and the weather. It resembled the ancient, nomadic days of the Nolanese tribes. The conviction that he'd inexplicably fallen into Nolan's past was strongest in the presence of the men who lived with the Badlands horses all year around.

Ertegan, Lurgit, and Demein were the most sociable of the horsemen who guarded the little bands of stallions, mares, and foals. On their feet the horsemen were clumsy as trolls but they were seldom caught walking. On the back of a horse the troll transformed into a hero. Their faces were dark and weathered. They wrapped their sun-whitened braids in brightly colored rags and strung the braids with beads and bells. Their moon-bowed legs marked them as a caste apart from the modern Nolanese man. Fighters they were, but they were neither soldier nor warrior. They could live without walls and cloth and fireplaces. All they needed was a horse, a knife, a handful of salt, and something to hunt. They called themselves the Old Men.

They came and went as they chose from the clefts and meadows of the Badlands. Most of their days were lived in company with Fulk's mares and stallions, and out of range of Old Nolan. They shared a mare's milk with that of her foal. Their travels were mysterious. At some time in his life an Old Man returned to his companions with a young boy. When the one who'd brought the boy into their society died, the boy took his finder's name and became a man. As far back as the Fulk bloodline went there had been a Lurgit, a Demein, and an Ertegan guarding the Fulk stud. In these modern times the Old Men seldom were seen off the properties of old-line Aristos.

They felt a genial contempt for Nolan's new men who slept behind walls and put horses behind fences. They believed that in his heart Fulk was like them. Without a Fulk there was no place for the Old Men to accomplish their lives. They had a passing respect for the Stablemaster as well. He doctored the horses skillfully, he knew which stallion had covered which mare all the way to the beginning of the pedigree, and most important, Powell put the horses' welfare above his own.

These three lived in the Badlands territory claimed by a black son of Deadly's, named Slayer. They watched the new arrivals from Three Trees carefully. Glennys they already knew.

Earlier that spring Ertegan and Lurgit had sat cross-legged under the necks of their horses the first day that Glennys rode into their camp in Powell's company. They had watched Glennys dismount and give Dodger's reins to Powell.

Slayer had kicked the young stallions out of his band at the end of winter. Now, with some mares already having foaled and coming into season again, it was the most dangerous time to be around him.

All the horses were edgy at that time of the year when everything was hungry. Like Ertegan and Lurgit, they were on guard against the predators attracted by laboring mares and newborn foals.

As Powell, leading Dodger, rode to greet Lurgit and Ertegan, Glennys walked toward Slayer. The mares lifted their heads, ready to spook.

Glennys talked to Slayer. He listened. They both stood still.

Lurgit had turned to Powell and said, "Is she brave or is she stupid?"

Powell's reply had been, "Neither. Watch."

Slayer walked over to Glennys and smelled her. She got on his back and rode, slowly at first, and then more swiftly. They circled the mares, who had relaxed.

"You've brought us a Stallion Queen," Ertegan had said slowly.

"No," Powell said impatiently. "I've brought you my apprentice."

"She's a Stallion Queen," said Lurgit. "There hasn't been one for a long time. And now it's too late. But we thank you all the same."

Glennys and the Old Men had chattered at each other that whole time of the spring tour in the Badlands.

Now it was summer, and she was back, and with her she'd brought two of Fulk's children.

Rampalli's harmonica played under the light of the moon, following the melancholy lines of their own pipes. The sad, swinging rhythms made the horses content. The next morning, after seeing the Dancemaster run through his daily sword exercises, Demein threw several short-bladed knives in succession at the tent pole where Rampalli and Hengst had slept. All of Demein's knives stuck in the slender target. Rampalli said, "I'm very impressed with your skill." He walked over to Demein, who was on his own two feet, to give the old man a congratulatory handshake. That handshake somehow turned into a slither knife that crawled invisibly from under Rampalli's sleeve. It sliced off a silver bell at the end of one of Demein's braids.

Unlike an Old Man, Rampalli didn't boast about what he'd done. The Dancemaster seemed to think of himself as a very comical fellow because he'd cut off a bell that hung just above Demein's right ear. "How careless my skinny little knife is! I might have cut my own wrist, or even your ear."

That evening Demein returned to the camp with another bell at the end of his braid. He presented the old one to Rampalli, as well as a curved gelding knife with a blade thin as an infant moon.

Stratton and Tykker were simply new men. Ertegan and the other two guardians paid them very little attention.

They were very polite to the Baron's children, but seemed to find them disappointing. "You'd think you were my father's daughter, Glenn, the way they fawn all over you," Thurlow said. "But you like me, even if they don't, don't you? You like me better than you like them."

At first Hengst was full of curiosity about everything in the Badlands, finding it all new and interesting. But as the days passed, he began to be sullen and withdrawn. Sometimes Glennys could get him into a more pleasant and hopeful state of mind. His moods were always blackest when Glennys and Thurlow were most friendly.

That summer in the Badlands, Glennys felt she was living the life she'd been born to have. The days were lazy, full of sun, wind, and grass. The horses lived their own lives, and the music of their calls to each other and to the guardians were the happiest sounds she'd ever known. The summer nights were still short and lighted by moon, stars, and campfire. Thurlow sorted her botanical specimens and told stories. Rampalli played his fiddle and his harmonica. The Old Men sang wordless tunes and played their pipes. Glennys and Thurlow would brush each other's hair, turn and turn about, while the music coiled around them.

There wasn't any work to do, as Glennys understood work. The horses fed themselves on hardy grass and their guardians gave them a supplement once a day of grain and the salt necessary to a mare in foal. They groomed the horses only enough to keep them familiar with the feel of man's flesh, and rode them often enough for them to remember their elementary training. They drifted over Slayer's territory as the band of horses grazed new ground.

There was time to ride a horse, play with a horse, watch a horse, talk with a horse. Glennys learned more about horse nature in her weeks in the Badlands than she'd learned all year in a stable. There was time to strip naked and swim in the small, warm Swallow Lake and doze under the trees on the banks above it. There was all the time in the world to ride alongside Lurgit and listen to him talk of the horses at the beginning of the world.

"It might be the beginning of the world all over again, here in the Badlands," Glennys said, "with just us and the horses."

"No," Lurgit said. "The beginning of the world was very different. We are at the end of it."

The Old Men particularly watched over the young bachelor stallion bands that ranged the Badlands. They had neither mares nor territory of their own. They were ever hopeful that a mare or filly would stray far enough from her companions that she could be kidnapped. If a mare was captured, the young stallions fought among themselves as to which one she would belong to. Often enough the mare was determined to have none of them. Frantic to get back to her familiar herd, she'd bite and kick. The top stallion would tear after her. He'd wound the young ones with rending teeth, pounding hooves, and his greater strength and weight. He'd want to punish the stray from his harem. But if she was not in season, particularily if she was an older, experienced mare, she would have none of that either. She'd kick the stallion in the head when he tried to bite her hindquarters. Frequently, while one stallion was retrieving his lost property, another top stallion raided the unprotected herd to expand his own. The Old Men oversaw these endless permutations of free-range horse behavior. Sometimes they intervened to keep the more powerful stallion from badly damaging a valuable younger one.

The Old Men also protected the horses from the Alaminites who came to cut lignite out of the sod and buy coal from the King's Mine. A young stallion, unaccustomed to being on his own, without the boss mare and the top stallion to think for him, was vulnerable to attack. He'd be lonely. Used to the Old Men, he'd trot up to a group out of congregational Soudaka. The Alaminites would bait the horse into terror and finally kill him. Since the conscription, the Old Men's work had been easier, if less exciting.

Lurgit explained all this one day to Glennys while they were riding. "The brown bear kills for food, so he doesn't kill every time. But the Lighters kill because they hate horsekind, just as they hate us. Lighters are afraid of the Old Men who guard the horses. Would you like to see a reason the god men are afraid?"

He threw back his head and showed his big yellow teeth in a laugh. He signalled his horse, which he rode bareback, to gallop. He slid around the horse's side smooth as grease. He was almost invisible. He hung on with an arm at the base of his horse's neck and with one heel hooked over his horse's back. A curious pocket gopher paid curiosity's price. Lurgit skewered the gopher with his knife as unerringly as the red-tailed falcon pierced her prey with her talons. Lurgit hardly slowed the horse as he retrieved his knife.

Glennys clapped her hands. "That's almost as good as what the Baron and Deadly do in the Sword Dance. Can you teach me how to do that?"

Lurgit said blithely, "You already can. A Stallion Queen is born knowing such a simple thing."

After the first twenty tumbles Glennys thought the Stallion Queen business was nonsense. On her back in the grass she said, "I thought Rampalli had taught me everything I ever wanted to know about knives, but I don't know anything at all. I can't even ride."

Lurgit dismissed her doubts with an airy wave of his hand. "A Stallion Queen has all the teeth and hooves of the horses at her command. She doesn't need a knife."

Lurgit was tirelessly patient helping Glennys to learn to throw. But first she had to master the barrel ride. The blue beads in his sun-bleached hair clicked and the little bells at the end of his braids tinkled, when he shook his head after Glennys's second day of falls. He seemed sincerely bewildered that Glennys still hadn't succeeded. He ran his hands over her legs. "They should curve like a filly moon. It would have been better to have backed a horse before you learned how to walk, while the leg bones were soft as cheese. By now your legs would have grown to a horse's barrel and you'd never fall off."

"Some Stallion Queen I am, Lurgit." Glennys lay on the ground and pulled in air around her words. "Believe me, if I'd had my way, I would have backed a horse as soon as I could sit up. It was my first wish. But I will learn how to do this," she grunted, "even if my legs are almost straight. Besides, Rampalli and Thurlow don't want my legs to moon-bow."

"That's because Thurlow is jealous of you. If your legs bowed, you'd be even more beautiful and then everyone would try to steal you away from Fulk's daughter. She is like her sire and wants to keep what she thinks is her own."

"I'm going to try a different horse. Maybe Dodger's barrel is too big." She sent him back to his own set, hobbled by the tents. The King's horses had to stay within sight of people at all times.

"You are a Stallion Queen," Lurgit pronounced. "Only a Stallion Queen could put her word on a stallion to go to a place and have him go there without him running for the mares."

"Just don't tell Powell I do that," Glennys warned. "He's told me not to."

"Powell is a good man," Lurgit said, "but he flinches from your Horse Sense as you say your mother flinches from your woman's body."

Lurgit touched her nipples, first one, then the other. His brown, weathered face was sad and tender. "The Horse Sense and your body blossomed at the same time because you are a Stallion Queen. You will have to choose a mate carefully because in these days it will not be easy to find a worthy one."

He snapped his fingers, and made the bells in his braids jingle. "Choose your mount. I want to see you fall off a horse again," he laughed. "You do it so well."

Glennys's farsighted eyes and Horse Sense ranged over the horses spread out over Slayer's ground. Her will teased a bay mare, who after a few moments gave up grazing and ambled across the grass to where Lurgit and Glennys waited. The bay was called Sparkstone and her conformation was more delicate than most of the others. She was smaller and her foals weren't as big. But the bay was smarter than most of the other mares. She was the elderly boss mare's favorite head-

and-tail mate to brush off flies. For all these reasons she hadn't been culled out of the herd. She was allowed to breed because her nature was fiery and she passed that trait on to her offspring.

Lurgit gave Glennys a pat of approval through the wide linen trousers she wore. "Tomorrow you will be successful. I can smell it on you. You can try three more times with Sparkstone and then you must quit falling on the ground for today."

On the second try Glennys managed to hang on to Sparkstone with her arm and leg in the proper place for several running lengths. Lurgit pronounced the practice over at that point. Glennys thought it was funny to be treated in a training session the same way she handled a horse. "Never let a horse stop work with a sense of failure," she remembered. "If he's going well, let him go with a sense of accomplishment."

Thurlow was calling her. It was time for their ride to Swallow Lake.

Powell had done all he'd been able to do for the stock back on Three Trees without returning to congregational Soudaka. No summer was long enough to make up for winter, and he felt all his winters were waiting to pounce on him. He'd sent a man from the King's Mine to Three Trees with instructions and then waited for the messenger to return. The man had showed up with the handlers and the draft horses. Powell was now on his way to Slayer's territory to join the others. He reread Cook's letter while his blue roan stallion, Stoner, jogged along over the pathless ground.

> *I am sorry to inform you that by the time Glennys and the King's horses were met by you, the young stallions here began to die. Our mules are healthy, though noisier than ever.*

> *As you instructed, the remaining handlers are gone with the draft horses. They will be able to earn something this summer at the King's Mine, as you suggested. We have no reserve here, either in cash or kind.*

> *We stay within the House except once a day. We*

*take such precautions as we can. I've slaughtered
all the poultry. Tell Glennys that her sisters are
healthy and the permanent staff grows fond of them.
If we didn't know they were kin to Glennys we
would never have found it out. They enjoy helping
me in the kitchen. The hired hands have gone back
into Nolan, from fear of the sickness and because
they were mad from the pests.*

*I've included the mail that has accumulated here.
You're a fortunate bastard to be where the flies are
few, the air is fresh, and so is the meat.*

*Lowell, bastard line of Fulk, Cook for Three Trees,
wrote this.*

Two of the draft horses had died on the road. Another had
come down sick but seemed as though he would survive.
Powell had made arrangements with the Mine's overseer for
the Three Trees horses to earn some cash by hauling coal for
the rest of the summer. The settlement around the Mines had
public houses where drinks, meals, and beds were to be had.
A man could also find female companionship in the King's
Pleasure House if this taste ran to desperate girls who'd not
been able to find a better way to feed themselves. Every man's
taste did run that way on occasion, he thought. The Three
Trees handlers would be content there, away from the sickness,
earning a second wage by driving the teams for the Mine.
The King's Daughters ought to make something out of that
wage.

Powell was at loose ends as only someone can be who has
too much work to get done in a day, day after day, and no
way to do it. His orderly mind juggled lists and priorities. He
tried to plan the best use of this empty time before the frosts
killed off the vermin that had something to do with the
sickness in Soudaka. There was elementary training for the
horses. There were the King's racers. There were mares not
yet in foal, because they'd dropped a foal too late in spring,
or the foal had died, or because they didn't like the stallion
with which they were pastured. He'd see to it they found
another top stallion more to their liking, or tease them into

mating. Three Trees needed a bumper crop of foals to make up for the loss of this year's four-year-olds.

After frost he'd have to go into Drake and negotiate a very large loan to replace lost stock, and buy food, feed, and seed grain. He was going to have pull the Alaminite women through the winter so they could raise food for Three Trees next year. Fulk was going to have to take emergency measures because his own people couldn't help him this year. They needed their Master's help instead. Let him rob one of Leon's loot lines. It wouldn't be the first time a Fulk had done that when it was called for.

The open, empty country began to soothe him. Powell's heart lightened in spite of himself. That was the Nolanese part of him, he thought, gladdened by the sight of Slayer's band of mares spread out around him. Here was the aroma of good, clean horse dung and the smell of wholesome horse flesh. The foals at play delighted the Nolanese part of his heart. He wanted to run races, eat, drink, and then snooze in the shade.

At first Powell thought Slayer was warning his Stoner to stay away from the mares. A cry made Stoner hop. It came from the rider of a bay mare, whose black legs were churning in a flat-out run, her mane and tail streaming like flags in the wind, as she swept by him. Glennys clung to the mare's neck, and her heel in a soft foal's hide sandal was hooked over the mare's spine. "Hey Powell, look at me!"

Her head was low on the mare's shoulder. Her hair had come loose out of the knot on her neck. The long, gold strands swept over purple clover and yellow colt's foot flowers that were crushed under the mare's hooves. Fear gripped Powell's throat.

The applause at the campsite made Glennys push Sparkstone faster. She sat up on the mare's back, and then slid to the other side just as the bay made a sharp, leaning turn.

Rampalli blew a shower of congratulatory notes on his harmonica when Glennys and Sparkstone trotted up to him. They waited for Powell.

Lurgit knew how to strut while sitting on the back of a horse. "She learned quick. Well, she learned almost quick. She had me for a teacher, an excellent teacher. Can you, Demein and the music man, teach her about a knife as skillfully as I can teach her to ride?"

Thurlow stood under the awning of the tent she shared with

Glennys. The lap desk on which she wrote out labels for the toads, worms, and plants she'd gathered at Swallow Lake was knocked on its side. She'd stood up too fast when she'd heard Glennys's wild yells.

Powell rode up to Glennys where she'd stopped Sparkstone. "The old Lurgit taught the Baron and me that trick when we were about your age. But we didn't have hair hanging down to our ass. It could have tangled in the mare's legs and around your neck. You could have been killed."

Glennys tossed her hair out of her eyes. Impudently she said, "I've got Gordon's Luck, Stablemaster."

Thurlow applauded again, all by herself. "You could have been one of my father's men, or even a barbarian, the way you rode into camp."

Glennys inhaled Thurlow's praise. It was given for once without holding anything back, without a reservation, no matter how tiny, of mockery. A gypsy breeze brought her Thurlow's perfume. The shirt Glennys wore was too small. A few inches of her brown midriff were bare. Powell saw her diaphragm muscles working as she breathed.

"Thurlow, want to go to Swallow Lake now?" She rode Sparkstone to the tent. The bay mare wore no saddle. Glennys put out her foot and Thurlow used Glennys's fingers and the arch of her foot as a mounting block. She wrapped her arms around Glennys's waist and whispered in her ears. Glennys laughed, throwing back her hair. Sparkstone left the others quickly behind.

Tykker had held his breath and now he let it go. Demein thought he looked very funny. "New man, I don't think your face is pretty enough for a Stallion Queen to want to ride you."

There was a short period of perplexed silence in the campsite. The Horsegirl had ignored her Stablemaster. The men wondered what he would do about it. Powell said, "So, this is how it is these days, since I've not been around to keep my eye on things."

Rampalli cleared his throat. "Well, what can one expect under the circumstances? They are young, it's summer, there's no one else their age, and that old Waterford Thurlow's going to marry won't care. He's an old-line Aristo."

Powell threw Stoner's reins to Stratton.

Rampalli said, "There's no news here." He raised his

voice. "The most important thing is that Hengst has killed his first white-tailed deer with a bow. One shot, the first shot. We're quite proud of him." He whispered for Powell's ears alone. "He, poor fellow, isn't proud of himself. Having not yet gotten the hang of what Glennys has already mastered, he's sulking in his tent."

"Is it Glennys or Thurlow who has mastered what he's trying to get the hang of, Dancemaster?" asked Powell. "Never mind answering that. As you say, youth and summer and there's no one else." He threw down the mail pouch from home. "We'll go through this together. I sure could use Muran right now. But business, like everything else, has got to wait until first frost. Never thought I'd see the day where I looked forward to winter. And this one's going to be a killer."

Rampalli poured two tin cups full of bitterberry kept warm by the campfire. He gave one to Powell and went to his tent. He didn't go inside, but called softly, "Hengst, Powell's here with the mail pouch. Have a cup of bitterberry with us and go through the papers and periodicals."

Powell could see that Hengst wasn't blooming like the rest of them out here. He looked unthrifty, out of condition, not in his body, but in his face. "Loneliness," he said to himself. "No one his age or his gender all this time. He doesn't dare to love the Badlands though he wants to, because it will go to Stogar, not him." Powell understood what it was to be of an old Aristo line, but not to be the Baron.

"Where are the girls?" Hengst asked. There was a faint aroma of brandy in his question.

"Swallow Lake," answered Rampalli.

Hengst looked at the disorder under the awning where Thurlow had been sitting. "They didn't take any of the water bottles or specimen jars. Tell Tykker to saddle me Dodger. I'm going to Swallow Lake too. I'll bring Thurlow her collecting equipment."

"I don't think Thurlow wanted her things," said Powell carefully. "I think this is a girls' party. They didn't invite anyone else."

"The lake doesn't belong to Thurlow any more than it does to me. It's my brother's property. Glennys is just a Horsegirl, nothing belongs to her at all. If I want to go to the lake I will, and I'm going to.''

"If you insist on going when you weren't invited take any other horse than Dodger. There's enough horses about to satisfy anybody's taste.''

Rampalli drummed his fingers on his tin cup after Hengst went to order Tykker to saddle him a horse. Powell picked up an issue of a St. Lucien journal.

"You know what he's going to find at the lake, don't you?" asked Rampalli.

Powell lowered the journal and looked levelly over the top. "He's going to find naked girls playing together, neither one of which he can touch. It happens to the best of us, Dancemaster. Thurlow's like her mother and Glennys is waiting for the Baron. Gordon's Luck be with her.''

Rampalli sliced some meat off the spitted pheasants roasting at a second fire. He put the meat on flat oatmeal cakes and gave them to Powell. "You must be hungry by now, Stablemaster.''

"Not as hungry as we're all going to be if the bank in Drake doesn't give Three Trees another loan, a big one. I think I'll take Hengst with me to Drake when I go. He's off his feed here. He'll get some new scenery. There's lots of young, pretty King's Daughters in Drake. And banker's daughters, merchant's daughters, lawyer's daughters. None of them will care he's a second son. That he's legitimate, registered old-line Aristo get is all that will matter to them.''

At supper Powell thought of how often they'd all been together for this meal. He understood the shift in the lines of tension that always had run among the three young ones. Thurlow was never as charming as when she'd gotten the cream that someone else wanted. If she wasn't so attractive in face and body she'd be intolerable. Glennys was different than before this Badlands stay, however. She'd discovered her body for the first time as something valuable, lovely, and full of delight.

Glennys had discovered something. Hengst thought he'd lost something. Powell pondered what Hengst might think he'd lost while Thurlow began the story of Eve and the First Stallion.

*It was at the Lake Ulanor that the lady saw what at first she thought was a deer without horns. But this deer had a long, hairy tail, a hairy neck, and wore a silver crown between its ears.*

*The Lady Eve asked the deer, "Who are you? Have you seen a child? I am looking for a girl-baby and no one, not the cougar, not the wolf, not the eagle, have found me one."*

*"I am Torgut, bred from stallions, and a stallion myself. If you want a girl-child get on my back—if you dare." Torgut's eyes blazed, he threw up his head and reared. He opened his mouth and showed all forty of his long teeth. His nostrils breathed out a smoke hot and strong. From the Lake Ulanor came a mist on the back of the wind and when it had cleared the Lady Eve was on Torgut's back, where he carried her for seven days.*

*Eve's daughter was also called Eve. On the day Eve was born, out of the west came an endless procession of horses: stallions, mares, and foals— for in those days the third sex, the gelding, hadn't been made—they were all Torgut's folk, and he led them. They came to pay homage to Eve, the daughter of Eve. Thus the human and the horse kingdoms were created.*

Hengst threw the dregs of his bitterberry into the fire. "That's the stupidest story I ever heard, and I don't want to hear more."

Glennys said, "You used to like the old stories. How come you don't care for them anymore?"

"Because they're lies that cheat. It was never like that and it isn't like that now. And it will never be like that again."

Hengst ran off into the night.

After a few moments Glennys said, "I think I'll go and find him. Don't anybody bother waiting up for me if you're tired and want to go to sleep."

She found Hengst under a solitary, low-spreading cotton-wood tree that hung on to the edge of a gully. The gully washed wider with every spring runoff and thunderstorm. She sat down beside him. She could tell he had been crying.

Finally he said, "All the journals from Old Nolan are full of it. The King's invited ballistics designers from Outremere to meet with his cabinet in St. Lucien. He's going to build a factory to forge cannon. Do you know what that means?"

While Hengst had brooded silently next to her, Glennys's mind had slipped back to the kisses in Swallow Lake. She didn't know what Hengst's announcement meant.

"Tell me, Hengst."

"You're too stupefied by my sister's charms to figure out anything. How much good is hiding behind a galloping horse going to do you when you're shot at with a cannon? Tell me that, oh Stallion Queen," he mocked. "Everything I've been taught to do, everything I've been taught to honor, is useless, dead. Sword dances, war horses are a mean joke. Guns and cannon are the war of the future."

"But," said Glennys reasonably, "horses are what make the Nolanese. Cannon or not, Aristos are going to want horses."

"Not war horses. A war horse isn't a child's pet, or a lady's mount, or a merchant's transportation. They don't race or pull loads. A war horse is an inconvenience in a rich man's stable. A horse soldier is an inefficient inconvenience against a bunch of slovenly men on foot setting off a piece of field artillery."

Glennys thought about it. Then she said slowly, "I hope the bank in Drake gives Powell the loan before the bankers figure it out, if what you say is true. War horses are Three Trees' collateral."

She put her arm around Hengst. "It will be all right. You'll see. Things aren't really black the way you're seeing them."

Glennys believed what she said because she didn't know what she was talking about. It was impossible to believe the end of the world was in sight when she'd just discovered sex.

# SEVENTEEN

Alam tested his congregations severely during the summer of epidemic and the harvestless months that followed. Necessity forced the women of Soudaka to accept unblessed seed in order to sow crops that next spring. There were no Reverends with revelations to explain why Alam saw fit to treat them in this manner. Though the husbands had been taken to foreign parts to fight for the hated Aristos, some golden-haired babies began to appear. The seed from which these babies had sprung was as unblessed as that from which grew the oats, corn, barley, and flax.

Three Trees provided the seed-grain. Powell had been more goaded than charitable with his help for the Lighter women, given out of Three Trees' bank loan and a mysterious largess from the Baron. Privately, he and Muran agreed that Fulk must have appropriated funds not originally intended for his personal use. But that shower of gold had paid off the loan's interest and part of the principal. It had allowed the Stablemaster to listen to Stella without strangling her.

Stella demanded, she preached, she nagged. It was Three Trees' obligation to provide for Alam's folk since the Baron had taken away their men.

Once he'd exploded, "Woman, the Baron's got nothing to do with the weather!" But Stella was merciless and cunning, just as she was in the marketplace. Alaminite women knew how to hide grain when Aristos plundered, but when nothing was left to plant they knew the Lord expected them to help themselves. They helped themselves by getting Powell to do it.

Stella invoked Powell's long-dead mother, who had been seduced at seventeen by Fulk's father. She appealed to the Alaminite blood in him, his better half, as she called it. Powell had never been so grateful as when the weather luck turned favorable and the Alaminite women could take care of themselves again.

There'd been two bountiful harvests since then. The congregations had made good progress paying back Three Trees what they owed for seed and restocking, but Powell still sat in the Library office and worried. It had to be the Alaminite side of him, he thought, that made him anxious. He worried about those babies. Bad weather or good, harvest or no harvest, the Post Stage ran out of St. Lucien into the County. Coal traders traveled to the King's Mine. Traders bought Lighter lace. There were visitors and the traveling hands from Old Nolan on Three Trees. A boy who'd been below conscription age when his father and the older brothers had been taken was now eighteen or older. Alaminite women got lonely on long winter nights, restless in the short summer ones, just like other women all over Mittania. So there were babies.

The congregations had held midnight atonements hidden behind the stone walls of the kirks, but the babies remained a fact of life that made up for the deaths during the summer of sickness and the winter of famine. Alam might be merciful to a woman, even if there were no Reverends to bring the revelation that great sins can sometimes be forgiven. "The Lord maketh good out of evil," and the babies were good to have when so many had died. But Powell worried. Alam might forgive, but would fathers and husbands, Elders and Reverends?

He worried about the Lighter boys who'd grown up without the iron authority of either father or Reverend. He worried about the women. Many of the congregational women sincerely missed their men. But Stella wasn't the only one of them who'd developed an authority of her own and was more content with it than she'd ever been with her husband's. Powell wasn't an imaginative sort of man—he left that for someone like Rampalli—but Powell did understand consequences.

There was peace in Sace-Cothberg. The Alaminite men were coming home. They'd want to find their houses ordered the way they remembered. Instead they'd find that small boys had become young men and that women who once had asked permission to sell their wool were now used to running the farmsteads on their own. This had all happened before and Powell was tired of it.

These were the things on Powell's mind this early autumn evening. He'd carried out his responsibilities to the very best of his ability. But the responsibility of three children growing into adults wasn't something he'd ever expected. He'd been content to raise Three Trees' horses, without wife or child of his own. But he was starting to feel a resentment against Fulk because the Baron had put his own children into Powell's care without so much as a by-your-leave. It was just like the small blackbird that put its eggs in the nests of other birds. Three Trees was Fulk's nest, not Powell's. But it was Powell's blood, his sweat, his care that kept Three Trees alive.

He rubbed his kidneys. There was a hot burn in the small of his back. He bent to the fireplace and lit the kindling. There'd been too many Soudaka winters, too many kicks, and throws, and falls, and bites from horses over many years for him to feel good. Wherever his bastard brother was tonight, Powell expected, hoped, Fulk felt the same misery in his flesh. He drank a large swallow of the cellar's best. It was his third snifter already this evening.

Out in the dining hall he heard the voices of Hengst and Thurlow rise. Their war was heating up again, a war which this year had had few cease-fires and fewer truces. Uncharacteristically, Powell slammed the Library door, to shut out their disregard for his privacy.

He was sick to death of juggling the demands of young Aristos against the needs of the horses. He could have been having peaceful days in the Badlands with his apprentice. Together they could have put the final touches on Leon's horses to get them into competition condition. Instead, he'd had to take the Post Stage into Drake to manage Hengst's latest indiscretion. This one had given a prosperous textile manufacturer's only daughter a big belly.

Glennys, with the Old Men's assistance, would have to handle the job with Leon's horses. She must welcome this time alone with the Old Men, time in which she could sink completely into her Horse Sense, with no other obligations, no matter how agreeably they called. He envied her and wished he were there with her.

Out in the Badlands Glennys could stay out of the crossfire of Thurlow and Hengst, too. Powell could never decide whether or not Hengst really wanted the girl or just didn't want his sister to have her. While Powell could sympathize with the boy, the problems of the young held no interest for him.

The summer of the epidemic it had seemed a good idea to take Hengst into Drake and introduce him to people his own age and sex who, if not his own breed and class, were prosperous and willing to have an old-line Aristo son as a familiar. Looking back, Powell still would have done the same. Hengst was unhappy, felt that he was worthless. Perhaps that was why he'd not done the simple, uncomplicated thing and found an actress or used the Pleasure Coaches that plied the streets with feminine goods. He'd gotten a manufacturing master's daughter with child while on recreational leave from Three Trees.

In Outremere the Baron had had a talk with Nathan Drake, Commander of Nolan's cavalry. Nathan's brother was Elliot Drake, Chief of Drake's First Bank. After Elliot sponsored an honorary dinner for the manufacturer, and after the bank invested in the manufacturer's new dye works, the pregnant girl was married off to one of her own cousins. Her name and child would never be written in the Fulk line records. The Fulk line had no use for the get that came out of a mating with a townswoman.

Hengst had remained welcome in the homes of Drake and able to mingle with the nubile daughters of Drake's masters. The fathers liked his company as much as their daughters did. It seemed that Hengst had inherited at least one of the lengendary Aristo skills—the power of seduction.

The unexpected difficulty had come out of Hengst's determination to marry the girl. Powell didn't think that was because he cared about her or the child. The marriage might have given him an opportunity to be something other than the second son of Three Trees, which belonged to his father and his brother, but not to him.

Powell thought about opportunity while he drank his fourth snifter of cognac. He was thorough and organized. He understood the importance of details. He could make numbers and percentages work for him. Those traits made him an excellent Stablemaster, but they were just as useful to a banker. Half Alaminite, half Aristo, born on Three Trees, all he'd ever known was the old Stablemaster and the Big House. The life his luck had given him was good, but he'd had nothing to do with the choosing of it. But who did choose? Your luck was your pedigree, the mating that produced you, and that held for old-line Aristos as much as it did for bastards. Case in point—the two siblings fighting outside the Library door.

Hengst barged in without knocking. He went straight for the decanter. "Leave me alone," he shouted over his shoulder. "I don't want to hear anymore about my privileges. You have your own."

Thurlow was after him like a wasp. "I'm not allowed to go anywhere except within the County. I can't talk to a man except in the presence of at least three of the people I see every boring day of my life. If I get pregnant before I marry, I'll be dead. My relatives would see to that, if I didn't myself. All except you, Hengst. You're not man enough to kill me. You're not even man enough to take me with you on visits to Drake."

"It's not allowed, Thurlow. And someone's got to run the Big House. You're born a girl and that's not my fault. But if you'd been male, you'd have been me, the second son. I know your opinion of second sons!"

Thurlow was almost panting, she was riding Hengst so hard. "Don't tell me your life is harder. How many children has my husband-to-be sired over the years that no one cares about? Yet he's allowed to have another pure, untainted brood mare to guarantee his pure, untainted bloodline. It makes me sick!"

Hengst's grin was a crooked line. "Just how pure you are is debatable. You and Glennys—that's having your cake and eating it too. You're too hungry for your own good, Thurlow. You'd eat the whole world if you could. You hold on to her so tight because she can be asked to a man's bed and you can't. But you're only a shadow that she kisses while she waits for our father."

Powell's bellow was just like the Baron's. "Stop it! Rattle your sabres all night where I don't have to see you or hear you. Both of you, you're ugly as Alaminite sin, face and tongue. It will be a lucky day when you two clear out of Three Trees. All year you've given the rest of us nothing but a pain in the butt. None of us can wait to see your backs. What do you think about that?"

There was blessed silence for quite some time during which Powell took away the second glass of cognac that Hengst had poured himself. For a moment Hengst became that beautiful boy who'd come lonely out of St. Lucien when eleven years old, and had followed him wherever he went.

"I apologize." Hengst made a short bow, one equal to another, exactly as Rampalli had drilled him.

Thurlow's neck tilted over her shoulder in a parody of naughtiness. Her eyes were half hidden behind the luxuriant fan of her lashes. She used the voice that contained hundreds of things. She could offer something with it and in the next breath pull it back. When you began to believe she was laughing at you, her voice said she loved you. The times you thought were going well between you, her voice turned away. Her drawl made Powell want to smack her pink mouth.

"I think, Stablemaster, that you are crude to say what you said. Nor would Glennys, if you were so rude as to ask her, say that's what I've given her."

Her stance was provoking. Her fingers stroked the supple, soft foal's skin skirt that clung to her long legs.

Powell rubbed the space between his eyebrows. He'd spent too much of himself on the Fulk line to back down from a seventeen-year-old girl. He threw Hengst's drink into the fire, which blazed briefly blue. But he wasn't so foolish as to argue with girls that age. They were so high-strung that only an idiot would try.

"Get out of here and leave me alone."

Hengst and Thurlow went. He flung some words at the soft leather that followed the planes and curves of Thurlow's back. "Hengst is right about you wanting to eat the whole world. I think your appetite is going to amuse Waterford very much. He's the right age to like it."

He'd had the last word. As foolish as it was in someone his age, he got a lot of satisfaction from it.

Aristos said that it was best to keep distance between the members of a bloodline just as it was best to keep distance between stallions. Otherwise there'd be no peace in a Big House.

Well, there wasn't any in this Big House these days. The blood was tangling, snarling, making knots where there should be straight connections. No wonder Aristos' birth drink was Blood Ale. Powell sipped cognac and worried about that, along with the Alaminite women's babies.

A little later a noise in the front hall indicated that Muran had come home from the first days of school in Dephi. He'd brought the mail pouch from the Coach, and news from town.

"Get ready," Muran said, with a smile of pleasure. "Three Trees is going to have a lot of visitors, and some of them are important, like Lord Duke Albany. Young Fulk—Stogar, I mean—is coming out to try running his patrimony before the Baron returns himself. The heir's bringing some friends, and Miss Thurlow's going to be pleased. Her Aunt Abigail is one of the visitors."

"You won't like the rest of the news," said Muran. Powell grunted, not having liked the first part of it.

"The first of the surviving conscription is being routed back on home," Muran continued, tapping the mail pouch. "We have messages about it in here. Mrs. Prochnow told me about it though, before I even looked inside."

Muran got a look of surprise on his face when he sampled what was left at the bottom of the decanter. "You don't usually drink yourself this fine or this much, Stablemaster."

Powell decided that Muran had earned the privilege of helping him worry. "Sit, down, Shoolmaster," he ordered. He opened another bottle. "Now I want you to listen to me. I bet you don't even know anything about what Stogar, the Fulk-to-be's like."

Muran left the "Shoolmaster" pass. He said, "Stogar's supposed to be a very promising, diligent sort of young man. I've heard that he's a modern sort, like me."

Powell poured himself another snifter and began. "The only thing Stogar and you have in common is a quick intelligence, and his is sharper than yours."

Powell was unsteady on his legs, yet he could manage to prowl about the Library.

"Think about Thurlow, as the Dancemaster would say, in her most provoking attitude. Compound it a hundred percent. Think of a man more seductive than Hengst because it's all coming to him. Think of a man more heedless than Fulk. Put all of this together without any influence from me," Powell said.

His words slurred not at all now, Muran noticed.

"Stogar rode a horse to death once, under my eyes, to see how long it would take," Powell added.

Powell came back to where he'd been sitting and fell to the cushions.

Muran was glad that his future didn't depend on Three Trees.

# EIGHTEEN

When Glennys read Powell's new orders she understood that the war in Sace-Cothberg was finished. The war, and Sace-Cothberg itself, had seemed chimerical to her, like the landscapes where legends happened. Now that it was over, the war was made real to her.

Powell's orders were to take charge of culling the Badlands' breeding stock. Without a campaign, and no immediate prospect of one, the production of Three Trees' cash crop, the war horses, had to be cut back. Instead of stimulating mating and foaling by whatever means, they'd do the opposite now. In early spring, before the mare's most fertile season got started, they'd reduce the number of horses again. Rather than concentrating on quantity, they'd try to improve the quality of the bloodline. That was an exciting prospect for a horseman. Glennys was highly gratified that Powell trusted her judgment enough to run the Badlands' culling.

She and the Old Men separated the least valuable horses from their bands. These included barren mares, some of the elderly ones, mares who didn't get along with other horses, and bad-tempered stallions who hadn't inherited the leavening of good sense to offset their fierceness.

It was a delicate business, the choice between those who must go and those who were to continue the line. A war horse had to possess the killer instinct, but he also had to know the difference between your horses and those of the enemy. It was a gamble, determining how a horse would turn out. A horse survived by its speed—it ran away from danger—yet it had to have the spirit and bottom to turn on the threat. The nomadic Nolanese tribes had realized long ago how valuable horses were in battles. In those distant days they'd already begun breeding aggressive horses.

Fighting horses didn't always have a steadfast nature. When a stallion began to thicken with muscle, or when he felt the mating urge, he could be too aggressive. He could hurt foals and mares, as well as rival stallions. If, as Thurlow said, there were men who'd fuck mud, Glennys maintained there were horses who'd do the same and try to kill it for good measure. A killer horse who was stupid was too dangerous and had to be destroyed.

But you couldn't always predict; a mare could throw two foals in two years from the same sire. One would grow up worthless and the other one would be the best horse a rider ever had. The Old Men studied the foals' natures from birth, looked to the bloodlines, and updated the herd book throughout development and training. Sometimes a seemingly bad horse, coupled with the right handler, trainer, or rider, could turn out to be superb.

Other horses were too timid for the profession they'd been bred for. If they weren't too high-strung, they could be sold to civilians as riding horses.

Glennys did her work conscientiously and she enjoyed it, except for killing the horses they couldn't in good conscience sell. They always knew, the ones you picked to take out, and they burrowed into the center of the herd trying to hide.

Sparkstone, the bay mare who'd helped Glennys learn how to ride like an Old Man, was an excellent partner in this work. She was handy, agile as a cat, and knew as well as Glennys what Glennys wanted. Sparkstone neither respected nor feared any stallion. She and Glennys always got their horse.

It wasn't until after the nights and mornings had turned chilly and the second frost had fallen on the grass that Glennys gave Sparkstone her final treats and said "so long" to the Old Men. It had been a golden stretch of days from the summer solstice until now. She'd not known anything better than this. At the end of this year she'd be sixteen and by the end of next summer she'd have her license. Then she'd be an adult. The idea made her flesh go hot and cold. Long before next summer's end, the Baron would be living on Three Trees. . . .

Except for Stratton, the handlers who'd come to take the culls to Three Trees and into Old Nolan were hired while she'd been in the Badlands. They were strangers. After the warm respect of the Old Men's company, the manners of the other men made her feel as though she were a bizarre acquisition of Three Trees. She was of interest because she was a freak. Stratton had been talking to the new men about her Horse Sense and they were eager to see it demonstrated.

She decided to leave the evening before the rest of them did. It was something she'd never done, riding across Soudaka alone. But she was almost sixteen and grown-up, and she thought it was about time to do as she liked.

She chose a barren black mare they called Witchy. The horse had good rhythm and a decent temper. Once she understood you meant business, she'd get down to it herself. Witchy, five years old and covered by several stallions, had never caught. She'd lost the privilege of a life in the Badlands. But she didn't have to suffer sterilization and she'd make a decent mount for a townswoman who wasn't afraid to ride something other than a rocking chair.

Soudaka that fall was as fat as the County ever got. The weather had been very good and there'd be a thankful Harvest Gatherin at autumn's end to praise Alam for his bounty. Orange pumpkins planted among the corn stooks absorbed the last nourishment from sun and stalk. They glowed like a miser's fantasy. Shoats scavenged among the box elder and cottonwood trees that made shelterbelts behind the more prosperous farmsteads. Pheasants ran over the oat stubble, exposing their scatterbrained activity to any eyes.

Mrs. Dieke had set her household to work spading up the garden already. This Alaminite wife wasn't going to get caught by the first big freeze. She waved at Glennys. She stepped to the edge of her garden and held up a bottle as an invitation. Politely, Glennys left Witchy hobbled on the road. Her riding boots slid down the long grass on the sides of the ditch between road and garden.

Since the year of flood and famine, the congregations were, if not exactly friendly, at least willing to pass the time of day with the riders of horses and those who lived on Three Trees. And some had done more than pass the time of day, Glennys knew. Otherwise Alaminite women wouldn't have those babies at their hips or toddling at their skirts today. Some of the sociability, of course, had come from the money, seed, and stock that Powell and Stella had provided the congregations. And some had simply come out of shared hard times.

Mrs. Dieke and Glennys exchanged weather news. Glennys volunteered the information that several handlers and sixty-three horses would be coming by tomorrow or the next day. She said the war was over. Mrs. Dieke already knew that, she said, as she gave Glennys a share of the cider in her bottle.

Back on Witchy, Glennys thought that on days like these she could almost feel fond of an Alaminite farm. However, autumn sentiment in the chill of evening wasn't strong enough to make her ask for shelter at a farm, even though it was her right. Without another rider for company, just the thought of sleeping in an Alaminite girl's room, putting Witchy up in the barn, made her skin creep. She'd learned to sleep rough in the Badlands. She was prepared for it.

As in the Badlands she lay on her back, arms under her head, and looked up at the constellation the Old Men called the Great Bear. Her thoughts were much the same as in the Badlands' nights. She considered the idea that, at least long ago, according to the Old Men, animals could change into each others' shapes. It made sense. Cats reminded one of owls with their reflective, intense gaze, their pointed, tufted ears, their flexible necks. Cats also made her think of gophers and rabbits sometimes when they sat up on their haunches with their front paws held in front of their chests. Horses, when ready to attack, sometimes crouched like wolves. When colts played with each other, their splayed legs and snapping teeth made them resemble a pack of puppies. A band of horses seeing something new would run away, but if the object were stationary, they'd come creeping back to investigate, like cats padding on their pillowed toes. There were hundreds of expressions that compared man's behavior and appearance to that of animals.

Through the nights before falling asleep out under the Badlands sky, Glennys had compiled these observations. She believed the Old Men were right. Once, when the world was new, flesh wasn't set rigidly for all time, but could change and flow like water does, until it finds its level. She wondered, if she went deep enough, if she matched perfectly with the right horse, could she leave herself behind? She didn't know.

The third day she was deep into congregational Soudaka. The grass was nibbled sheep-short. It appeared as peaceful as it had been in the last three years, but the feel was different. No one waved to her, or offered to talk about the weather. There was a buzz of tension, like riding through a mist of gnats. She recognized the tension. It had been absent for a long time, like the Alaminite men had been absent.

Witchy was reluctant to move along the road. They were going upwind and the mare's nostrils cracked, releasing her breath in a sound like a light wooden door hitting the frame in a breeze. Ahead of them was a stand of apple trees. Then Glennys understood Witchy's reluctance.

A black bear, its glossy fur wobbling over pillows of fat, reeled out of the trees into the road. He vomited a bellyful of apple skins and pulp. He hoisted himself up to his front paws, and like the drunk he was, weaved back to the trees and the windfalls. He gave a powerful swat to the trunk of one, and sat down fatly, apples raining on his head.

Bears got sick when they gorged on apples, just like people. The cider left in their stomachs affected them just like applejack did a man. He was an inebriated clown who made Glennys laugh. She thought Rampalli would enjoy this. The bear wasn't any danger. Witchy could outrun him in her sleep. Black bears didn't often eat flesh in any case. But they could be dangerous if all their senses were working and they felt threatened.

Glennys thought it odd that no one was gathering apples today in prime season. The tension didn't disappear as she left the bear behind. It got stronger, like an itch left unscratched, as they alternately trotted and cantered towards the village of Durl.

Durl's one street was empty. No one was putting on winter shutters or strengthening the chicken coop roofs for the snow to come. Two windows on the west side of the kirk were open and she heard the call and response of an Alaminite service. A man's voice began to preach. It was a voice that belonged to someone who was a lot older than most of the men left in the County. The voice was practiced in congregational exhortation. It promised punishments and atonements for the sinful, heathenish ways of its lapsed flock.

"Without the vigilance of your shepherds you've gone lusting after the heathen, brought dogs among the flocks, listened to the seduction of woman. Even within my own house, my own house, my wives and my children, the vileness has spread." Reverend Durl had come home.

Why did they have to come back and ruin everything? Glennys thought. There was no more joy in the ride. She put her heels to Witchy and made her work. "What's inside those stone walls," she muttered to Witchy, "is crazier than a drunk bear."

The next day, when dusk was a smoky blue glow, Glennys and Witchy turned into the access road at Three Trees. She breathed deeply the smell of home. The comforting odors of horse settled into her chest. She was back in Nolan, safe from congregational Soudaka.

There were hordes of dogs. Lights fluttered gaily in and out of the stables, back and forth between the barn and the Big House. That must be how a field of fireflies would look, she thought. It was one of the things in Old Nolan she would like to see.

Something in her mind stirred, something that had been still for a long time. It was faint, barely trembling over awareness, as a dragonfly skated on quiet water. Witchy reached for the bit when the hands on her reins lost interest in her mouth. That pulled Glennys's attention back to the horse she was riding.

"Who are all these people?" she asked a stableboy.

"Young Fulk's friends and their serving folk," he said, and shrugged. "Ain't it lively though?"

"One Fulk's enough for me," she said. The pastures and paddocks were full of strange horses; so were the stables. "Just where does Powell think we're going to put the culls?" she asked Tykker. "Why didn't he warn me that Three Trees was making jubilee?"

Below the surface of her questions was a tautness, an expectation, as though a much-longed-for thing was about to be presented to her as a gift.

Tykker took Witchy's reins. "Powell's got it figured out—apprentice. You're not Stablemistress yet, and the old boy's got all his senses full and active. He didn't invite these people. It was the heir's idea, and his right. It's a nice change, that's what I think. I'll take care of your horse."

He wrinkled his nose. "You want me to help you clean up? You smell like an Old Man."

"Button yourself, Tykker," she said.

"You're probably crawling with Old Man lice anyway," he said.

No horse in hand, she was drawn to the Long Stable. The feeling was strong. The herdmaster's loose box wasn't empty.

He'd been waiting for her, she understood, as he licked the palm of her hand, twisted his black tongue around her wrist in their old greeting. "What a horse you are, Deadly. Why didn't he tell me you'd been hurt? You saved his life, didn't you?"

The clean, springy straw rustled under her boots. Her mind threaded into his like a many-eyed needle with different colors of silk.

The night the barn burned he'd put a claim on her as no other horse had done. He was even more impressive now. The gashes on his chest and belly weren't fresh, but bore thick scabs. The shallow scar on the side of his neck, where a ball of shot had gouged a path through the thick muscle, was almost healed. He was missing the furry triangle of his left ear. He hadn't died. Life still burned in him strong as summer sun. His eyes were clear. He stood solidly on all four feet, holding his head high.

He'd lived through that, the ocean-trip out of Sace-Cothberg, the trip across Old Nolan. Deadly was a horse of horses. But he was so terribly thin. The sight of large patches in his coat, between the scraggly areas where his winter coat tried to grow, made her sad, but it added to her admiration. He'd done his job under impossible conditions and he'd lived through it.

A young man came into the box with a pail of warm mash. "Ah, you're here. Now I can forget about this bag of bones that's been hanging around my neck for weeks. He's been nothing but a big pain in the ass since we shipped out of Tourienne. I had to put him in his own chariot pulled by a team of draft horses and watch him all the way here. But now I can pass the responsibility over to you."

"Any decent man would have been proud to have had that duty. Who are you anyway?"

"I know all about you, Horsegirl. I'm sorry to learn you haven't returned the interest. I'm your master—or will be when Dad kicks the bucket. Until then you can call me Lord Stogar, like everyone else does."

She examined her future Baron. His blood showed, of course. With a narrow, long body, high forehead, long arms, and big hands, he was a Fulk get, but not as young as Hengst and not as developed as the Baron. She hated him.

His voice, which carried a stone behind every chuckle, offended her—though she'd found the same quality intriguing in Thurlow. The smell of him, mingled with the musky scent he wore, irritated her nostrils. His careless manner, shown in the way he offered Deadly the mash, as if he didn't care whether the stallion wanted it or not, made her believe he wasn't a horseman. The satin trousers he'd chosen to wear in the stable confirmed her impression. The little hairs on her neck rose in warning.

"Where's Powell? If you despise your father's horse so much, Powell would be glad to take care of him."

Stogar said, "But he's leading some of my guests on a sunset trail ride. I'd have gone with them but I had to plan the menus for our evenings' dinners."

We eat dinner at noon, Glennys thought. At night we have supper.

"Dad said you'd get Deadly back into condition faster than anyone else. He wants more foals out of him. His belly was chewed up too, but let me show you something."

Stogar took Glennys's hand and pulled her toward Deadly's hindquarters. He squatted gracefully in the straw.

"See. Here, touch it. The stallion apparatus is fully intact and functional."

Glennys pulled her fingers out of his. "Oh no you don't, Sir Stogar. That's the oldest stable lecher's trick there is."

She put her hand on Deadly's nose, quieting the stallion. She fought against her desire to throw Stogar out of his own stable. "Was it a battle that did this to Deadly?" She forced herself to be calm.

"It was a stupid slaughter, not a battle," he said, "no matter what the old-timers say. Dad was determined to show that a cavalry charge could break a line of artillery. That Deadly's still alive is supposed to prove it. My old man is sitting in a cuckoo nest. He's trying to get Leon to give Deadly a decoration for bravery on the battlefield. He thinks you and Deadly are going to make the future weapon that can take on cannon. Now, he surely doesn't think Deadly's going to fuck you? Does he?''

Glennys thought Stogar was grotesque.

"Maybe he does think Deadly's going to fuck you. When it's high horsing season, the Horsegirls get awfully excited, I've heard," Stogar said.

She turned on him, teeth snapping like a horse's at a fly. Deadly whistled. His front legs danced in a sickly parody of his old spirit.

"Fighting filly, ain't you," Stogar said cheerfully. "I've heard about that too."

She hated him. He didn't belong here.


Powell found her in the stable office where she'd quartered herself. Her little room upstairs in the Big House had been taken by the maid of Lady Abigail Withey, the Baron's sister-in-law. It also housed a pack of Lady Abigail's precious little dogs who never shut up and messed wherever they stood.

"Mostly I'm going to sleep in Deadly's box. He wants me around," she announced.

Powell's long legs were stretched out in front of him. He was going to be sleeping in the stable office as well. Stogar was in his room because Duke Pierce Albany was in the Master Bedroom. Powell offered his apprentice some of the sparkling Tourienne Winebow he'd hooked out of the dining hall.

"Young Fulk hasn't impressed you, has he, Glennys?" Powell remarked. "He's going to be your Baron, you know."

"I've got a Baron already," she retorted. "Do you like him? The Baron, I mean, not that other one."

There could be a long answer to that question, Powell thought, or a short one. "Yes, I care a lot about my half-brother. We grew up together."

Rampalli knocked. "Thought the fine folk would keep you

playing the violin all night," Powell said, pouring another glass of Winebow.

"You seem to have tired them out on that ride," Rampalli said. "The pheasant shoot tomorrow calls for an early morning. Fowling pieces here on Three Trees, I can't believe it. I've been moved to the attic and it's cold up there. I've left my little brazier heating up the box of stones, so it was an opportunity to welcome back our apprentice properly."

He bowed formally, kissing her hand and both cheeks. "Welcome home, my dear. The Badlands air, as always, seems to have agreed with you. But you should have stayed in the Big House, with the other young people."

Glennys scowled. "I'm not wanted there. I don't want to be there either. Thurlow's perfectly content with her Aunt Abigail."

"Like that, is it?" said Rampalli. He hummed a tiny fanfare. "I'm going to give you some advice, Glennys. It's your business to take it or not, just as mine is to pass on the benefit of my experience. You should mingle with them, if only to make an appearance. They may seem foolish, but you won't lose anything by being pleasant. They might be able to help you someday, when Three Trees needs help. Muran doesn't belong with them either, but he's there, standing in a corner, waiting for a chance at conversation."

Glennys mimed retching.

"That's exactly how I felt, and behaved, for years. In the end, when it was too late, I learned it had done me no good. My example of integrity had no influence, and the wealthy and the powerful were still the means of my livelihood. Thus, I end my days on this place, aptly described by Miss Thurlow as a 'half-garrison and half-horse farm,' far away from the ballet and opera for which I'd kept my integrity unblemished."

Rampalli's cheerful laughter sparkled in the little building. "It doesn't matter in the end, Glennys. Those people don't even notice you've licked their floor, they're so used to doing it themselves."

He perched gracefully on the ancient, worn desk. "But all the same," he grinned wickedly, "I had some times I'd never want to change, putting some of them in their place. I never did pop the cherry on compromise and I've been free."

He threw up his head, opened his arms wide, and began an

aria from a Langano opera. "Let them call me rebel and welcome, I feel no concern from it. But I should suffer the misery of devils, were I to make a whore of my soul . . ."

The other two looked skeptically at him. It was probably their Alaminite blood, he thought with a sigh. Laughter didn't come easily to them.

"I see you two don't have my sense of humor. I confess, when I was your respective ages, neither did I. So I'll say no more about deep and puzzling matters. I'll have another drink." He did have a drink, about half a bottle's worth.

Cook came in, bringing Glennys some clean clothes fit for dining with fine folks. "Stella just guessed that you'd grow over the summer and she was right. I hope these fit you." He'd also brought along another two bottles of Winebow. He began to grumble about what the people up at the Big House wanted from him. "It's not them so much I mind. It's their bloody servants. They don't understand how decent people do things. We don't have servants here. We have hands."

Muran knocked next. There was barely room for him to stand in the crowded stable office. "Can I have a horse, Powell? One that goes well in the dark but isn't too sparky?"

"Take a horse, Schoolmaster. Take three. We got more useless horseflesh standing around here eating their fool heads off than a granary's got mice."

"That's settled then. I've got to ride back to the School tonight because Lord Hale's snoring in our bed." He nodded toward Rampalli. "It's just as well. The Lady Abigail's going to visit tomorrow afternoon and I want to make my preparations. The boys and girls that have been with me these last years have been willing pupils and I'm proud to show off their progress."

Glennys's mood was still sour, despite the sweet Winebow. "Enjoy showing off then. Give the St. Lucien lady a good round of declamations, lightning arithmetic, and a spell-off. It's going to be your last good term, Schoolmaster. I heard Reverend Durl preaching in his kirk on my way back to Three Trees. He's just the same as before he left."

Muran said, "Truthfully, I don't care. This is my last winter in Soudaka. Next spring I leave it to the tornados and droughts and floods and blizzards. The Reverends can have the County back, and the childrens' minds too. I've fulfilled my duty with interest just in time. Reverend Tuescher's in St. Lucien.''

Glennys had tilted her wooden chair on its back legs against the wall. Her feet hit the floor hard. "Rat shit."

Muran said, "If you'd eaten in the hall instead of the kitchen you'd have heard he's paying a big fine to the throne for the troubles back during the conscription. He paid it in raw *silver*. There's legal maneuvering yet, but he's coming back to Dephi soon. The war was expensive and Leon's looking for money for artillery factories. The rumor is that Tuescher's going to provide some of it."

Powell scratched the stubble on his chin, usually carefully shaved twice a day. "The King's building cannon and Fulk's trying to get battlefield decorations for his horse? I don't understand what the world's coming to."

Glennys grabbed her sleeping roll. "You can find me in Deadly's box if you want me. I'll get you a horse saddled, Schoolmaster, and send the boy around here with it."

Muran said, "Don't forget to see your mother first thing in the morning. You've been gone since the solstice."

All the way to Long Stable the words Muran had said the night he'd rescued her mother and herself from the stone-cold kirk throbbed in her head. "You need money and powerful friends to get along in this world."

The moon shining overhead was orange as a pumpkin. "I need horses to get along. Horses like Deadly."

The blood sang in her veins. The Baron would be home soon, the Baron would be home soon, her blood told her over and over again. He'd make Three Trees its proper self again and Stogar could play with himself.

# NINETEEN

The annual autumn horse fair in Gordonsfield was the one that counted if you owned, bred, or trained war horses. Glennys wandered through the deserted lanes that separated the picket lines of magnificent horseflesh. It was the final morning of the fair. In previous years, the lanes had been crowded with eager buyers and traders even on the last day. This year, when every breeder and trainer was dumping his stock, it had been a buyer's market and no one had bought. Everyone was waiting to see just how far the Eidel throne backed those who believed the day of cavalry was finished.

In other years, when money briskly changed hands, the fine fall mist made the sellers alert and busy. Today they'd retreated into the spirit houses before noon. Horsemen were masters in the art of drinking today's bad luck into tomorrow's good fortune. These last days there had been more business for the tack and trappings sellers than for the horse traders.

Glennys patrolled the area traditionally claimed every year by Three Trees. Handlers and grooms, dressed in the livery of the Equine Academy, led away the last of her horses to a new life. She felt a twist in her guts, like a twinge of colic, seeing the young stallions go. She'd helped train them herself from the spring they'd been foaled. But her guts would have been really sick if they'd had to destroy the stallions. Three Trees couldn't afford to keep eighty young war horses who had nothing to do but fight and eat. Powell hadn't made a profit on them, but at least he'd sold *their* crop. The knackers and the hide dealers had full, fat looks; they'd acquired unscarred, well-fed goods for the asking.

The fairground wasn't a happy place; the stallions weren't her responsibility now, and she was starving. She was ready for the spirit house called the Tribe and Bow where Powell and the Academy's Captain Tulliver had gone. Inside, the spirit house was steamy, full of the smell of horse dealers, trainers, and breeders. Horsemen always believed that luck was about to turn in their favor. It was a gay, furious bustle, like the fair as a whole was not. She saw Powell and the old Captain seated at a big table on the owner riser, placed like a small stage above and to the side of the crowded room. Powell and Tulliver had it to themselves, though there were plenty of well-wishers and gossip-seekers stopping by. Everyone was very interested in the fate of the Baron's petition for Deadly's decoration. Powell knew no more than anyone else.

She greeted Captain Tulliver and Powell, and pulled out a chair for herself. The atmosphere of a horsemen's spirit house always made her feel good. "Your men are taking the horses away and a fine bunch of young stallions you've got for yourself," she said to Captain Tulliver. Despite Rampalli's advice she knew she could get along with important people if she wanted to. Tulliver liked her, she could tell.

Powell put a good face on it now, as he handed over the formal bill of sale. As the seller should, he stood the buyer good brandy. "Three Trees' loss is the Academy's gain. Your health, Captain Tulliver, and to Gordon's Luck, may it be with Nolan, as it ever has."

"To your health and your good chance," responded the Captain. But he didn't have the glossy, satisfied face that belonged by right to someone who'd gotten the best part of a horse deal.

"Bloody artillery and cannon might work, or it might not, but it tain't what a proper cavalryman of Nolan can be proud of." He spat over the railing. "That's my opinion of guns and munitions of every kind. The world's getting to be one too much for me, but I don't say that because I'm looking at my eightieth winter. I say it because the foundation of our honor's jeered and fleered these days. The young twerps holding the King's ear aren't old-line and they have only envy, not sympathy, for the good old ways that made Nolan great. How a man conducts himself with his weapons on the back of his stallion is the only thing that counts. Anything else is just flimflammery thrown up to distract attention away from the fact that those Cabinet Ministers can't ride!"

Tulliver stood up on legs that had a small tremor in them. He and Powell had been in the Tribe and Bow since mid-morning. The Captain pulled his sword from the scabbard. "A toast, Horseman! A toast to Deadly who destroyed the gunners of Nemour's cannon emplacement without rat-assed infantry. To Deadly!"

Glennys joined the toast, as did the entire room. It was Burning Amber brandy and it set a fire in the belly that almost made her believe every word old Captain Tulliver uttered. But Deadly had barely survived that charge. Every other one of the Baron's men had died and so had all their horses.

"So," said the Captain, looking at Glennys. "Powell's apprentice is a Horsegirl. Good to see that Three Trees ain't afraid of the good old ways of doing things. Most of these breeder-trainer families, they don't bring their line up like the Fulks do, no they don't. The others have sold out, they say they don't have the land and the hands to do it anymore the way it should be done. It shows in their horses, yes it does. They're product, not breeding. That's why Fulk and Deadly could do what no one else has done. The Fulks, the Waterfords, the Elys, and the Gordons are about the last of the old kind, our kind, left."

Powell said, "Three Trees' way of doing things needs a lot of hands, a lot of food, a lot of country. The Alaminite crops, the Old Men in the Badlands, and the demand for our horses, is a real delicate balance. If we lost even one of the three elements, I'm afraid that would be end of the Fulk stud."

"You certainly don't foresee such dreadful luck, Stablemaster?" the Captain asked.

Powell shrugged. "Look at the price you gave me. Stogar—young Fulk, that is—believes in the modern ways. Who knows what's breeding at the back of fortune's wind for Three Trees these days? But I can assure you," the Stablemaster said dryly, "that the Baron sees things as you do."

Powell changed the subject, which he'd gotten heartily sick of during the course of the horse fair. "The Baron put Glennys in charge of getting Deadly back into breeding condition. She's been about married to that stallion since Stogar brought him back to us. Or maybe it was more like pulling a new mama away from her sucking babe to get her to come along to Gordonsfield with me. It's hard to tell the difference between marriage and motherhood in her diligence."

She flicked a bit of brandy at Powell's clean-shaven face. "Don't make me out to be more horsy than I am."

She was good-natured about it, but there was something in Powell's words that she didn't like; they sounded a bit too much like Stogar. It was only around Deadly that Stogar didn't bother her. Otherwise, wherever she was, there he was, insinuating, courting, mocking. Deadly didn't take kindly to anyone else teasing his property, which he'd decided Glennys was. Stogar didn't take kindly to not getting his way. It was a characteristic all the Fulks shared. She would have liked to have gone back to the simpler life of the Badlands, but there wasn't anything for her to do there now. And horsy or not, a winter in a sod shanty wasn't appealing.

Powell said that the Old Men made a pet out of her. Stella said that the Three Trees folks spoiled her. Stogar said she had an opinion of herself that was much higher than it should be.

The horse fair in Gordonsfield had been a change of scene that Glennys had enjoyed very much, even though the market had been a bad joke. Old Nolan had a lot of charms, she thought, including men her own age who liked talking horses as much as she did. She waved to the Gordon's Stablemaster's apprentice across the room where he talked with the son of a small independent trainer. That father and son were looking for work. Their short picket line had gone to the hide dealers.

Her food arrived and she dug in with a good appetite that thoughts of Stogar couldn't dull. Stogar was a talker who wanted people to listen to him. Glennys listened to Stogar as little as possible. Muran thought Stogar had sound financial sense.

One of Stogar's favorite topics was war. As far as she'd been able to follow him, wars were slippery events. Even if your side won, you could lose. You could lose your life, your limbs, your fortune, and your luck. But even if your side lost, there were always individuals who came out of it better than they went into the war. If your luck ran strong, you escaped, life and limb intact, and your fortune improved. This ability to do well out of a war, win or lose, was part of the luck that made old-line Aristos, Stogar maintained. It wasn't horses that made an Aristo, but battle luck. The Gordon line was an example that proved it. Since the old days a Gordon had never been seriously hurt in a battle.

A team of broadside singers let in a rush of fresh air and pulled Glennys's attention back to the Tribe and Bow. These singers were prosperous, as she could see, glancing down from their tall, horsehair hats to the rolled cuffs of their soft, expensive ankle boots. The band included gitar, drum, curly horn, bass fiddle, and a hurdy-gurdy.

> *Cannon cannot frighten*
> *Fulk's fiery fighting steed*
> *Listen now and you shall know*
> *Of Deadly's deadly deed!*

"King Leon, may he live forever, has just presented Deadly the Decoration for Distinguished Battlefield Bravery. And here we are, the Gordonsfield Broadsiders, prepared—already! —to sing you the history of it all!"

No wonder this broadside team was popular, Glennys thought, as the Tribe and Bow crowd cheered, pounding its glasses against the tables and the bar. They worked fast, if they could make a song out of the news so soon. They knew the song's perfect audience as well. Before the team had completed tuning, the pretty little soprano's tambourine was full of scrip, which soon made her half-bodice full-swollen, as she tucked the paper money around her breasts.

Powell shouted at his apprentice through the racket. "We're caught. We're obliged to make them a present for this performance, and not in scrip but in coin. That's the way it's done." He shrugged. "Never mind, that's their job. For whatever it's worth, it is good news. Maybe their ballad will be popular and whip up support for Nolan's cavalry."

The Tribe and Bow patrons, at least, adored it. The entertainers settled in for a long session. They'd won this audience's acceptance, and outside, the skies opened to pour down rain in earnest. No one was going to leave and the doors opened regularly, admitting more drinkers. The team would eat well for a while out of this performance.

Though Powell requested an immediate reprise of "Deadly's Deed" and gave the broadside team a roll of forients for the honor of Three Trees, he was restless. He was anxious to start the journey back home.

They paid off the handlers who'd helped them bring the stallions to Gordonsfield. Powell apologized for having no more work. "Sorry about this, fellows, but the war's done with and it's a fallow time for war horses."

They took the Post Stage. It was faster than herding and horseback. It got colder and more barren the closer to Soudaka they got. Powell was gloomy company all the way to the Coach Inn in Drake, where he had to meet with Lady Abigail. She'd taken Thurlow into the textile town to shop for the yards and yards of material necessary for the wedding next summer. It was more economical to buy there than in St. Lucien, Lady Abigail had said. But she wanted money, and until Powell came back from the horse fair he'd refused to release funds. He also needed to deposit the Academy's draft for the stallions in the bank.

Lady Abigail met them in her carriage. Glennys and Powell stood in the chilly afternoon wind while her little dogs yapped at them from inside without ceasing. She told Powell all the places he needed to go with her. During a pause in which Lady Abigail got her breath, Glennys asked, "Is Fulk home yet?"

Lady Abigail spread her fan and opened her eyes wide, eyes that looked exactly like Thurlow's though Abigail was so much older. "That's hardly the concern of this person, I should think," she said to Powell. She seemed to assume that directing her remarks to the Stablemaster was as far as she dared condescend. After all, he was on fairly intimate footing with many of the important people of Drake, whom she could barely tolerate herself.

Powell asked her the same question. "Is the Baron on Three Trees yet?"

"Civilized people know that the opera, *Deadly's Charge*, is about to open at Queen's Theater. A young coloratura from Langano sings the Baron's role dressed in war gear. It's going to be the sensation of the season. My brother-in-law is giving the singer dramatic coaching."

Powell rubbed his chin. "I see," he said.

Glennys didn't see. How could a bloody opera be more important than coming home to be with Deadly himself?

Powell got up on the box with Abigail's driver to go to the bank. Glennys was pointedly not included. She had nothing to do until he returned and they picked up their connection for Dephi. She was cold in her short jacket, long shirt, and leggings. Without Powell's company Drake seemed grotesque and unfriendly. Not many people in this town seemed to go on horseback. There was a lot of traffic though; there were carriages, traps, gigs, and buggies, as well as drays and cartage vehicles.

She might as well see what there was to see, she thought. Hunched inside her jacket against the wind, her half-gloved hands in her pockets, she set off on her own two legs. It was disorienting to go somewhere for no reason, even more so to go without a horse. Drake smelled of money, she thought. But it wasn't horse money.

She finally gave in to the numbness of her senses, created equally out of the cold, the noise, and the noseburning reek of the big textile mills on the Devil's Falls River. Hungry, thirsty, and with only a little money to spend, she went into a hole-in-the-corner cook house.

She began to realize that the other customers were staring at her after she drank off the first serving of mulled ale. She looked around and discovered she was the only female in the place who didn't wear a skirt. She unfastened the frogs at the bottom of her jacket to display the gelding knife she wore in a sheath under her navel. It had the same curve as her calves. Let them look at the knife as well as her legs. It didn't matter that she used it mostly to open burlap sacks of feed and cut leather. It was sharp.

She waited a long time for her stew. It was mostly potatoes, and the meat was horsemeat. The street outside the open door was deep in shadow by then but the proprietor, saving his pennies, didn't close the door and light a lamp. There was a rumble of masculine voices overhead through the low ceiling. As she ate, the voices began to sound familiar to her. If she never heard Tuescher again for a thousand years, she believed she'd recognize those tones. The floorboards of the second story creaked and the rickety staircase rattled as the voices came down to street level. Glennys slumped deeper into her dusky corner.

Tuescher halted at the bottom of the stair. His hand reached up to his deep-brimmed hat. It wasn't the Bishop's Hat but it was top-heavy in the crown in the same way, as though the Seeking Stone had found a new home.

He looked a little different. His beard was neatly trimmed and styled into a point. He wore a good black suit and an embroidered satin weskit. There was lace at his throat and at his bony wrists. He looked rich. His oldest son Ezekial was with him. And behind Ezekial was Stogar.

Glennys had become a full-grown woman since Tuescher had last seen her, but as he stared into her corner she believed he knew her. He'd always know her, just as she'd always know him. She waited.

Stogar glanced in her direction, without seeming to see her in the gloom. "Come along," he said to Tuescher, "or it will be too dark to see the mill."

As soon as she thought they were far enough away, Glennys paid her bill. She walked directly back to the Coach Inn yard, returning in less time than her wandering away had taken. She paced around the yard, waiting for Powell and wondering what possible business Stogar could have with Alaminites.

Powell arrived barely in time to catch the connection. "Thurlow sends you some dinner and her greetings," he said.

"That's nice of her," she said without any display of interest. Glennys could count on her fingers and toes the number of words Thurlow had addressed to her since she'd returned from the Badlands.

"Aren't you pleased to be going home?" Powell asked after several miles had raced by without a word from his companion.

"I suppose. I liked Gordonsfield though."

"You aren't thinking, by any chance, of leaving Three Trees and going into Old Nolan?" he said carefully. "It's not done, to go through an apprenticeship on Three Trees and take off for somewhere else. There's no place for you in Old Nolan, you know."

"There might be," she said. "Captain Tulliver said I could work for him at the Academy any time I wanted to."

Powell snorted. "Old Tulliver's in his dotage. They're pensioning him off next year. Gayfyrd, who will be taking over his duties, isn't an old-time Aristo and has a low opinion of Horsegirls. Three Trees is it, my girl.''

"You sound like my mother, before the Baron came and took me away. She said I had to marry an Alaminite and have babies," she said sharply. But the thought of Deadly and the Baron seized her. "Don't worry, Powell. I'll stay on Three Trees and help you, you know that.''

"That's good, then, because as these bones of mine worry me and my kidneys ache, I need you more every year.''

Deadly made Long Stable's joists vibrate long before their mounts carried them into the stable yard. He was back at weight. His winter coat was coming in, thick and shaggy now. Some of the bald patches had disappeared, though the thickest scars would always stay bare. Until they began to mate him in the spring, Glennys understood, she was the only herd of which he was master. A stallion without horses to dominate or work to do got lonely and bored. He'd made friends with a half-grown hunting cat while Glennys had been gone, but the cat wasn't as entertaining as his Horsegirl.

The Baron's children, and all the guests except for Duke Albany, had left. But Cook was in as foul a temper as Glennys had ever seen. "They'll be back in another few days, wanting this, ordering that.'' He muttered often about retiring to Drake and opening his own cook shop.

Muran wasn't spending as much time at Queen's School as he had in previous years. "With the men and the Reverends back, the children aren't learning with the will they had for their work before.'' But the Schoolmaster was happy, writing letters to everyone he could think of in St. Lucien and at Seven Universities, dreaming of the position he'd get and the life he'd lead, once he got out of Soudaka for good.

Rampalli was as sweet and courtly as ever, though the cold bothered him even more intensely than it had in previous years. But he was enjoying the Duke's company.

It was hard to believe that Albany was almost ninety years old—he looked younger than Rampalli. That was attributed to his blood, which was as ancient a lineage as the King's, and to his family's wealth, which once had rivalled the throne's. Albany had known every ballerina, every opera queen. He'd spent time in the cities of Outremere, especially in

Tourienne, where he'd lived much of his youth. He'd taken the Silk Road and explored the Kafir continent from which the blackamoors hailed. He'd even been to the Saquave Desert below the Rain Shadow Mountains. He owned an immense spread of land in the Saquave, granted to his family long ago by Royal charter.

Glennys was most interested in the Saquave. He told her, "I keep my lands there because no one wants them. They're considered good for nothing except hunting. So the charter is about all that's left of what I used to own. My travels, my collection of paintings, and St. Lucien's Academy of Fine Arts have eaten everything else."

"What about the ballerinas you kept, your other concubines, Duke?" asked Rampalli.

"Now those ladies are the basic necessity to support life," Albany said. "You must expect to pay for what you receive. I don't begrudge them the money they got from me, no indeed."

Harvest Gatherin was imminent. Reverend Tuescher had returned to Dephi kirk and his farm. He preached roaring sermons that for now concentrated on Alam's desire for his Kingdom on Mittania, not Alam's horror of heathens and their ways. Albany had gotten Rampalli to create Alaminite disguises and take him to a sermon. He hadn't been able to persuade Glennys to join them, however.

Still Stogar, Hengst, and Thurlow stayed away. The Baron did not come. Autumn's winds opened winter's generations-old battle against the Big House.

There were no young stallions in the stables and last shift stable duty was removed from the schedule. After supper they gathered in the Master Bedroom around Albany's huge fire. Though out of the proudest bloodline in Aristo Nolan, Albany himself was interested in persons, not rank. Cook shook up huge batches of popping corn in the Master Bedroom and drank more than anyone else. "This is where I started—you too, Powell," Cook said every evening.

Glennys was fond of Gustave, the Duke's parrot. The bird measured sixteen inches from the top of his coral red head to his coral red tail feathers. The rest of his body was gray. His shiny black beak could shred one of the Duke's ebony-handled hairbrushes into toothpicks in a few hours. Even more than brush handles and popped corn, Gustave liked wine. When he got tipsy, he became lecherous and preened and courted his own image, reflected in the huge mirror behind his perch.

"Like Gustave," stated the Duke gaily, as he winked at Glennys, "I too am lewd and obscene when full of wine."

On the contrary, thought Glennys. Even more than Rampalli, the Duke's manners were always just what were called for and in perfect keeping with whatever company he kept. Stogar was the one who was lewd.

"Gustave is older than I am," Albany said. "He and I are now trying to see everything we missed the first, second, third, and fourth time around. This is the first visit we've ever paid to Alaminite country. Now tell me a story. Tell me stories about Soudaka and all of you who live here. Who goes first? You, Cook Lowell? Or the Stablemaster? And you, Schoolmaster, are you remembering everything you hear?"

Glennys did find these evenings pleasant. But it didn't make her stop wondering when the Baron would return.


# TWENTY


The first light snow had fallen and melted away before the Fulk children returned to Three Trees. The Fulk carriage hadn't been used since their mother's time and it was the excuse for their extended visit in Drake. The carriage had been refurbished inside and out. The chassis had been rehung and balanced over smaller wheels and modern springs and axles. Abigail had gone back to St. Lucien in her own carriage in time for the opening of *Deadly's Charge*. She preferred to meet her brother-in-law again on her own turf of the capital's theaters, Thurlow had told Glennys.

However, Stogar had brought back three young manufacturing heirs to Three Trees. Erloff, Tufts, and Wheeler were youths who had as much social ambition as industrial aspiration. The opera, *Deadly's Charge*, had turned out to be popular. So they'd begged to come to Three Trees and see the horse who'd inspired it, since they couldn't get to St. Lucien and the theater. As far as Glennys could tell, not one of the three ever bothered to pay a visit to Deadly's stable.

Tykker had acted as driver of the carriage. He didn't seem to mind changing from a war-horse trainer and handler to a carriage-horse driver. He liked the Drake men's generous tips. They'd come inside the carriage with Thurlow. They'd brought one groom to care for their horses but he was a townhouse groom who couldn't handle Three Trees' horses. All he understood were soft, stable-standing geldings. Glennys reworked the stable duty schedule. Four new matched black carriage horses and a dozen outsider geldings, bred to carry fashionably dressed men on a social ride, changed everything. If the Baron brought company back with him, she and Powell would have to take on grooming chores themselves, short-handed as Three Trees was now.

"You're getting soft, old girl," Glennys told herself, just as Powell came into the office.

"Look at this—Stablemistress," he said. "I wanted you to see it before I sent it off in the mail pouch."

There was a packet of paper in Muran's clear writing and a letter on the top signed by Powell. The letter stated that Glennys, born and bred in Soudaka County, trained at the seat of Three Trees, had completed five years of apprenticeship running a breeding farm. She was fully capable to train stallions, geldings, and mares of any breed under the saddle. She could cipher, read, and write. She was an honest worker and performed all of her duties carefully and cheerfully. A draft from the bank in Drake was enclosed for one hundred silver forients to pay the license fee. Her eyes got wide. That was as much as Stella got from her daughter's wages every year.

"Muran's made two copies of the papers. One is for the Library in the Big House, and the other is for you," Powell informed her. "The license from the Horseskillers Association should arrive sometime this winter and make it official. Cook's got to make a dinner every night because of our guests, so we've decided to make one of them a jubilee in your honor. If you're willing, let's have your mother and sisters here at the table with us.''

Glennys was doubtful. "I don't know what to say. It's Harvest Gatherin in their world. Stella might be at the kirk in Dephi.''

"Don't worry about your mother," Powell said. "You've worked hard for five years and satisfied those you've worked for—most of the time. You've got steady, honest, hard work for the rest of your life here. We know Stella approves of that. I'll drive Cook's cart to the farm myself and pick them up tomorrow evening.''

Powell cleared his throat. "Thurlow's got you something new to wear. She bought it herself out of her allowance and paid to have it made up. It would please her if you'd wear the outfit at your jubilee. You've been turning into a slattern again without Thurlow after you every day.''

The last part of what Powell said was true—as far as it went. But she preferred to smell of horseshit around Stogar. It wasn't something she'd discuss with Powell, or anyone else. But they had eyes in their heads, didn't they? They should know that he was bothering her.

On the other hand, she'd listened to Albany and Rampalli discuss opera singers and ballerinas—their style, their teachers, their clothing—every night. Whoever she was, Glennys hated that coloratura soprano from Langano. Good clothes, like good horses and good horsemanship, got respect. That was the way of the world. Thurlow could provide the clothes. But the horsemanship was her own. She'd lay big money that the coloratura couldn't slide around a galloping horse's barrel and kill a pot-gut. What was screeching at the top of your lungs compared to training a stallion to kill?

Yet, and yet. She hadn't worn skirts since her last ballet class with Rampalli. That had been before summer solstice. So, for once, though Deadly wanted to go out, she left him in the north pasture and didn't heed his demand. Deadly was a horse, after all. The Baron was a man. She went up to the Big House to get a bath, brush up on her manners, and ask Rampalli to run her through some of the ballroom figures he'd tried to teach her. She told herself she was doing all these things because her mother would approve of such behavior.

The next evening it was like old times between Glennys and Thurlow. They took a bath together and dressed each other in the Lady's Bedroom. Glennys was giddy from breathing perfume and new, becoming clothes. Her hair was silver in the light from the spermaceti candles. The long strands left free in front of her ears and down her neck teased and distracted her while she fastened little gold rings to her ears with tiny silk ribbons.

Thurlow and Glennys both wore dusky rose satin. The skirts were smooth and rich as cream. The bodices were gathered below their breasts, instead of the old way, at the waist. Their shoulders were bare. Glennys followed every gesture and movement Thurlow made.

The dark-haired girl paced the floor while they waited for Agatha to come up from the kitchen and tell them it was a quarter of an hour before dinner was served. Suddenly, Thurlow stopped, with her skirts gathered in one hand. "Glennys, I'm going to tell you something that's still a secret. Promise you won't say anything until the time comes, will you?"

"What is it?" Glennys asked.

"I'm going to get out of here. Before the winter's gone, before the wedding. My Aunt Abigail is getting the Waterfords to invite me to live with them in the St. Lucien townhouse before the wedding. I hope I live that long! I won't stay here another minute more than I have to. By the time Rue's here, I'll be gone. I'll make an heir for that old man as fast as I can—the first night, if I have my way. And then, then I'll be free to live my own life. He can pay for it, but I'll do as I please!"

Glennys said, "I hope your plans come true, Thurlow. You were meant to shine in St. Lucien. Look at how beautiful you are."

Both of them stood fascinated by their own images in the floor-to-ceiling mirror, the one that was a double of the mirror next door in the Master Bedroom. Thurlow turned and leaned her head towards Glennys's shoulder. They kissed.

Glennys said, "Neither of us is interested in that anymore, are we?"

"We've outgrown girls' games," Thurlow said.

Agatha's pattens on the backstairs announced her arrival.

Her blue eyes sparkled, and her sweet, fiery breath told a tale of a bottle of Burning Amber open in the kitchen.

Thurlow gave Glennys a little push to go ahead down the hall to the front staircase. At the top, Glennys paused. She blurred her vision. She pretended that instead of Powell waiting to take her arm at the bottom, it was the Baron.

The others were seated in the drawing room. They got to their feet when Albany and Powell brought in the ladies.

"How fine your clothes are," exclaimed Debbie, when Glennys kissed her.

"I'm a Horsegirl still," said Glennys. "Don't tell anybody, but I'd feel better in my riding leathers."

That was a fib. Tonight she liked being dressed as Thurlow was.

Stogar brought her a glass of wine from Agatha's tray. "Congratulations, Stablemistress. I expect you'll do as well for me as Powell's done for my father."

For once Glennys could look him straight in the eye. Fine clothes were both an armor and a weapon, it seemed. They could make even crude men behave well in a drawing room.

Becky said, "Our father's never coming home. Reverend Tuescher says he stayed in Outremere and has a new family. He's not a member of any kirk anymore and it's your fault. He scolded *mother*." Becky was in awe of that.

Glennys thought that her sisters had had an easier time of it than she'd had at their age. They didn't have a father around who hated them, or Tuescher as that father's watchdog. Deborah had never even heard about the walk with stones and the congregation's sticks.

Glennys caught Muran's eyes and lifted her glass to him. Without the Schoolmaster what would her life have been?

Unlike the days with Stogar's earlier Aristo guests from St. Lucien, tonight Three Trees kept to the old custom of everyone sitting down to table at once. Guests, hired hands, permanent staff, all ate together. The people who served were help, not servants.

By the time Cook escorted in the five-layer cake in honor of Glennys's five years of apprenticeship, they'd all become merry with food and wine. Rampalli played a cadenza on his violin.

Muran leaned over and whispered, "When your birthday

comes you'll be an adult in Nolan. You can go wherever you want. You can work wherever you want. The Baron will be here by then, but promise me one thing tonight. Promise me that you'll remember you can go wherever you want when you're an adult.''

The table was cleared. Then it was dismantled to make room for dancing. Powell had moved into a soft chair in front of the fireplace. Glennys came and sat on a stool in front of him. The satin she wore rustled. It released a faint reminder of Thurlow's fragrance. ''We, I mean those of us who live on Three Trees all the time, don't make jubilees of our own very often, do we?'' Glennys said to her Stablemaster.

Powell watched the shadow from the fire flicker over the skin knitted neatly to Glennys's shoulder bones. After a time he said, ''No. But everything that's done here has been done before, and will be done again. This old House has seen everything.''

He was talking to her in code, Glennys thought impatiently. Rampalli's violin had set everyone's senses flying. She watched Erloff dance with Agatha. Cook danced with his own little girl. Her feet tapped the floor. Why didn't Powell ask her to dance? This had been his idea. He was the one that wanted to celebrate the completion of her apprenticeship now, before it officially was final.

A hiccuping snore escaped Powell's throat. When Stogar asked her to dance, she did.

They waltzed by firelight. They cooled off with sparkling Winebow. The dance, the light, the excitement, worked a transformation on time. It seemed much later than it was when Stella said she wanted to go home. Glennys lost track of things but found herself running down the front stairs again, this time in her riding clothes, out to the stables. Stogar, it seemed, had offered to ride the girls and Stella to the farm in the gig. Thurlow, Hengst, and the good friends from Drake were coming too.

Glennys had never ridden before when her senses were elevated with wine, but Deadly seemed satisfied with the state of his rider's abilities. He flew over the ground as though they weren't bound to earth, the road, or anything material. They didn't wait for the gate on the access road to be opened but leaped over it in a tremendous bound. It seemed as though

Deadly's hooves never touched the ground again until Glennys found herself in front of Stella's house.

Glennys was surprised to learn she'd never saddled Deadly. When she slid off his back she found the ground less solid than his back had been. Her feet had trouble walking straight. Stella sent the girls into the house immediately and the others moved politely out of ear range.

Stella said, with that mixture of regard uniquely her own, made partly of compassion and partly of Alaminite righteousness, "Daughter, you are drunk. The time's long gone when anything I say to you is heeded. But if you've got any smattering of the good sense Alam gave you, take that brute and get to your bed. How you can think to ride a beast like that in your state is beyond me."

"Yes, Mother," said Glennys, her eyes blinking from the smoke of the torches. But she had no idea what she'd agreed to. She wanted to get back on Deadly and ride again. She wanted to sink into that smooth, rocking rhythm that elevated them in the dark, leaving all of this far below.

They were all riding together now. They were going somewhere, but she couldn't remember where it was. On the road, one after another, Stogar, Wheeler, Erloff, Tufts, tried to ride at her side, but Deadly was having none of that and outdistanced them all. Once Hengst called her back to the group, and their horses stood still while Glennys and Hengst took long swallows from his flask. Good old Hengst. He always had a drink ready when you wanted one. It was Burning Amber and it was magnificent. She pushed the flask back at Hengst churlishly then. After drinking, she'd found out that another drink wasn't what she wanted. She didn't know what she wanted. They kept riding.

"We've come almost to Dephi," Glennys said, wondering why. Coal fires had been set around the ice frozen out of the brown, shallow water standing in the bend of the Shoatkill. She counted carefully. There were seven of them. But three times that many were pacing through the trees or skating on the crick. Stogar dismounted and went by himself through the trees.

Glennys was fascinated by the contrast of Deadly's black nose and Willi's white one as the two horses touched muzzles. "Now we'll find out what Stogar's up to," Thurlow

whispered. "He thinks the rest of us are too drunk to understand what's going on."

"I know," Glennys giggled. "He's doing business with
the Alaminites." It was as though that realization was a
counter-spell that broke the one she'd been riding under.
Glennys separated from Deadly. Her vision narrowed, but the
field deepened, and the colors that showed in firelight reap-
peared. Her hearing and sense of smell had become human,
not the grand symphony of a horse's.

Stogar was talking with the Coals of the Lord from Dephi
congregation, the men without farm and family of their own.
Ezekial, Reverend Tuescher's oldest son, who had been on
campaign with Fulk's men, urged his companions to be friendly.
Glennys, as well as the Coals of the Lord, began to understand that Stogar and Ezekial had planned to meet now when
the unmarried men gathered together to drink at the end of
Harvest Gatherin.

"Come on over," Stogar called back to the mounted people at the edge of the trees. "We're all friends here, or we
should be."

The Drake men dismounted. "I'm not a friend of a Tuescher,
now or ever," Glennys said fiercely. It wasn't the Burning
Amber in her talking. "Thurlow, he didn't mean you, but the
Drake men. Stay here," she ordered.

"And deny my curiosity? Look at that brute," Thurlow
said, pointing at Ezekial. "He'd still be over six foot without
his boots on. No Aristo has shoulders as wide and full of
muscles as he's got. His beard looks as soft as my furs."
Thurlow purred.

Ezekial was imposing. He stood in the chill night air with
his black suit coat over one shoulder, his white shirtsleeves
rolled up and straining over his biceps. Thurlow dismounted
and Glennys caught her scent.

"You think you're going to flirt with an Alaminite? A Coal
of the Lord?" Glennys was amazed that even Thurlow would
go so far. "A Coal of the Lord has never even heard the word
'flirt.' He doesn't know your game, and even if he did, he
wouldn't play by the rules. You can't play with someone who
doesn't understand the rules."

"Oh, I don't think so, Glenn," said Thurlow. "A man
always understands this game. And if not, you teach him.

He's a bit more of a challenge than Tufts there. Lady Eve,
but these Drake men are dull! They don't understand anything
but money and compliments.''

"I thought that was what you liked," said Glennys.

"Not their way, I don't," said Thurlow. She threaded her
way over to the light.

There was food though no one was eating. The Mule-Kick
jugs had been popular and so, now, was the brandy that the
Nolanese men had brought with them.

"What's this about, Zeke?" demanded Stoltenow, one of
the Bohn sons excused from conscription. "You said we'd
hear something that was going to improve our future and all I
see is more strong liquor to fuddle a man's mind."

"It is about the future," interposed Stogar. "Yours and
mine. Ezekial, your Bishop's son, can see it. So do these
sons of Drake's richest men. The future is three things:
gunpowder, cannon balls, explosives. Most of you here, like
Zeke and me, have seen it already in Sace-Cothberg. It was
munitions that made for the negotiated end of the war, not my
father's famous, foolish ride on a battered old nag.''

Wheeler passed around more brandy. He said, "There are
empty mills in Drake, next to the Devil's Falls, owned by my
father and the fathers of my friends. None of us is bound by
the old traditions of Aristos. You're the fortunate ones who
came back from the war, and a lot of you brought back a little
cash in your pockets. But not enough to buy a farm. You
might buy one wife, but where are you going to get the
money for the land? If you invest in our plan, not only will
you get wages from working the gunpowder mills, but you'll
get a share of the profits according to what you put in.''

Ezekial refused the brandy. He put his coat on and stood on
a tree stump so that all his brethren could see him in the
flickering light of the bonfires. "My father, your Bishop, has
spent long days and nights seeking for Alam's revelation in
this. And Alam says, *do it*! It's fire. It's light. It's a part of
the Lord's essence. Stogar is the Baron Fulk's heir. When the
time is fulfilled, this Aristo has promised that he will open the
Badlands to sheep and to farming. From the sale of wool,
with new farmland, with the profits that come out of the
factories in Drake, we can afford to move from this little
place to one much greater, which my father's found for us. It

will take long years of prayer and labor to properly prepare. But it will happen. Those of us who are worthy will make Alam's own Kingdom, where there will be room for all of you and as many wives and children as your upright ways find favor in the Lord's sight to possess.''

Glennys wasn't drunk anymore. How much Stogar despised his father, she thought, to plan something like this. No horses in the Badlands, that's what sheep out there meant. Where sheep grazed, the grass never grew tall and deep again. Their stools left in the grass contained worms that infested a horse's guts and made him weak and unthrifty. No war horses on Three Trees, that's what Stogar's plans meant. She was a breeder and trainer of war horses. The little jubilee in the Big House was supposed to celebrate that, but Stogar had been planning to ride out here and present this grotesque plan for Alaminite approval the whole time. The Baron would never ask Alaminite approval for anything. Just what was she supposed to do as Stablemistress on Three Trees when Stogar was Baron? Hold the reins of carriage horses?

Stoltenow said, ''Zeke, you brought me out into the cold night to listen to this daydreaming? When I could have stayed warm in the kirk basement? These are Mule-Kick fantasies. Shares and profits? We pay taxes and Alam's tithe. That's enough for me.''

A stocky man named Kesker said, ''Well, Brother Bohn, not everybody has a pa with more land than's good for him, a fortune made from lace, a smithy, and a cooperage. Let Zeke talk.''

Ezekial swung his hard body in Stoltenow's direction. ''*Your* father daydreams, Brother Bohn. My father has revelations.''

Stogar said, ''Hold on, my friends. This a new idea and some of us who stayed safe at home during the last war don't understand things as quickly as those of us who risked life and limb, slept out on the ground, and ate slop together.''

Wheeler stepped into the full light. ''I'd be willing to be a partner in this enterprise. This could make all of us, Alaminite, Aristo, townsman, prosperous in our own right, and independent of our fathers.''

Erloff picked up where Wheeler had stopped. ''I'm a blunter-speaking man than Wheeler here. But none of us three is an

Aristo bred to the top line. We're merchants, bred to the bottom line, like a farmer. But you don't know us. So you don't trust us. I've heard there's a competition that the Coals of the Lord hold. It helps you find out whether or not a brother belongs. We'd like nothing better than to go chug-a-lug with you. We may not be as strong in the back and shoulders, as you, but I think you'll find our heads are just as strong as yours. I call it! Chug-a-lug with any three of you. Are you ready?''

More than three volunteers stepped up from the ranks of the Coals of the Lord.

Glennys tugged at Thurlow's cloak, trying to get Thurlow to come away with her. "You don't want to see this," whispered Glennys. "Six men upend a jug of Mule-Kick apiece and drain 'em dry. Even the winner will end up on the ground spewing his guts out. The rest of them will be in the same condition pretty quick—just to keep the brethren company."

"My brother brought me here. I'm perfectly proper and safe," Thurlow said. "And I haven't found out whether or not Ezekial knows how to flirt. He's not going to go—chug-a-lug."

Glennys said, "I doubt that Stogar cares about your safety or decency, Thurlow. He's turned on all of you by what he's proposed here tonight." But she shrugged and left Thurlow where she wanted to remain. Glennys had no interest in a bunch of Alaminites throwing up. She no longer felt that Thurlow was hers to protect either. A year ago it would have been different.

Hengst spied her wading through the rattling old bullrushes. She was going back to Deadly. "You leaving us?" he asked. "I'll go with you, if you like. I never had the opportunity to tell you, but I thought you were lovely tonight, waltzing around the dining room, all dressed up like a girl."

"Thank you, though it doesn't seem so important since your brother is busy making plans to take away my work. But you can bet the Baron won't let him put Lighters in the Badlands."

"You're right, of course." Hengst grinned. "It'll make for interesting times in the Big House this winter, won't it?"

Glennys could have cried, except she was so angry. "Can you imagine the Badlands without young stallions and the mares and foals? There'd be nothing for the Old Men to do but die of broken hearts. How can Stogar even consider replacing horses with sheep and farmers?''

Hengst asked, "Do you remember that night in the Badlands when I said things had changed and that everything I'd been taught was useless? You said it wasn't that bad. Now it's your turn."

"Your father won't allow Stogar to change a bloody thing."

"You put a lot of faith in my father, Glennys. More than I can."

From beyond the crick bank they could hear a chorus of male voices chanting, "CHUG-a-lug! CHUG-a-lug! CHUG-a-lug! CHUG-a-lug!"

Glennys didn't want Hengst with her. She wanted to ride alone. She and Deadly covered a lot of furlongs before they headed back to Three Trees. She'd never gone as deeply into the Horse Sense as she did with Deadly. He was a close match for her. She pushed hard tonight, tried to make Deadly's legs, his power, his swiftness her own. The world was black and grey. Their sight ranged ahead, to the side, and back to their flanks. Their blind spot was directly behind them. They ran too fast for anything to catch them. Above, in the dark night sky, only the white owl ranged. It wouldn't attack anything larger than a newborn lamb. They flew over fences, ditches, piles of stones. But she'd had all this before, with other horses and with Deadly. It didn't satisfy her. Gently, she disengaged from Deadly. She remained as anxious and edgy as before they'd pounded over Alaminite fields. It was the first time the Horse Sense had failed her. Maybe she was outgrowing it, she speculated, as she cooled Deadly down.

There was a strange stallion in Long Stable. By the shape of his ears, the distinctive black points and bay body, she could tell he was out of the Waterford line. Deadly's long, sharp whistle of greeting wasn't for that bay stallion.

"If it's Deadly, it must be my Horsegirl that's been riding him," said a voice out of the shadows.

The blood rushed in all directions out of her center of balance. It subsided as quickly as it had climbed, leaving her dizzy. This wasn't how she'd imagined their first greeting, but it was right.

"Give me the kiss of welcome."
"Gladly, my Baron. Gladly."

Glennys missed her morning stable shift the next day, and the day after, and the day after that. Powell grumbled, but he didn't dare complain to her face.

# TWENTY-ONE

Hengst had predicted an interesting winter for the Big House. This was the first time that all of them—Fulk, Stogar, Thurlow, and himself—had lived under one roof. The Fulk family's unification was contentious, and it was brief.

For Hengst, the winter seemed to last forever. He and Thurlow didn't even keep up a pretense of lessons with Muran anymore, and Muran only came from the School to visit. Hengst would be a cadet at the Equine Academy as soon as the festivities of Thurlow's summer wedding were over. In the meantime, he just spent the days as though they were cheap money that bought nothing but cheap goods.

At least Stogar had given him something to do that seemed worthwhile. In secret, the two of them worked at the language of shoulder arms, artillery, gunpowder, and infantry command. Stogar had convinced his younger brother that these things were the keys to his future.

Hengst looked through the doors standing wide open in the west wall of the dining hall. This morning, bright sunshine had interrupted the clouds and drizzle of early spring. The fresh breeze cleared out the musty odors of winter and the equally musty memories of the arguments that had taken place while Stogar was still on Three Trees. As soon as the Baron had returned, Duke Albany had gone off to Langano, so the Baron and his heir didn't even have to be polite to each other.

The unacknowledged reason that the Baron had thrown

Stogar off the place was the partnership Stogar wanted to
make with Reverend Tuescher. Alaminites were despised tools.
The war horse and the sword were the foundation of Fulk's
honor. The Baron didn't disinherit his oldest son, as he
threatened. But he sent Stogar away without funds. "That
will teach him where his honor comes from and who is master
here," the Baron had declared.

There were threats and insults from the Baron. Many of
them. Stogar didn't care for spirits in the tradition of the
hard-drinking Aristo. That helped him keep his temper and
control his tongue when his father didn't. But Stogar did
share the Aristo's tradition of lechery.

The official reason Stogar's days on Three Trees were
finished was that he tried to raid his father's bed. It had been
a blustery day. Glennys had been breaking in two very young
stableboys fresh from Nolan. She told them the stable rules.
She drilled them in the characteristics of the horses. She was
good at taking new hands around. She'd never forgotten what
it had been like for her. Of course, none of the children she'd
taken in hand was as green as she'd been. She remembered
that as well.

She'd introduced the stableboys to Deadly. He was more
patient with people as an older stallion than when he was
younger. The boys wouldn't have much to do with Deadly.
But she wanted them to check that he always had plenty of
fresh water. When she came out of the stallion's loose box
the new boys hadn't understood that it was their obligation as
the least of the hands to fasten the gate behind someone like
Glennys. They were in a hurry to get their empty bellies on
up to the warm House for supper. Stogar had cornered Glennys
alone in the area where they stored hay and straw inside Long
Stable.

It had been funny, Hengst thought. Stogar scrambled to
safety on top of the covered ricks of hay piled against the
north wall of Long Stable. But not before Deadly's teeth had
taken out a chunk of Stogar's right buttock. The clamor had
brought everyone running. The whole place saw it. The Baron
had found his excuse.

"I'd rather tell the world my son was too hot in the crotch
to respect his father's bedright, than tell the world he wanted

to make money out of gunpowder with Lighters,'' he'd told Glennys.

Glennys was glad to see Stogar leave. With him out of the way for a while, life was blissful. The Baron satisfied her. It didn't cross Glennys's mind that her lover had known countless women and that what he taught her in the Master Bedroom wasn't new to him, as it was to her.

After Stogar's dismissal the Waterford invitation to Thurlow arrived. The ceremonies for an old-line wedding taking place in St. Lucien's most magnificent Fortune House were as long and orchestrated as a full-length opera. Thurlow had to learn many rituals before her wedding day, and would need coaching to get them right.

At the beginning of Rue, Fulk prepared the carriage to take Thurlow and her trousseau to St. Lucien. Hengst had never guessed that Glennys could screech as wildly as even Thurlow could in her most inspired moments.

"Escort!" she screamed. "You think I'm too stupid to know what's going on. You're using the Waterford invitation for an excuse. You're going back to that bloody opera bitch. She's got red hair, doesn't she? If she came around here Deadly would stomp her in the ground. And she dared to pretend she rode a horse like him. The closest she ever came to riding anything like Deadly was when she rode on you!"

There was no privacy in the Big House. Glennys wept for days and everyone could hear. Powell was furious. It was the coldest part of winter and his best hand wasn't working. He scolded her. He took away her privileges. She didn't care.

Glennys got thin and pale and silent. It made no difference. The Baron went to St. Lucien long before Rue was over. He didn't even send messages in Marche. He hadn't come back until yesterday afternoon.

Last night Glennys took all the presents he'd brought for her and thrown them out the Master Bedroom window. But Hengst found himself disappointed in her after all. The rejection of his father's gifts wasn't followed by a slamming of the Master Bedroom door. Instead, the House's inhabitants were entertained by another sort of noise entirely.

Rampalli and Agatha came through the garden and into the

dining hall. They were carrying all the things that Glennys had thrown out the night before.

"I guess she's going to want these after all," giggled Agatha. She laid a handsome pair of spurs on the table. "But if she didn't want the perfume, I would have loved it. The garden wall over there smells like the flowers in summer evening. Just a few splinters of crystal left to tell you what it was. What it was, was expensive. And she's still a-lying there in that bed of the master's after all that. And he's come down hours ago."

"Our Horsegirl's got as much temperament as an opera queen. Last night was worthy of a prima donna," remarked Rampalli.

Hengst was puzzled. "The whole time he was gone she said she hated him. She wanted to see him dead."

"She meant it too," said Rampalli. "But he came back to her so she hates him no longer."

"Women," said Hengst. "They don't make any sense."

"It's sex, not women, that's not sensible," said Rampalli. "I've seen men just as crazy for the same reason. It's the most powerful force in the world. So of course it's the most mysterious one."

Hengst said, "I've been thinking, Rampalli. I've had nothing better to do all winter. I'm starting to believe that sex is hardly ever sex. It's really something else."

"Aha!" laughed the old man. "You finally understand that it wasn't pretty faces, sweet legs, and fine bosoms possessed by those Drake daughters that attracted you. It was really their brilliant intellect. Now you're at the beginning of wisdom."

"Don't be sarcastic with me, Rampalli, because I'm too lazy to care when you poke fun at me." Hengst yawned. He threw the dregs of his chocolate into the fireplace. "I think I'll get the Horsegirl out of bed and ask her what she thinks."

"She'll tell you, Sir Hengst, that what she's doing isn't sex, but love. Women believe in it. Especially women her age. Good thing for men, because otherwise they'd have an even harder time getting them into bed. Sex is too powerful, too scary for them. But love, love is romantic."

Muran joined them, having just ridden over from Dephi.

"Aren't we worldly-wise and cynical this morning," he said, having overheard Rampalli's last remarks.

"Why shouldn't I be?" Rampalli asked. "I know more about love than any of you. It was my country, along with Tourienne, and certain other traditions in Outremere, that invented love. You barbaric Nolanese never heard of romance until you sailed to Outremere with your horses. In those days all you knew was a man and his horse, or a woman and her horse. And all you had was sex."

Muran just smiled. "I take it that Glennys has made it up with the Baron."

Hengst slipped off and ran up the front stairs two at a time. Glennys was half-dressed and seated cross-legged in a tangle of blankets at the end of the bed. It was large enough to hold the entire Fulk family. She was facing the mirror and looking at herself from under half-masted eyelids. Her strongly muscled arm pulled the Baron's brush in long strokes through her hair as though she had barely enough strength to accomplish even that light task. There was a tray on the bed table with half-eaten food and a half-empty bottle of brandy on a clothes press. Next to it was some dried-out cheese, bread, and fruit preserves.

Though Hengst hadn't knocked before coming in, his appearance hadn't disturbed Glennys at all. Her lips were swollen and curved in a lazy smile.

"What a lazy-bones you are," he said. "Sun's been up for hours and you're still in bed. What if I told your mother?"

"Don't you dare say a word! It's none of her business," she exclaimed, rousing into her everyday, daytime self. "Fulk said I should take my time. He'd make it all right with Powell. Powell's lectured me enough about Fulk. If my mother gets started, I don't think I can stand it. What do they expect from me? I'm a King's Daughter. Stablemistress or not, I can't expect to marry. Do they expect me to live celibate all my life? I've got the right to do what I like."

She got lazy again. "We're going to spend the summer, except for Thurlow's wedding of course, in the Badlands with the Old Men and Deadly. We're going to start breeding better war horses than ever."

"You won't be going to Thurlow's wedding," Hengst said bluntly. "Was last night worth having him leave you again?"

She looked at him with that blankness that belonged only to a girl in love. "It's better than anything in the world. It's even better than when I matched with Deadly's senses and flew between earth and sky. You're not between anything when you're matched with the person you love. You recognize the territory when you're belly to belly again, but you can't remember it afterward. You can only remember that it happened and that it was better than anything. That's why we rule over nature. We can choose procreation for horses, or deny them. We can have this whenever we want, for however long we want it, and without procreation. With horses, it's only when the cycle comes around, then it's over—quick."

Glennys gazed at Hengst quizzically. "You ought to know, old friend. You've been doing this a lot longer than I have."

"Not with anyone who loved me," he said.

"You didn't love any of them either, did you?"

"You know the answer to that, so why bother asking?" he said carelessly. "Love is an idea, says Rampalli."

With the arrogant callousness of someone who is young and in love toward someone who is neither, Glennys said, "What does he know? Love comes to you out of nowhere. It's not an idea invented by a poet. Someone rides into your life and your life changes forever. With him, you don't need anything more."

"But what happens if you lose the person you love, or if one of you falls in love with someone else? Then what?" Hengst prodded.

"Unless one of you dies, love is forever, and the one who is left will never love again," she stated with all the assurance possessed by someone who doesn't know what she's talking about.

"I think you're loco, Glennys," said Hengst.

She stretched her arms over her head. She arched her back until her breasts jutted straight at the ceiling. "I've been loco a long time. I'm used to it. Only a crazy lady like me can smell with a horse's nostrils, hear with a horse's ears. Only a crazy woman like me can tell that a mare is horsing before the stallion learns it, knows whether that mare wants that stallion, or that stallion wants that mare, before they try to kill each

other in the stallion shed because it's a wrong mating. And
Fulk and I are going to use that craziness to make the greatest
war stallions the world has ever seen! Powell hates what I can
do. He never wants me to use it. But Fulk does.''

"You had a horse shot out from under you, Glennys. If
anyone knows, you should. The day of the war stallion is
over.''

Glennys grabbed the rest of her clothes. She marched to the
door stiff-legged as an angry tomcat. She turned back to face
him. "Hengst, you were my first saddle partner and I haven't
forgotten that. You're the best of your father's children, I
think. Maybe, someday, you'll want to be father to one of my
daughter's children.''

It wasn't because she'd suggested he sire a child on a
half-sister that made Hengst feel sick. They were horsemen,
Aristos. Inbreeding, though not as common as it had been,
was used among the old lines on occasion, the humans as
well as the horses. The older peers complained that they had
lost too many of the Aristo traits because inbreeding wasn't
done enough. But it was shocking that Glennys was so foolish
as to believe what she could do would keep the Baron by her
side or that they could change the world. He felt as rotten as
if he'd drunk brandy all night. He looked for a cure.

In his own room he went straight to the clothes press.
Secreted at the bottom, inside a handsome pigskin case, was a
flintlock sporting gun. Stogar had appropriated it during one
of his own adventures in Sace-Cothberg. He'd presented it to
his younger brother along with the matching powder flask
shaped like a globe. The stock of the gun was inlaid with
silver wire. The butt silver plates were cut out and engraved
with trophies of the chase. There was a sliding safety-catch to
the rear of the cock. The striker incorporated a pan-cover
operated by a lever behind the steel. The lock worked on a
spring action, released by a trigger. The flint showered sparks
onto the gunpowder in the pan. The sparks ignited the powder
that fired the charge in the bore, propelling the bullet toward
the target.

Flintlocks didn't have the range or accuracy of matchlocks,
according to Stogar, but they were more reliable to fire in the
damp. You could carry such a gun already loaded. Like
Stogar, Hengst thought it was a sure bet that the new director

would have the cadets work with different sorts of muskets at least as much as they'd work with swords, shields, and lances.

Hengst saddled his own horse, a steady black stallion named Arrow. Smoky had been retired two years ago. He rode northeast along the spring-full Shoatkill Crick until he was several miles from Three Trees. He tethered Arrow securely. He went by foot several furlongs to where he and Stogar had set up a target and the forked rest for their pieces back in early winter. After Stogar had first demonstrated the flintlock to him, Hengst had found it necessary to construct a shoulder buckler of thick padding as protection against the recoil.

It wasn't a sword, but the barrel supposedly had been forged out of the blades of several captured Nolanese swords. As soon as he held it in his hands, sword or not, Hengst knew that this was a weapon with which to kill. There was a signature by its maker, Lorenzoni of Firenze, on one of the silver cut-out plates. It felt good in his hands. All those new words—trigger, safety-catch, striker, bullet, rammer—were still awkward on his tongue and in his mind. But this weapon gave him the same satisfaction as did blades made for cutting, thrusting, and parrying.

If more than one enemy came your way, you could pick off one and use your trusty sword on he other, he thought. There were endless possibilities here, none of which had been covered in his studies of deployment and tactics on the battleground. Trying to get a grasp on just what these possibilities were sure beat sitting at home on his butt, drinking brandy, and mourning over the blindness of a silly Horsegirl who thought she could make the world into what she liked.

Nolan would have a new army. And he, Hengst, old line of the Fulks, was not going to be left behind. He was determined to have a high place in it. He wasn't going to be a horse breeder. There'd never been the least chance for that to begin with. But he was a warrior bred and born. There was always a place for someone who was skilled in all the parts of the killing business.

The deafening blast out of the flintlock's barrel ripped off the willow buds from the twigs. Hengst saw that his charge had gone wide of the canvas target. He started the lengthy reloading process. The blast had cheered him right up. Knowing you were responsible for a really loud noise just made a man feel good. He was going to be at the top of his class in everything at the Academy. Between his old-fashioned father and Rampalli, and his modern, ambitious brother, he'd been taken care of. There was a place in this new world for him. By the end of summer he'd be in it. And his callow youth, imprisoned on Three Trees, would fade away like a dream in the bright light of the Academy and St. Lucien.

That morning Hengst wasn't the only one who found glimmers of a bright future in loud noise. In Drake, on the left bank of the Devil's Falls, Stogar and Ezekial had set up a demonstration. It was for the fathers of the men who'd gone chug-a-lug with the Coals of the Lord at Harvest Gatherin. It was also for the benefit of Reverend Tuescher and Banker Drake. The other man present was Acker from Fulk's regiment. He was a full colonel now.

Stogar, Ezekial, and Acker rolled casks of powdered nitre, charcoal, and sulphur in place. They'd stripped off their upper clothes and sweated in the bright, spring sun. All three of them were already turning brown.

They lined up three different field guns to face away from the Devil's Falls and toward an empty lot. "This is bloody clumsy work. These artillery carriages aren't exactly what I'd call easy-rolling, you know, Stogar?" panted Acker.

"The problem we're going to want to solve here isn't the artillery but the charge. That one we'll leave over to the King's foundries and the Outremere forgers he's imported," replied Stogar. "Our interest is the biggest profit—the ammunition. And to get them back there who's got the money bags to want it too." Stogar's chin indicated Elliot Drake, Chief of Drake's First Bank. The banker stood a little in front of Reverend Tuescher and the three manufacturing masters.

Stogar wiped his face. He straightened up and put on his shirt and vest. He turned to the Drake men and Reverend Tuescher and made a graceful speech thanking them for coming out from their business today.

Then he began his presentation. "A master gunner mixes the powders just before using them. The problem is that when the powders are pre-mixed, and then transported, the transport separates the three elements.''

Stogar carefully opened a marked barrel that had the words "St. Lucien" painted on it. He crowbarred several staves down, like a boy peeling a tightly closed flower. His audience could see that the charcoal, sulphur, and nitre had separated into rippled layers.

"So you've got to mix your charges on the spot. But that takes too long. Battle conditions change and you're caught with your pants down. That's how my father's regiment won that infamous engagement for which his horse got a decoration. Re-mixing in a hurry is dangerous too. I'll show you.''

Stogar put on face, arm, and chest protection. Ezekial had opened the other casks, and quickly Stogar prepared a tiny charge of the proper proportions. In the process there came a quick, dry flash that made a louder noise than anyone had expected from such a small amount.

"We want to make a powder that can be transported already mixed," Stogar said. "As well as immediately manufacturing ammunition for the King to buy.''

Elliot Drake eagerly asked, "What'll it sound like with a real charge in one of the pieces you've brought here? Don't make us wait around all day, boy, show us!''

Slowly and deliberately, Stogar made up a charge. Acker obligingly loaded an iron ball into the field gun. He ran back behind the muzzle, far away from where Stogar was standing. Stogar held a burning cord, ready to bring it to the touchhole.

It took several minutes for the townsmen's ears, virgin until now to gunpowder explosion, to recover. Then they laughed and cheered wildly, as though they would match the charge of the gun with their own voices.

Drake, Wheeler, Tufts, and Erloff shook hands solemnly. Then they began to pound each other's shoulders. They breathed the air deeply into their lungs. In the sulphur they could smell money.

"We'll talk business thoroughly tomorrow at the bank, but today I'm going to stand you all to a grand feed. This will bring more profit into our town than all the cotton, wool, and satin put together," declared Drake.

The banker turned to Reverend Tuescher and shook his hand again. He slapped his shoulder, though the Reverend didn't return the effusion. "I'm delighted that you're with us in this. What you've deposited last fall will give you an equal partnership with all of us. You have your ways, and we have ours, but profit and loss statements have their own rules. Good business is good business."

Tuescher smiled stiffly and touched his hat. He allowed himself to be borne off to dinner.

When the company staggered out of the Taffeta Drake three hours later, Tuescher appraised Stogar. There wasn't a trace of spirits on the breath of the young man. The two men stepped out of ear range of the others, who were talking about fowling pieces and other guns for sport.

"Now, boy," Tuescher said crisply, "there's a matter of you proving to me and to the Lord that your intentions toward my people are just what you say they are. The banker may worship my money, but we're still bloody Lighters and you're still fornicating heathen Aristos. You put this plan into motion yourself, you and Ezekial. But without my backing you're going to be a field hand, not a full partner. Your father's seen to that."

Stogar had been waiting for this. "What will satisfy you, Reverend? I'm prepared to do whatever you like."

"I think you must reveal that the Badlands are open to sheep and farming. Many years from now, when you come into your own, you may change your mind, or forget your promise. Alam must have proof now that you stand behind your promises. The Lord tests us all in many ways, and if you expect the Lord's help through me, you too must go to the test."

Stogar said simply, "I have every intention of proving my devotion to this business before the summer arrives."

In the privacy of his carriage Acker asked Stogar what Tuescher had to say. "Proof. He wants proof that the Lighters can run their bloody sheep over the Badlands. I'll give it to him, and gladly. And if the sheep find that Badlands grass is disagreeable and die, that's no problem of mine. War stallions are a business no longer, but we're Aristos and we'll always ride. There will always be horses in the Fulk Badlands."

"I never expected anything different," laughed Acker.

"I'm leaving for Soudaka the day after tomorrow to find

'proof' for Tuescher. This is a clandestine operation. I'll go alone. You can wait for me here.''

"Gordon's Balls, Stogar, you're a hard man," said Acker, shaking his head in admiration. "I bet I can guess what you're planning."

"Maybe you can, maybe you can't. Keep your bets to yourself in either case."

As almost always happened, the first few fine days made the gardener optimistic, and she put out seedlings in the kitchen garden too soon. The fine days turned into a heavy, freezing thunderstorm that was followed by a blizzard. First the sprouting plants were washed away, and then they were buried under eight inches of snow. Though it was winter weather, Glennys's blood ran hot and fast, much too hot and fast for Muran's taste. He wished she would be more discreet. He was trapped in the Library office, invisible as he was, behind the stacks of books and files. He'd been sorting through them as preparation to leave Soudaka for good.

Fulk had been calculating breeding lines when Glennys came in. He had the pedigree papers of all the Badlands mares spread over his big desk and the floor. Neither of them knew he was there, Muran realized to his sudden discomfort.

It soon became clear that Glennys was tempting Fulk to leave his work and go upstairs with her. If he looked through the space between two towers of books he could watch her try to seduce the Baron. He resolutely kept his eyes turned down to his own work.

Glennys was an adult. She certainly was willing. Muran didn't disapprove of the difference between her age and Fulk's. Nevertheless, he did disapprove of their connection. The difference in fortune was too great. Muran didn't see that Glennys could get a bloody thing out of her liaison that would better her fortune or her condition in life. That she wasn't carrying a child already could only be luck, he thought.

Fulk put his arms around Glennys. He rubbed his chin through her hair, and then pulled her into his lap. "You were such a bitty thing that first winter," he said, "but you still aren't too big for my knees."

Muran deliberately knocked the heavy volume of *Aquaria: Mimic Seas for the Young Lady's Drawing Room, the Romance of Natural History*, to the floor. It fell open to illustrations of sea serpents. Muran didn't want to hear them talking together. It was too distasteful. But more distasteful would be walking out of the Library in front of them as they were now.

The Baron put Glennys out of his lap, and turned back to his papers. "Glenn, ask Powell to come in here. I'd like to hear what he has to say about the look of the Ely stud from the south of Old Nolan. He must have seen their crop at the Gordonsfield Fair."

"I don't see why you need Powell for that," said Glennys sullenly. "I was there too, and I saw the Ely horses as much as he did. I can tell you anything you want to know."

The two in the front of the room changed. They began a comfortable, meandering discussion of horses. They talked about placement of eyes, the shape of heads, depth of chest, length of leg bone. Muran was able to get some work done. He got deep in a variant version of the Stallion Queens' history, as Glennys had heard it from the Old Men in the Badlands. He turned up the flame in the lamp above his small desk. He realized it was quiet in the front of the Library. No, not entirely silent. He heard tiny moans and a deep chuckle.

"Your belly's still flat," observed the Baron. "Aren't you ever going to catch?"

There was a thump, as though someone had gotten quickly to her feet. "You ask me that question about a thousand times a day. Is that all you care about? I've told you that I don't want children—yet."

"You know my plan. I want you to have children immediately," Fulk said impatiently. "Why else do you ask me to do this—and this?"

"Because I love you!"

"I'm sick of all this talk of love. What matters is that life continues. Love was invented by clerks because they've got nothing between their legs. You rouse me, that should satisfy you."

Muran put his hands over his hot cheeks and rolled his eyes to the ceiling. Why hadn't he gotten out of here when he'd had the chance, embarrassment or not? This was far worse.

"We're not horses," said Glennys in a voice that had the steel of a stallion's battle shoes in it. "Do you or do you not love me?"

"The two of us can make the horses of the future. Deadly's

the best stallion that ever came out of any Aristo's stud. We can breed more like him, and then go on from there, making larger and stronger ones. But Deadly's been hurt badly in his career. He's not a young horse. When we take him to mate in the Badlands he'll need all the help you and the teaser stallions can give. He has to cover fifty mares in a few days. You will match with him when the time comes, keep his excitement high and strong. And when that time does come, I'll be there for you. It will be a mating better than anything I've shown you yet. If you're not pregnant before, you will be then!" the Baron boasted.

"Tell me, Sir Fulk," Glennys said, her words like silk running over ice now, "what's the big difference between what you want out of me and what the bloody Lighters want out of women?"

This was treacherous terrain, Muran knew. Whenever Glennys compared something with Alaminite ways she was dug in like a mule.

"You're as stubborn as a stinking mule about getting your own way, just like your mother," the Baron said impatiently.

It was a growl that recalled the Baron's own that came out of Glennys's throat. "What do you mean—just like my mother?"

"I mean what I mean!" the Baron shouted. "You're just like her."

"What are you telling me?" Glennys demanded.

"That the only way you're different from your mother is that you don't believe in her religion," the Baron answered.

"The only way you could know *that*," Glennys jabbed, "is if you'd had my mother in bed."

"But I did," smiled the Baron. "Often."

Muran heard his heart beat four times, then four times again.

"You should have told me. Someone should have told me. Why didn't anyone tell me?" Glennys cried.

"What does it matter?" the Baron shouted again. The ground was dangerous so he charged over it. "Sire mates with mare and daughter in the same season—if we so choose. Why should you care?"

Muran clenched the sides of his desk, as if that way he could hold the world together for Glennys.

"Everyone's lied to me and I was too stupid to see it! My mother uses my money, you use my body, Powell uses my hands! Who cares about ME?" Glennys cried.

Muran braced himself for a chair to be thrown through the window. She'd done that before when they'd fought. What he heard was the Library office door open and then the front door of the House. He heard the chink of her spurs as she went down the porch steps.

A scream wrapped around the House. Deadly added his scream to Glennys's, and then, one by one, each of the horses on Three Trees joined in the fury of the Horsegirl.

# TWENTY-TWO

The full moon was reflected off the crust of snow and ice left over from the storm. It made the night bright as day. Glennys shoved a bit in Deadly's mouth. She didn't pick her way delicately through his senses. She brutally bent him to her purpose. She was riding to battle and the ground was her mother's farm. She felt the moon above her head and howled at it. She pushed the old stallion relentlessly to the top of his speed.

She and the black horse were clearly visible on the white ground to those who watched Three Trees. At the access gate they saw Deadly rise to leap without a proper collection. He went over, but stumbled. His rider pulled him up. The watchers saw a cold glitter in upraised hands pushed through golden hair. Glennys had taken the gelding knife she wore and hacked off her braids.

Deadly was an old war horse. He smelled strangers as he turned in pointless circles. His rider, lost within her private, blackened landscape, was blind to the witnesses of her act. When she raked Deadly's sides with her spurs to send him galloping once more, it was the Baron's body she tore. When she jerked on Deadly's bit, it was her mother's mouth she bloodied, that mouth that never told secrets. A tiny part of her cried out against hurting the stallion. Still, she struck out to hurt. She revelled in the blood and gashes on Deadly that were invisible on her own body, but just as surely there.

Three Trees' staff had roused as if the place had been attacked.

The Stablemaster hit the yard in time to see Glennys on Deadly, racing into the dark. He felt his heart break. Three Trees' assault came out of a passion that he'd only been able to discipline, but never quench. But the real cause was the Baron, whom he'd never been able to discipline at all.

"You fornicating idiot, what did you do to her? I worked with her so hard, so long, so this madness wouldn't happen. You come back when and how you please and she tears the place apart!" Powell shouted.

A storm of horses had kicked free of their bonds. They broke out of the stables, screaming with the outrage put into them by a girl not yet seventeen.

The Baron stood in the center of his stable yards. "I knew she had the power to do this. I had to find the key. I can put this to use! A dozen girls like her, a regiment of stallions, and I can take an army!"

The horses pastured outdoors threw themselves against the fence railings. The first assault fell heavily. Powell heard the unmistakeable snap of leg bones giving way. "There's no point to it! Only destruction! I rode her on a short rein for years, trained her to understand self-rule and duty so this day would never come. In one night, Fulk, you've ruined over five years' worth of *my* work! What did you do to her?"

"I didn't do one bloody thing, you bastard. She just figured out that her mother once had been my mistress. Stella wasn't the only one, not even then."

The Stablemaster turned his back on Fulk. He gathered his forces to calm and silence the horses of Three Trees.

"Powell, where is she?"

The Stablemaster shouted over his shoulder. "You're so proud of bedding women but you don't know a thing about them. She's probably going to kill her mother."

• • •

On the small rise west of the Big House were three cotton-wood trees. Underneath them were two nervous Alaminites and an intensely interested Stogar.

Elder Beal made the Circle of Alam. "It's a witch's sabbath down there."

Ezekial demanded, "Stogar, what in the devil's name is going on?"

Stogar was fighting with his own horse, who struggled to take off like a demon out of the pit when the Three Trees horses went berserk. "It is a witch's sabbath, Elder Beal. The Horsegirl's shown her colors at last. That's not the Baron on Deadly. No one else except his bedmate would get up on that demon-spawned stallion. Alam has smiled on our venture after all these nights of waiting in the cold. See? That's the Baron going after her. For once, he's alone. Between the moon and the snow he's a target that can't be missed. I'm tracking him. You can follow or not, just as you choose."

Deadly was mad. His rider was full of battle fury and they were riding to battle charge, but the enemy was behind them and to their flanks. His training and his instincts were divided. His training told him to turn and charge those behind him, but one of them was his master. His instinct was to keep running. Deadly ate the ground, not in a gait or a charge, but in full runaway.

They crashed through the budding lilacs, heading straight to the front of the house. It was a solid obstacle for Deadly. He reared and struck the door. He shattered it like an ax splinters a skull.

"Mother, you knew what he was when you sold me to him. Get out here and talk to me! Talk to me!" Glennys screamed.

"If I hadn't 'sold' you,' you'd have run away to him anyway." Stella's voice was as high and shrill as her daughter's. It cut through Glennys's rage as no one else's could. Stella spoke in the tone Glennys had always obeyed, the tone that had never brooked nonsense from children.

"Don't you ever talk to your mother like that again. Get that horse away from the house. You've terrified your sisters."

The red, hurtling wave of Glennys's anger hit the dam of her mother's authority. She groped for control over herself and her horse. The battle-mad, runaway Deadly took all of her capacity. She backed the stallion from the house as she looked down at Stella.

"You took the Baron for your lover. You hid it from me. But Father knew, didn't he?"

"It was my sin. It is none of your business," Stella said sadly. "It was a long time ago and it's a matter that's only between my God and myself now. Alam's forgiven me."

Stella was clearly outlined against the light in her kitchen there on the steps to her house. She could hear as well as Deadly and Glennys the thunder of hooves. The Baron pulled up his horse, bravely getting between the fire of the girl and her mother.

"Here's *our* lover, Mother," Glennys sneered. "Tell me again that your sin is not my business."

The light that spilled out of Stella's shattered home revealed the Baron's face. He sat at ease on his charger, one knee bent around the pommel of his saddle.

"Ladies," he said. "Easy now," he coaxed. "Stella, sweetheart, calm down. Glennys, back Deadly off. There's no need for the two of you to quarrel over me."

Stella looked up at him, her eyes wide from the shock of what he'd said. "You think this is—two women fighting over *you*?"

The small muscles around the Baron's mouth quivered. "You've kept it down a long time, but Stella, you're still the woman I knew once," Fulk drawled. "And Glennys is your daughter."

Fulk couldn't suppress his amusement.

"Do you see how foolish he is, Glennys?" Stella shrieked.

It was intolerable to see his face. Glennys and Deadly moved in.

Stella struck first. "You couldn't keep your hands off your own daughter! I didn't think even you could be so dirty!"

His mouth froze in its half-smile. The Baron jumped from his saddle and grabbed Stella's shoulders. "And how was I supposed to know she was my daughter?" the Baron snarled. "This is the first I've heard of it. You never told me. You didn't want me to know!" he said, shaking her.

"You didn't want to know!"

Glennys clapped her hands over her ears, and her head twisted from side to side, just as her mother's was doing now, trying to block out what she'd heard. She tried to smother the surge of pride that her father was a horseman, not a farmer. But stronger than pride of blood was her desire to hurt them both, as they'd hurt her.

Which did she hate more, her mother or her father? Glennys told Deadly to charge them both. No horse could obey two different orders at the same time. Deadly reared in protest.

The night shattered along lines of noise and light. They smelled heat. Stella's breast sprouted tendrils of blood. She sagged like an empty sack of flour on the steps of her house.

Deadly leaped above the ground, and twisted head to tail in mid-air. A crossbow quarrel hissed from the west side of the barn and struck the Baron's back with a force that knocked him on top of Stella's body.

Deadly, buffeted by conflict, seized on the one thing he understood—his rider's fury. He raced away, over the black and white field, toward the figures that ran from him. He leaped over a huddle of bleating sheep behind the barn, landing in a flat-out run that slammed Glennys's teeth together over her tongue. The pain took her out of herself. She followed it down into Deadly's flesh and matched with him, flowed into him.

Her own eyes were closed. Deadly advanced on Elder Beal, dodging the heavy blows thrown by the Elder's bewildered mule. The stallion's huge jaws fell on the Elder. It tasted like the smell of sheep. The enemy fell under his hooves.

There were still two more, running away from him. One wasn't an enemy because he smelled like the Baron. But that one pushing a mule toward the brightness in the grey field of Deadly's vision was not an ally.

Ezekial looked over his shoulder at his pursuer. What he saw was the embodiment of a pious Alaminite child's nightmare of being dragged into hell. He drew a long knife and threw himself headlong under Deadly's belly, slashing up and out. The stallion kicked away in a *capriole* above the ground. On his back, his knife still clutched in his fist, Ezekial stabbed up into the flesh between Deadly's forearm and the point of the horse's elbow. The Alaminite rolled out from under the hooves unharmed, slick with the blood that was the result of his first wild score. He scrambled on all fours, desperately searching for his feet.

Deadly screamed and screamed. His neck curved back, taut as a bowstring. His head punched out, backed by hundreds of pounds of bone and muscle, striking Ezekial's spine, knocking him sideways. As the man fell, the stallion's jaws clamped on his right ear and cheek. Deadly shook the body, dangling the man like a rag doll washed and hung out on a line to dry in the wind. The flesh ripped out of Deadly's grip. Deadly stomped on the broken Alaminite.

The human part of Glennys shoved against her Horse Sense. That thing that made her Glennys, not Deadly, recoiled and sickened. Glennys's revulsion broke Deadly's stride in a horrid, wrenching spasm, like tissue torn from tissue. She was vomited up, out of the Horse Sense, thrown out of Deadly. As they separated, she could feel the agony of the wounds in the horse's body.

Blood poured out of Deadly above his forearm. The thrust had gone deep and severed tendons. The shaft of his cock was deeply scored, following a jagged path that had finished with a piercing of his testicles. His head hung down, his nose touching the bloody ground. She knew how much he hurt, but now she didn't feel it.

She had to do many things. She began by slapping snow and ice from the ground directly onto the wounds in Deadly's body. She worried that the ice carried the taint of sheep and pig droppings that would poison him. It was a different world that she'd emerged into from the Horse Sense.

She felt deaf, and dumb, and blind. It was only her own nose, eyes, and ears that told her things. Deadly was telling her nothing.

She was aware of her hands as she tried to tend the stallion. These hands, these fingers, she'd seen them all her life. They were like Powell's, like Cook's, like Hengst's, and even like Stogar's. These were the hands of the Fulk line. Horse Sense had told her much. It hadn't taught her about her mother and father.

She'd wanted them dead, but now she wanted them alive. But Stogar had really wanted his father dead and killed him. He'd done it. She'd smelled him when she was matched deep within Deadly.

She left the old stallion and ran to the house. Debbie was with Stella, who was soaked in blood, but still breathing. The Baron wasn't.

"The devil's loose tonight," Debbie sobbed. "Ring the fire bell, get help. Becky's too little. Who can help Mother?" she cried. "Mother's the one who helps."

"I'll get Cook and Powell," Glennys promised.

The Waterford stallion that the Baron had ridden was spooked. He'd stayed close to his dead rider because it was the only familiar smell on the place. He didn't want this stranger that smelled of the dominant Deadly to come near. Time meant everything and Glennys was stumbling after a shy horse. This was the future, she thought, this is what it's like for everyone else when a horse is afraid.

She went through the motions of what previously had been only rituals. She breathed evenly, deeply, and rhythmically. She approached the bay slowly, deliberately, quietly. He'd let her approach. He'd sniff at her and then swing on his quarters away from her, ears laid back. She grabbed at the dangling reins and he kicked sideways at her. She was a stranger, an enemy. Glennys couldn't bend him to her purpose.

She sat down and talked to him. She distracted him with oats. She talked to him.

"Please let me touch you. I need you. Let me have my way with you." Her mother was dying and she was talking to a horse. She was a monster.

Debbie and Becky had dragged all the blankets from Stella's bed. They arranged them around her to keep off the cold.

"Ride for Cook, Glennys. Don't just sit there!" Debbie cried.

"Shouldn't we get Mother inside?" Glennys asked.

Debbie said, "It's bad to move her. We have to wait until the blood stops. But it's as cold in the house as it is out here. You broke the door."

"What did you do to my mother?" Becky demanded, her face smeared with blood and tears.

"I didn't do it, I swear. It was a gun. Like with a bow and arrow, it can hit things from a distance."

"It's against Alam's law to kill people unless they're bad. This was a terrible sin," said Becky.

• • •

That was what Glennys heard her sister say when she swung into the bay's saddle to get Cook's help. She'd killed two men tonight, and neither of them was the right one.

Cook believed that the bullet that had entered Stella was still in her. "She can't heal until we get it out and I've no experience with this kind of thing."

Hengst showed him what to look for, exhibiting bullets for the flintlock made by Lorenzoni of Firenze. It was Powell, whose huge, sensitive fingers, so skilled at groping in a horse's birth and anal canals, at investigating the softness inside hooves, who went to work seeking the bullet.

"Good thing she's a big-breasted woman," grunted Powell softly. His pincers held a lead bullet. "All that flesh on the right side of her chest, along with the distance from which it was fired, softened the impact."

After many days they began to believe that Stella would survive. Glennys worked the farm. She went to Three Trees once, the morning they buried the old Baron. His coffin was put among the others of his line under the hill on which the cottonwood trees grew. None of his regiment, none of his peers was present. Neither was Thurlow. It was too far to come in time for the burial. But Stogar was there and no one asked how he'd heard the news so quickly in Drake.

Stogar stood next to the vault in the side of the hill. He spoke the only words that were said over the Baron's dead body. "We treat our dead good here and we always will." Stogar administered the *coup de grâce* to lame Deadly himself. The sick old horse received his end with dignity.

Perhaps, Glennys thought often, Deadly went to his grave with the same relief that she took back with her to her mother's farm. She couldn't make herself stay on Three Trees, no matter how much Powell cajoled or ordered. The keening of the Old Men who'd ridden in from the Badlands couldn't be borne. They were keening for what she'd lost as much as they were keening for the Baron.

Stogar had brought the banker with him from Drake. "We know who killed my father and my father's horse executed them," he said. "There's no question now of allowing Alaminites any part of our business currently in hand. They're fortunate that I'm not a vengeful man." They took Hengst away with them. He never got the opportunity to tell Glennys farewell.

She couldn't meet Powell's eyes when he came to see her on Stella's farm. He discussed the planting of Stella's fields. He offered to loan her a draft team to plow up the fields. She refused. "I can't stand to be around horses, Powell. It's gone, the Horse Sense. It hurts too much, even with those who could never hear me."

Powell came again and again, trying to persuade her that she could work in Three Trees' stables. Finally she told him. "I smelled him. It was Stogar who killed my Baron. You know I tell you the truth when I say I was with Deadly and I smelled the man who is the Baron now. I can never go back to Three Trees."

She plowed behind the oxen. She planted the garden with her sisters. She did the heaviest farmwork by herself. The family didn't have her wages now. It was only their dawn-to-dark labor with arms and backs that would put food into their mouths.

Along with the Horse Sense all the brightness in her world had vanished. It was another kind of blackness the day she saw Reverend Tuescher coming at her across the field where she worked. She fought back but couldn't escape his wrath. He beat her skillfully with an economy that she dully realized through the blows and kicks was severely disciplined.

"I shan't kill you," he panted, when he'd finished. "I prefer to leave you to suffer knowing what you are, knowing that you are forever cast out from the decent folk."

What she knew was that he didn't dare kill her. Everyone believed it was his son and his oldest friend who'd murdered Fulk. If he killed her, everyone would also believe it was vengeance. It was against the law for anyone to kill in Soudaka except when it was the Baron's execution as the representative of the King's Justice. Before, in the days of the Horse Sense, Reverend Tuescher wouldn't have been able to get near her.

One of the Bohn wives who helped them with Stella's care came to where Glennys lay in the furrows. She'd brought a pan of water, cloths for cleansing, and bandages, as well as wine. She made the Circle of Light over the girl. She said,

"Alam forgives those who repent," and took the oxen back to the yard.

Unhappy though she was, the crops and the garden grew. The chicks fledged their wing feathers. The piglets were weaned from the sows and squealed over the trough. Her mother's farm reached for summer and Stella mended.

Glennys had fed Stella her meal every evening. Now that Stella was stronger and could feed herself Glennys still carried in the tray, even though she'd rather have been anywhere than in her mother's bedroom. This was the hardest thing. Glennys had two families and belonged in neither one. There was no one to talk to and no one to talk to her, about anything.

In that time of the year when the sunset is long, Stella put out her hand and said, "Can you forgive me?"

Glennys murmured a lesson from catechism class. "The sins of the fathers are visited upon their children, unto the third and fourth generations."

Stella smiled faintly in the lingering light. "New generations are born every day and each one makes its own sins. The story didn't begin with me. It certainly didn't begin with you. As well as our guilt, we make our own innocence."

Glennys's hair wasn't long enough to cover her face. She wanted to flee but she had to remain. Otherwise nothing could ever begin again.

Stella said, "Alam walked with my father and gave him all the love he needed. Mother died when I was very young. From the moment I saw Fulk, I was his. I expect it was the same with you."

Stella waited for the question she knew Glennys would ask. "Why did you give me to him then?"

"I had to. You weren't like your sisters. You were too much Fulk's child. I was sure he knew that he was your father. I never realized that a man like Fulk couldn't be bothered to count the days between when he'd last seen me and the news that I was married and a mother. But he never thought of me at all until he heard I had something he might want."

"I loved him," said Glennys. "I thought he loved me. He didn't."

Stella said, forcing the words out, "Glennys, I am so sorry

that you must suffer because you made your father into your lover.''

"But I don't suffer from that!" Glennys cried. "I don't think of him as my father. I think of him as a man who made a fool out of me. I suffer from that. I suffer because I had a life and I don't have it anymore and I don't know what to do now.''

Stella, who had been leaning forward to hear Glennys's words, leaned back on her pillows. "Fulk was your father. It was a sin," she said weakly.

"But I didn't know it, and neither did he," Glennys said. "I didn't sin. I was stupid.''

She lapsed into silence.

"You aren't what you were before that terrible night," said Stella. "Deborah speaks as a child but children see truth. The devil was abroad and in all of us. Alam can help you, Glennys, if you allow him room in your heart. Don't be angry.''

"Alam can't take the place of what I had in the Badlands and the training ground," said Glennys.

"You are grieving, Glennys. You've come into worldly knowledge. Worldly knowledge does not give a woman peace or give her comfort, or a purpose. You will only find that in Alam's hands.''

Glennys was surprised to find that she'd gotten some comfort out of her mother's words. It wasn't the comfort of Alam, but the belief that her mother didn't despise her. Her mother believed they had shared a terrible thing but that they deserved to go on living.

"What matters," said Stella with satisfaction, "is that you've come back to me and the farm where you belong. Both the farm and I need you. And you will find the Light of Alam here. The Lord works in mysterious ways, praise the name of the Lord.''

Over the next days Glennys's sense of time returned. Thurlow was wed to the Waterford line now, she'd think. Or, Hengst must be a cadet by now. But the farm could give her no pleasure, as working with the war horses had done. And that was gone forever. They had no purpose anymore.

* * *

One morning before the first summer harvest Muran drove into the farmyard in Cook's cart. Glennys came out of the barn. She leaned against the pitchfork and watched the School-master put on the brake and secure the pony.

"I hadn't planned to stay out here so long. I've been contractually free since the spring. But Stogar gave me a bonus on top of the one Fulk promised in my contract with him if I'd do business here and then go to Drake and read his bank contracts for him. This is farewell."

Stella invited him into the house for a cup of bitterberry. "I don't have the time, but thank you. I came to ask Glennys to ride into Dephi with me to take a stirrup cup at the Coach. Cook will ride in later and pick up the cart."

Suddenly Glennys felt she had to go with her old School-master and get off the farm, even for a little while. "I'll come. Let me wash and comb my hair."

She took the reins of the pony when Muran handed them to her as if it was the most natural thing in the world that she should take over this task. They didn't get very far before Glennys halted the pony and got down.

"Is there something wrong, Horsegirl?" Muran asked in-nocently. "I harnessed him myself."

"You put Knees between the shafts. He's got the bit up in the front of his mouth instead of where it belongs. He's always been good at that trick," she said. She adjusted the bit's cheekpieces that were supposed to extend below the horse's lips and prevent the bit from slipping through its mouth while the pony was driven into a turn.

She looked into the back of the cart before ascending. There were a couple of trunks, mostly full of paper and books, if she knew the Schoolmaster. It was a surprisingly small amount of baggage for a man who'd spent so many years in Soudaka County.

They drank in the public room of the Coach Inn while they waited for the Post Stage. Muran talked about the position he'd accepted as assistant to Duke Colfax, the Minister in charge of the Office of Inquiry. "Stogar, I mean the Baron Fulk, as he is now, gave me another recommendation to go with old Fulk's," he informed her. "It seems that Stogar and the Duke became friendly in Sace-Cothberg."

It was good to hear talk about the world beyond the farm

again, she thought, even if Stogar was a part of it. They drained the pitcher quickly and Glennys leaped up to get another one. She'd forgotten she wore skirts, not riding leggings. She tore her petticoat on a loose nail in the bench. She swore. She'd not done that in weeks.

"By the fornicating Luck I hate these clothes and I hate it here!"

"I think we discussed that a long time ago, didn't we?" Muran said. Both of them laughed just a bit then, because, considering how the world wags, what else could they do?

The Schoolmaster said, "Rampalli hates it too, now that you're all gone. But his contract gave him a place here until he dies. He doesn't think it will be too long now either. He's awfully frail."

The Schoolmaster looked at her very seriously. "But it's different for you. You're an adult. This is Nolan. Unlike those old countries Outremere, Nolan's people are free. You don't have to stay where you were born, even if you were born a farmer."

"You're still trying to teach me lessons, even in the last minutes before you wipe the dust of Soudaka County from your feet forever," she said. But she smiled.

"I've got something better to give you than advice," he said with a grin. He took out a roll of forients. "Your last wages. Powell asked me to give them to you, not to Stella. Here's your license from the Horseskillers as well."

She didn't hesitate. She took them.

"St. Lucien's full of horses. All kinds of horses. You should be able to find something you can do with them, until you find something else you might like better," he said.

The Post Stage was ready to leave. Mrs. Prochnow came out of her living quarters to scatter table scraps to the chickens in the back. She hissed when she saw Glennys. She put up her fingers to ward off bad luck.

She remembered Powell's words the night of her apprentice jubilee. He was right, she thought, everything that happens here, has already happened more than once.

She waved to Muran as the Post Stage's three teams

changed leads out of the turn and picked up speed. If you want to go somewhere fast, she thought, you have to have a horse.

**The city of St. Lucien
beckons Glennys,
as she enters
a world of glamour
and intrigue in
*The Stalking Horse,*
coming soon
from Ace Books.**